Visiting
Fellow

Visiting Fellow

a novel by
Dave Williamson

TURNSTONE PRESS

Turnstone Press
Artspace Building
206-100 Arthur Street
Winnipeg, MB
R3B 1H3 Canada
www.TurnstonePress.com

Turnstone Press gratefully acknowledges the assistance of the Canada
Council for the Arts, the Manitoba Arts Council, the Government of
Canada through the Canada Book Fund, and the Province of Manitoba
through the Book Publishing Tax Credit and the Book Publisher
Marketing Assistance Program.

Printed and bound in Canada by Friesens for Turnstone Press.

Library and Archives Canada Cataloguing in Publication

Williamson, Dave, 1934-, author
    Visiting fellow / Dave Williamson.

Issued in print and electronic formats.
ISBN 978-0-88801-576-1 (paperback).--ISBN 978-0-88801-575-4 (epub).--
ISBN 978-0-88801-577-8 (mobi)

    I. Title.

PS8595.I564V57 2016   C813'.54   C2016-901664-1
                                               C2016-901665-X

For Linda, Jim, Wendy, and Laura

Visiting Fellow

1.

HARASSMENT

It was the only message in Wally Baxter's voicemail: "Hi, Wally. It's Erica Mead. The new sexual harassment officer. Please give me a call at 2777."

Wally began to sweat. He thought of the time he'd gone to the pub with his students. He remembered the young woman who'd French kissed him when they'd both had too many beers. And there was the one in the miniskirt who'd sat on his desk—on his side of the desk. But those events were years ago. Was somebody dredging up a past indiscretion and reading something abusive into it? Wait. Valerie Clark had come into his office the other day; hadn't their hands touched when she gave him her paper on Riel? Had she read something into that?

He dialed Erica Mead's number. As expected, her recorded voice came on; no one answered live anymore. "I'm not able to take your call right now. Please leave your name and number and a detailed message after the beep and I'll get back to you, or press zero to speak with my assistant."

"Hi, Erica," he said. "It's … um … Wally Baxter, returning your call." He gave her the time and his number.

Wally wished he hadn't hesitated—that *um* before his name. It smacked of guilt. He tried marking a student paper. Zena Sereda's. He thought he could smell her perfume. He bent his head to sniff the page. My god, what was he doing?

He stood up and moved the pile of first-year papers to his side chair. He'd tidy his desk. He threw away a brochure for a conference in Newfoundland. He looked briefly at a flyer for a book called *Quebec: Distinct or Defunct?* and ripped it up.

His phone rang.

"Baxter here."

"Wally. Thanks for getting back to me. It's Erica Mead." He liked the sound of her voice. He liked the friendly tone of it.

"Yes, Erica. Uh … um … hello."

"Could you meet me sometime in the next day or so?"

"Right now if…"

"Right now would be great. My office?"

"Sure. Could you tell me, um, is this…"

"Nothing about you, Wally. Why, do you have reason to be concerned?"

"I beg your pardon?"

"Just a little joke, Wally. I want to ask you a few questions about someone else."

Relieved, Wally put on his topcoat and walked in the cool February air over to the Administration Building, that picturesque but impractical old building that marked the centre of campus. He walked up the worn stone steps, entered, and went up more steps to Erica's office. She came out to greet him. Her assistant gave him a benign smile and went about her business at her computer. Erica, in black-framed glasses, sand-coloured pantsuit, and black shirt, shook his hand and showed him into her office. He sat in her loveseat, wondering if they called it something else in the office of a sexual harassment officer. She closed the door.

"I have to swear you to secrecy," she said, sitting in a chair beside him and crossing her long legs. "It's a clear-cut case: female student accuses male prof of giving her a failing grade because she won't grant him any favours, i.e., she won't let him get into her pants."

Wally felt his lip curl slightly. He detested the use of *i.e.* in speech. It took no more energy to say *that is*—the words *i.e.* stood for. He considered *i.e.*—which was an abbreviation of the Latin term *id est*—to be acceptable only in written reports.

"The prof is a colleague of yours," Erica continued. "I'm involving you because you have a reputation for being fair-minded and trustworthy. All I want you to do is answer a few questions; you don't have to answer them if you don't want to."

Wally had been a valued member of several committees, like the controversial one a few years ago on smoking policy and the one developing the University's new vision. He agreed to cooperate. Erica told him who the accused was, and he wasn't surprised, though he didn't tell Erica that. Wally had heard the guy had been boffing students for years. But Wally believed the guy had integrity and wouldn't give an *F* for anything but academic reasons, mostly because the guy was rarely rejected. Wally told Erica none of this. He answered her questions.

Her interrogation lasted no more than four minutes. "That's it," she said.

"While I'm here," said Wally, "could I clarify something?"

"Certainly."

"What if I'm talking with you and you take whatever I say to be an advance?"

"Do you mean *me* or a hypothetical person?"

"Let's take you and me for an example. Say I'm horsing around because I'm in a good mood, and you regard it as chatting you up."

"The key thing is whether the advance is wanted or not wanted."

"But what if I don't intend it as an advance?"

"What matters is how I perceive it. There's no such thing as an unconscious or unintended pass. If I like what you're doing, there's no problem. If I don't like what you're doing, I'll let you know. If I let you know and you persist, we have the makings of a problem, i.e., you are beginning to harass me."

There was that *i.e.* again. Wally wanted to say, Could you give me an e.g.? Instead, he said, "What if you like what I'm doing at first and then you change your mind?"

"There is no point of no return. As soon as I decide I don't like what you're doing, you have to desist."

"Surely that depends on perfect communications." Wally was warming up to the subject, to his own articulateness. "Normal human interaction isn't like that. We misinterpret and misunderstand all the time; is there no margin for error?"

"The signals we give are seldom so subtle that the other person can't read them. Of course, there can be misunderstandings, but then one of us should be ready to acknowledge them."

"And apologize."

"Yes."

"Let's say you take whatever I'm saying or doing as a pass, and you want it to be a pass, and you think you're encouraging me, and, when you realize that what I'm saying or doing isn't a pass, you're disappointed. Might you not report me to get revenge?"

"A mean-spirited person might do that, yes; that's why we have to study a case thoroughly."

"Then there's the whole question of power, and who really has it, one over the other, and how it's used; there's a lot to this harassment business."

"Maybe you'd like to discuss it further sometime."

"I would."

She looked directly at him. "Over dinner?"

He smiled. "Sounds good."

"Good, but it would be unwise for us to be seen in public while this case is still pending."

They waited until Erica had made her report to the president. She was not obliged to tell Wally what decision was made, and he didn't want to know. A rumour persisted that an independent panel would re-evaluate the student's paper and that the prof would be suspended. But it was

May now, and faculty tended to lose track of one another as summer approached.

With the case officially closed, Wally phoned Erica to see if she was still interested in dinner.

"Absolutely," she said.

"Uh … you know I'm divorced."

"And I'm single."

"I thought we should clarify that."

"Good for you."

"When would you like to have dinner?"

"Tonight?"

"Well, yes, sure. Rae and Jerry's all right?"

"Rae and Jerry's it is. At seven?"

"Fine. I'll make the reservation."

"And I'll drive, i.e., I'll pick you up."

Ugh, thought Wally.

"I thought it might be good of me," Erica said, "since you helped me on the case. But then I'll be the designated driver, won't I?"

"It's all right, *I'll* drive."

"You want to drink, don't you?"

"I'd like to…"

"So would I. Look, I'll pick you up, and we'll take a cab home. My sister can take me to my car tomorrow; she owes me."

After speaking with Erica, Wally left his office and went to pick up his mail. There was one letter, one he'd been anticipating. He took it back to his office and tore it open.

Dear Dr. Baxter:

Thank you for your last letter. Don't apologize for communicating by fax; it actually makes a lot of sense. I suspect it is also cheaper. We have at last acquired a longed-for plain-paper fax of great sophistication, relatively speaking. I think the old one was coal fired.

Our summer vacation is December, January, and February. The academic year begins in the last part of February and ends at the end of November. In the middle of the year there is a three-week vacation, which always falls in July and divides the academic year into two equal semesters. The first semester thus runs from late February to July, with a mid-semester break of one week that coincides with Easter.

I would like to confirm that you will be here for the first part of the semester, arriving about February 20 and leaving on Easter weekend.

The flat is quite big enough for two; there is a study as well as a bedroom. Would you confirm, please, if you are bringing your wife with you and if you require a double bed? As noted in our information sheet, the college provides board and lodging for the Visiting Fellow and spouse.

There is a parking space for a Visiting Fellow's car, and, in my opinion, it is always preferable to have a vehicle. I would avoid the major car-hire companies, however, and after arriving negotiate a deal with one of the low-cost firms that specialise in five-year-old vehicles.

As far as your obligations are concerned, let

me say that you will be able to call your time your own, except for one or two talks on your specialty, which I understand is Canadian Studies. There is a rather active Canadian Studies association here, and they will want you to make a guest appearance. We also hope that you will join us each Monday and Thursday evening for high-table dinner.

The airport is about twenty kilometres away from Hobart. I would like to be able to pick you up myself and I would find it most convenient to meet you either on an early morning flight or a late afternoon one. It would give me pleasure to do this. I would hope that you could arrive by 20 February because we have Fellows' Dinner that night, and this would be a very good opportunity to introduce you to the students.

While the time in question is several months from now, we do like to pin down details well in advance.

If you have any questions or need for further information, please do not hesitate to ask. We want to do everything we can to make your stay with us meaningful and enjoyable. (By the way, you asked in a previous letter if the singing group The Seekers was still active here and if one might be able to see them. I must say I do not have the foggiest notion.)

With all best wishes,
Yours sincerely,
Dr. Dennis Lockridge, Principal,
Jane Franklin Hall,
University of Tasmania

Wally had met Lockridge through Arne Davidson, a professor in the English Department. Davidson had been the first Canadian invited to take part in Lockridge's Visiting Fellow Program. When Wally met the Australian in September 1995, Lockridge was on a bit of a tour to spread the word. Wally's interest was tweaked by the coincidence that his own doctoral dissertation was on John and Jane Franklin.

"So you would be interested in coming to Jane as a visiting fellow?" Lockridge asked over lunch in the University of Manitoba Faculty Club.

"Very much so," Wally said, though he hadn't thought a bit about it until then.

"Then please send me a letter expressing that."

The three of them talked about what a visiting fellow did: lived in a flat right on campus; made himself accessible to students and staff—as tutor, guest speaker, advisor, someone who had expertise on the country he came from; spent most of his time on his own work, in the writer-in-residence mode; immersed himself in the life of the college, but that obligation was never meant to be onerous.

When Lockridge was back in Tasmania, he sent a package of information to Wally, and Wally quickly responded with a formal request to be considered. In November, Lockridge wrote, "extending an invitation to you to come to us as a visiting fellow." Wally had some difficulty understanding that that was the extent of the selection process. But Davidson assured Wally that he'd likely passed Lockridge's test at their first meeting; Lockridge was apparently fond of saying, "What better criterion than good lunchmanship?"

So it was clinched, his plan to get away from the dreariness of his daily life and go to the other side of the world, at least for a couple of months. It was a good way to spend his sabbatical, but February 1997 was still nearly a year away.

He decided to answer Dr. Lockridge before he did anything else. One thing he had to clear up was Lockridge's assumption that he was married.

Dear Dr. Lockridge:

I will definitely plan on reaching Hobart and your most hospitable college by February 20. My sabbatical begins at Christmas, but I will take some time to wrap things up here. I hope to visit the mainland before going on to Tasmania.

Please forgive me for not having made it clear that I will not be accompanied by my wife. What I mean to say is that my wife and I were divorced some years ago.

I will be alone, I would still prefer a double bed.

I look forward to two productive months. I will make whatever presentations you or the Canadian Studies group may want me to make. I hope to work on a book about Canada's attempts to emerge from the shadow of the United States.

Thank you again for this opportunity to see and work in a different environment as a visiting fellow at Jane Franklin College. (And please forgive my query about The Seekers.)

I will be in touch again as the departure date nears.

Sincerely,

Wally Baxter

Wally waited for Erica to pick him up in front of his Osborne Village apartment building, an odd place that had high ceilings and broad doors and had once been a hospital. It was a pleasant evening, and he was dressed in a suit. He always wore suits to Rae and Jerry's, partly because it was a suit kind of place and partly because he didn't want to look like the typical professor—tweed jacket with leather elbows and baggy creaseless pants. One thing he didn't like doing in a suit was standing out on River Avenue waiting for someone. Erica was late. He kept looking east for her car; she'd said she drove a green Corolla, and sometimes he looked west past the Gas Station Theatre, as if she might be coming the wrong way on the one-way street. He wondered what had happened. Maybe she was trying to phone him while he was down here waiting. He went inside and ran upstairs to check for a phone message.

The door opposite his opened.

"Hi, Wally." It was Miles, his tattooed young neighbour. "Lock yourself out?"

"No, no. Just forgot something." Wally fumbled for his keys.

"I was just going to see if you were home. We've got pizza coming and I'm a bit short."

Typical of Miles, always living on the edge. He claimed to have spent eight months the previous year up north with Manitoba Hydro, making lots of money, but Wally had heard he'd been in Headingley Jail. Miles never had cash, and here was Wally with his hand already in his pocket.

"What's a wild Australian dog, five letters, the first two are B and I?" This came from a female voice inside Miles's apartment.

"*Bitch*," Miles called back. He smiled.

"It's *dingo*," said Wally. "The B must be wrong."

"*Dingo!*" Miles called.

"How much do you need?" Wally asked.

"Would thirty be okay?"

"You remember you owe me a hundred and thirty." Wally took two twenties out of his wallet and handed them to Miles.

"Whoa! That's great," said Miles. "Got a poker game going later so I'll pay you tomorrow. Hey, come on in and meet Stacy."

"I'm late…"

"Oh, come on. I want you to meet a real classy lady."

All right, he'd go in. He was always amazed at the beauty of Miles's women friends. Everyone knew Miles knocked women around, yet his reputation seemed to attract young women, not repel them.

"Hey, Stace, meet my very clever neighbour, Wally Baxter."

"Hello, Wally."

Stacy was, as far as Wally could tell from her slouched position on a futon, tall, perhaps twenty-two or -three years old, and gorgeous. She wore a long turquoise satin shirt, and Wally couldn't tell if she was wearing anything else. She had a newspaper folded crossword up, more or less in her lap, and her pencil hand was running through her long brown hair, rearranging it this way and that. Wally shook her free hand.

"Hi," he said.

"You're sure it isn't *bingo?*"

"It's definitely *dingo*."

"Then what's a Mexican place if it isn't *abode?*"

"*Adobe. A-d-o-b-e.*"

"*Adobe!* Of course." She rubbed out the word.

"It was nice to meet you, but I have to be on my way…"

"Aww … can't you stay and help me with this?"

"Yeah, stay, Wally. There'll be lots of pizza."

"No, no." One part of Wally wanted to stay, especially now that he'd been stood up by Erica. But he'd better check downstairs or call her. He headed out.

"'Colombian capital'?" Stacy called.

"Bogota!" Wally called back as he scampered down the stairs.

He met Erica coming in the outside door.

"Where have you *been?*" she said. "I've been honking and I'm parked at a bus stop…"

"You're late. I went back in to…"

"*I'm* late?"

They both had steaks and baked potatoes and manhattans and a bottle of Canadian pinot noir. Wally was mildly surprised that Erica liked Rae and Jerry's, where all the servers were women in identical unflattering red uniforms. But that was precisely what she liked—the fact that the women's attire didn't cater to sexist men. They discussed how easily a dinner date could fall off the rails because of some silly circumstance like somebody's clock being a few minutes out, and wasn't it good that two educated people were able to acknowledge that these things happened and there was no sense getting your shit in a knot over it. Erica had used the term *i.e.* exactly seventeen times, but Wally was beginning to see it as the flaw that made this woman bewitching, the way a mole becomes a beauty mark on a gorgeous face.

Sixteen days and three dates later, Erica invited him over for Sunday brunch. She said she'd like to try two new recipes, one she'd discovered and the other she'd created herself. Though they hadn't yet kissed, Wally thought they'd had some stimulating conversations; one had gone on for five hours, and the manager of the restaurant, a quiet little place in St. Boniface, had been forced to beg them to leave. When Erica called about brunch, he thought he detected a change in her tone. Was it sexist to think her voice was huskier? Whatever it was, he liked it.

2.

A MARRIAGE

Wally's marriage to Marjorie lasted eighteen years and hadn't seemed all that bad.

They met at the University of Saskatchewan, where they were both on the staff of the student newspaper, *The Sheaf*. That was after Wally had taken his legendary bus trip. As a grade twelve student in Saskatoon, in 1971, he had a friend who read Kerouac and wanted Wally to get out and discover the world with him. For months, they planned a summer jaunt to California. When the friend's father insisted he stay home and work instead, Wally told his parents he was going off on his own, and he was astounded that they consented. They said they'd never done anything so adventurous and they wished they had; this was the best time for him, when he was young and had no responsibilities. It was too easy—their consent almost took the fun out of it—but he did take off, by bus. His mother gave him snacks wrapped in waxed paper with notes that said things like "Beware the evils of alcohol" and "Take baths, not showers." Somewhere in Montana, a young woman boarded the bus and sat down beside him. At first, she terrified him with her friendliness, telling him she was a dancer hoping to catch on in Las Vegas and accepting one of his apples. He grew to like her, her throaty laugh, the musky scent of her. She took one of his sandwiches and laughed at the note that was wrapped into it: "Don't be too kind to strangers." Darkness fell, and, as they passed through towns, her eyes and her lipstick gleamed in contrast to her smooth dark skin. He couldn't believe what she wanted to do in the middle of the night, and, with the people near them either sleeping or ignoring them, she proved how flexible she could be, her sleek legs embracing him. When he looked back on the experience, he credited her not only with taking his virginity but also with helping to raise his consciousness of racial strife. When she disembarked, disappearing into the Vegas glitter, he realized he didn't know her name, and he worried for days that he'd caught something from her. Soon, though, he chose to see her as a happy experience, the highlight of his trip. When he returned to Saskatoon, he was anxious to increase the awareness of the civil rights movement. That fall, as a University of Saskatchewan freshman, he joined the staff of *The Sheaf* to put his views into editorials. On the fourth or fifth press night, he met Marjorie Sangster—white Anglo-Saxon Marjorie—who still lived at home with her parents, as did he. She liked listening to stories of his bus trip to California. They started to see each other, or date, or whatever the term was then, and they drove down to Regina for Roughrider football games, often with another couple. On the way home from one of those jaunts, with Harry Klassen and Jill Newton in the front seat, Marjorie surprised him by fondling him while Jill was talking. The next time they were alone, in the basement room of her parents' home on Wiggins Avenue, with the parents out at a party and her sister out babysitting, they made love on the shag carpet in the glow of a fake fire. He'd always remember the way her dark hair blended into the shadows, the way the light danced on her flesh.

They were sweethearts and lovers for the next few years, gaining a reputation for their hard work on student committees; if you wanted a function handled properly, you put Wally and Marj in charge. They promised their parents they wouldn't get married until after graduation. The summer they got engaged, just before their senior year, they went on a two-week trip to Europe. He'd always remember the morning Marjorie sat naked in the gabled window of an attic room in Paris, the sun highlighting her upthrust breasts, her bare nipples still moist and erect from their lovemaking. Posed there, she rivalled any painting of a nude he'd ever seen. From his supine position on the lumpy bed, he asked, "Aren't you worried someone might see you like that?"

She said, "It feels *good*, you know? Not caring, not worrying." She'd become reckless that way, and restless. He attributed it to their being away together, unmarried and unsupervised in the City of Love. They spent a few days driving "on the wrong side of the road" in the UK, and their favourite spot was Festiniog in Wales, where Marjorie charmed handsome labourers in the village pub. At the end of the two weeks, they faced the reality of going back to their studies and decided it'd be best not to move in together and, unsure if they could stand to live apart, they returned to their separate rooms, feeling like recaptured felons.

They made it through their senior year, trysting when they could, and they got married in 1975, shortly after graduating with their bachelor of arts degrees. They wrote their own vows. Harry Klassen played the guitar, and the ceremony took place in the bandbox near the stately Bessborough Hotel, where they spent their anticlimactic wedding night. They went to New York City for a five-day honeymoon, seeing the sights in their matching Yellow Cab sweatshirts. In the middle of a cloudburst one evening, they hurried arm-in-arm across an intersection, Broadway-musical playbills their only shields against the downpour, and Marjorie didn't miss her handbag, didn't know she'd dropped it into a puddle half a block back. When a young man overtook them and grabbed Marjorie's arm, both Wally and Marj were frightened, sure they were being mugged, until they realized that the fellow was holding the handbag under their noses. He'd seen it fall, he said, and he'd picked it up. They thanked him effusively, getting soaked in all the time this took, Marjorie hugging the fellow and kissing him on his stubbled cheek, Wally seeing the good deed as an omen that their marriage was blessed.

Back in Saskatoon, Marjorie encouraged Wally to pursue a graduate degree, saying she'd work and postpone children until he had his doctorate in history. He was accepted into a master's program at the University of Minnesota in Minneapolis, where Marjorie landed a job as a secretary and bookkeeper on campus while Wally drew a stipend for assisting his professors. They lived in an apartment near the campus, one with a Murphy bed that often threatened to flip back into the wall when their lovemaking was too vigorous. Their third-floor window overlooked a church steeple, and they noticed a pigeon perched on the cross every morning and evening. Marjorie swore it was always the same pigeon and she named it Jesus. "Morning, Jesus," she'd say when she got up, and Wally saw the bird as another good omen. They went to Gopher games, drank moderately at parties, and smoked the odd joint with new friends.

After Minneapolis, it was off to the University of Alberta in Edmonton for Wally's doctorate. His thesis looked at the significance of John and Jane Franklin in the development of Van Diemen's Land—the future Tasmania—and what drove John to his ill-fated Arctic expedition. Wally knew Marjorie was bored, waiting for the day when his studies would end and they could start a family. They had a little place near the campus, and every night they walked over to Whyte Avenue for coffee or a beer. She landed a good job in a bank. Time seemed to move slowly, and, one night, as they prepared for bed after several drinks and he got amorous, Marjorie said, "Wally, I'm fed up with fucking for the fun of it."

And just like that, she gave up on her original vow, and Wally, who was nothing if not accommodating, felt they were close enough to his goal; why *not* start a family? So Marjorie went off the Pill, and it seemed that now that they had a purpose, sex was better than ever. She was six months pregnant and joyfully crying when she watched

Wally receive his PhD. He hoped to find a position at either the University of Toronto or York in Toronto but the best offer came from Seneca College; at least it was still the Big City, and he thought he could settle in there and keep watching for openings at the universities. Marjorie was due in September, so she thought she'd better stay in Saskatoon to have the baby; that, after all, was where her parents and her doctor were. Wally took a small apartment on Finch Avenue and walked to his classes. Marj would say for years after that she programmed her body to give birth on a weekend; Wally got the news that she was in labour on a Friday night and made it home Saturday in time for Geordie's grand entrance into the world. Not long after that, an offer came from the University of Manitoba, and Wally snapped it up. He gave Seneca a couple of months' notice and wasn't due to start in Winnipeg until January, so he had time to spend with Marjorie and the baby and to look for a house that he eventually found in St. Vital, across the river from the campus.

By the following fall, Wally wanted to work on another child. "Geordie needs a sibling," he said, his heartbeat quickening with the memory of those all-too-brief nights of conception and Marjorie's rebooted enthusiasm. But Marj was disappointed with motherhood. Impatient with the demands of a tot, she wanted desperately to get back into the working world, maybe set up some kind of business of her own. Yet she felt it wasn't right to farm Geordie out somewhere too soon; sounding like a martyr, she said she'd wait until he was in school for full days. She wasn't too thrilled with Wally's marking papers and planning lectures night after night, but she rallied behind him when, in 1984, he got into trouble with the administration for conducting a survey that proved how little university students knew about Canadian history and geography; some even said the premier of Manitoba was Ronald Reagan. The survey itself—given to first-year students in arts and science—would've been all right if Wally hadn't leaked the results to the media. The local daily had fun with the fact that 18 percent of those surveyed thought the Group of Seven (Canadian artists) were members of the FLQ (Canadian terrorists). Upper administration did not appreciate the front-page headline "Canada Test Stumps Frosh." But Wally did succeed in getting Canadian Studies included in the curriculum.

As life calmed down and Geordie started kindergarten, Marjorie met the mothers of his classmates and grew envious of the ones who were wives of businessmen. She wished Wally had been an entrepreneur. He worked so hard; if only he could've been channeling that effort into profit-making enterprise. Why couldn't he be a *capitalist?* He said he thought *she* wanted to go into business. She said she'd only feel right if they could *both* be businesspeople; she hated to see him doing such *unmanly* work. They became embroiled in arguments about the rut they were in; Wally argued that it was the rut they'd been preparing him for through all those years of graduate school. They were invited for dinner by the parents of Geordie's pal Josh; the dad, Buzz Forsythe, ran a local car dealership. Buzz was such a good-looking and funny guy, Wally couldn't blame Marj for conversing with him most of the evening and envying him and his wife, Trix, for their two brand-new vehicles, which she insisted on seeing and test-driving. Marjorie said nothing as they drove home in their old Chevy Citation. Geordie said, "Dad, can we get a big new car like Josh's?"

By the time Geordie was in grade four, Marjorie had tried a few jobs and, for all Wally knew, had tried a few affairs. None of the jobs—account executive in an ad agency, office manager for a few dentists, TV station promotions coordinator—seemed to be the kind of thing she aspired to; and, if she was seeing other men, she must have been meeting them for nooners, and they weren't making her any happier. She said she thought she could find what she wanted if she were on her own. She told Wally she'd been thinking of leaving him for a long while. He said he wasn't surprised. Geordie was in junior high school when they finally agreed to split up. He was so precocious, they let him choose which parent he wanted to live with, and he chose Marjorie because he said her life had "a better infrastructure." He of course knew she'd be staying in the house and he'd be able to keep his room, and, besides, she made way better meals than Wally did. Wally rented an apartment in Osborne Village and agreed to take Geordie out for dinner at least once a week.

Wally wasn't surprised when Marjorie became head of the service department at Buzz Forsythe's dealership. She did start overtly seeing other men, yet events over the first year of their separation kept throwing her back with Wally: Marj's mother's illness, Geordie's school play, a break-in at their house. They'd get sentimental and end up in the sack. Wally would spend the night, but something—a call from Marjorie's latest boyfriend, a disagreement on how to handle Geordie, the ton of papers Wally had waiting to be marked—always sent Wally back to his creaky apartment.

Early in 1993, Bill Horton asked Marjorie to marry him. She accepted and quit her job with Buzz, hoping to get into some kind of business of her own. The odd thing was, Bill Horton wasn't the businessman Marjorie supposedly coveted. Bill Horton was a social worker. Wally didn't discuss this change of heart with Marjorie; perhaps she believed that social workers did more for the public good than either businessmen or professors. All she would say was that Bill Horton was "real together," and she and Wally went to their lawyers, and a divorce was arranged, but not without a lot of maudlin tears.

3.

MORNING OF THE IGUANA

On Sunday morning, Miles popped in to tell Wally he was going away for a few days and he had this assortment of flowers that he hated to throw into the garbage; would Wally like it? Wally thought it'd be a romantic gesture on his part to take flowers to Erica's; if she saw it as an advance, then so be it. He took them—a profusion of roses and carnations and lilies—and Miles let him borrow the vase. There was an unstated hint that the flowers would retire some of Miles's outstanding debt.

"Did you hear the weather report?" said Miles. "It might snow today. Snow in May? I'm outta here."

Wally went out in his favourite shirt, a pullover, good pants, and a reasonably unscuffed pair of loafers. He wasn't sure how to prop up the vase and the flowers in his Honda Civic; he ended up tying a plastic grocery bag around the vase and putting that in a box with scrunched-up newspapers all around as packing. He then strapped the box into the passenger seat.

Erica lived in a condo on Pembina Highway, near a bend in the Red River. You could see St. Vital Park on the other side. When Wally got there, five minutes early, there were no spots available in Visitors' Parking. He parked the car in an open spot reserved for the handicapped.

Leaving the flowers in the car, he buzzed Erica's number.

"Hello?" came her voice in a burst of loud static.

"Hi, it's Wally."

"Come right up, lover," he thought she said, but he might've been mistaken because of all the static.

The buzzer to open the door was activated.

"Wait, Erica?"

She didn't answer. The buzzer was still going.

"Hey, Erica!"

No answer. He'd better open the door. Before he grabbed the handle, the buzzing stopped. She was going to think he was a dolt for not opening the door. She might think he was nervous. Maybe she was a little anxious herself. How was she to know he was parked in a spot reserved for the handicapped? He buzzed her again.

"Hello?"

"It's Wally. Can you tell me where to park?"

"Park?" More static. "Visitors' Parking, Wally." He thought that was what she said.

"It's all full."

"Where's your car now?"

"In a handicapped spot."

"You can't leave it there," he thought she said, and something about a casserole; or had she called him an asshole?

No, maybe she'd told him to park out on the street if he had to.

He went outside. It was starting to rain. A young man came out behind him and Wally watched him walk to a car in Visitors' Parking.

"Are you leaving?" Wally asked.

"Nope."

The young man got into his low-slung Mustang, started it, revved it, lit up a cigarette, and turned on his stereo, loud.

What had been a sprinkling of rain became a shower. Wally eased his car out of the spot reserved for the handicapped. He could feel the young man watching him drive out of the lot and onto the street. He didn't like the idea of parking on a major thoroughfare like Pembina Highway. There was a motor hotel with a popular beverage room just up the road. Since today was Sunday, he thought they wouldn't mind his parking on the beverage-room parking lot; to be certain, he stopped at the main entrance of the motor hotel and ran inside to ask someone if it was all right. The young woman at the front desk smiled at him.

"Hello," Wally said. "I wonder if..."

She held up her hand and he noticed that she was wearing a headset telephone. "I'll be glad to send one up as soon as I find one," she said.

Wally had to wait for what seemed like a long time before her conversation ended and he made his request. She waved him off as if to say he could set up the Red River Ex on the lot for all she cared. He thanked her, went outside, and drove his car to the end of the lot closest to Erica's condo. He thought he could take a shortcut through some grass and a hedge that separated the motor hotel from the condo. It was pouring now. He wished he'd brought an umbrella, but it would've been difficult to carry the flowers in the box and an umbrella, too. He fumbled with the seat belt, finally released the box, lifted it out of the car and slammed the door. He hoped he could get to the condo before the flowers were ruined. He couldn't run with his burden, so he walked as quickly as it would allow. What he hadn't been able to see from the parking lot was that the grass on the other side of the hedge was sparse, more mud than grass. There was no opening in the hedge, so he had to go around it and then still walk through the mud. When he reached the condo canopy, soaked and splattered with mud, the flowers bent and the box a soggy mess, he remembered that he hadn't locked the car. It wasn't smart to leave a car unlocked these days. Car thefts in Winnipeg were at an all-time high; twelve- and thirteen-year-olds lurked nearby, perhaps just over the bank of the river, waiting for guys like him to leave their vehicles unattended, and then they'd jump in, cross a couple of wires, and whip around town on madcap joyrides. Wally had been putting off buying an anti-theft device; the least he could do was lock the car. He set the box down in the area between the outside door and the locked inside door and he ran back over the mushy course to his car. He locked it. By now, the rain had turned to wet snow. He trudged back, his hair matted over his eyes, his shirt, sweater, and pants drenched, his good shoes filthy. He felt chilled to his marrow. As he reached his destination, he noticed that not only had the young man who'd said he wasn't leaving left, but also there were

two other spaces vacant in Visitors' Parking. He picked up
the ruined flowers and rang the buzzer.

"Hello?"

"Hi. Believe it or not, it's Wally."

"Where have you been?"

His shoes wiped a hundred times in the condo lobby but
still muddy on top, Wally presented himself at Erica's door.
Her frowning face softened when she saw him. He noticed
that she was wearing an orangey caftan and black tights.
He smelled perfume: Sandalwood maybe.

"Flowers, Wally," she said. "What a shame; let me see
if I can save some of them. Oh, lilies! Don't you love their
deep throats?"

She took the box, which was now little more than a
shapeless cardboard bag, and rushed off with it somewhere. He stood there, afraid to go in. He was creating a
puddle on the corridor broadloom, like some comic-strip
character. He took off his shoes.

He called into the apartment, "Can I put my shoes…?"
But he let his voice tail off because he didn't know if she
could hear him.

"Come in and take everything off," she called from
somewhere. "I'll get you some towels."

Wally entered and closed the door. He had hoped he'd
be taking off his clothes in Erica's apartment this morning,
but under much different circumstances.

"Here, this'll warm you up," said Erica.

Wally sat in her living room, in one of those low-slung

easy chairs that you fell into with little prospect of ever being able to get out. He'd wrapped himself in the three beach towels that Erica had produced. There were about thirty-five plants in the room, and a fish tank that had no water in it, only some foliage and what he believed was an iguana. He knew people in Winnipeg who kept ferrets, but this was his first lizard.

Erica handed Wally a glass filled with something brown. He touched the glass, found it hot, almost dropped it, and wrapped both hands around it. He took a sip.

"A hot rum toddy," she said. "How is it?"

"G-good. Thank you. I'll stop sh-shaking in a m-minute."

"I didn't start the eggs or anything." She sat down on a dining-room chair.

"I'm s-sorry about this."

"Don't say that, okay? Don't blame yourself for something you have no control over—i.e., an act of God."

Ah, yes, *i.e.* It warmed him as much as the drink.

"I've got a tracksuit that might fit you," Erica said.

"I don't think I could get into one of your…"

"No, no, it isn't mine. A man I used to date left it here."

"Oh."

"Want to try it on?"

"No, it's okay, thanks."

"You're going to eat brunch in those towels?"

"My clothes are in the dryer; can we maybe wait for them?"

"That dryer takes forever. Come on, let me…"

"No, look, I'll be okay…"

"Oh, I know. You don't want to try on the tracksuit because it belonged to someone I used to date."

"All right, maybe I'm old-fashioned or something. I mean, I come over here today feeling pretty good about myself, and I run into some weather and that sort of … Well, I just can't put on some other guy's clothes, okay?"

"Okay!"

"Okay."

"Okay, then."

"Is that green fella over there alive?"

"The iguana? Yes, very much alive. And he's a she. I call her Sheena."

"After The Jungle Girl?"

"No, after the singer."

"How do you know she's a she?"

"The vet told me. He thinks she's carrying eggs. Do you want to hold her? She likes being held, i.e., she likes the warmth of a human body. You just have to watch out for her tail."

I.e. had lost its endearing quality. Maybe it was his situation—wrapped in towels and feeling stupid—but her saying *i.e.* suddenly grated on his nerves.

"I'm not really into iguanas," he said, "but I'll bet she's interesting to watch. Have you seen her shed her skin?"

"I think she's always shedding some part of it. Sure you don't want to hold her?"

"Not right now, thanks." He looked at Erica, standing up now and posing in a way that he found downright provocative. "Under normal circumstances, if I hadn't run into such lousy weather and hadn't wrecked the flowers and was still feeling as good as I was earlier, I'd be glad to hold her. But to be honest, I would've much rather held *you.*"

"Oh, ho!"

"What does that mean? *Oh, ho?*"

"It seems you've just moved our interaction to another level."

"I suppose I h-have."

"Tell me, Wally, are you harbouring an urge?"

Wally wished he wasn't sitting in this giant sponge of a chair. He made a mighty lurch and ended up on one knee on the floor, doing his best to keep the towels around him.

"I … I'm going to level with you," he said. "I came here today with more than an urge. I came here today with a *condom.*"

She smiled. "You came here with a condom. In your wallet, I suppose, with your keys and shoes in the bathroom."

"Right." He put the other knee on the floor so that it didn't look as if he was going to propose.

"Well, I'm not surprised, to be frank. The flowers sort of gave it away, i.e., they're kind of over the top. The question is, Do I *want* our relationship moved to this new level?"

These *i.e.*'s were making him feel aggressive. "No," he said. "I would say the question is, Would you have wanted this move under normal circumstances? If I wasn't chilled to the bone and waiting for my clothes to dry."

"So what you're posing is a theoretical question."

"All right, yes."

"Okay. If you hadn't got soaked and you were here with me, fully dressed, and you made this move of yours, would I go along with it?"

"That's the question."

"If I didn't go along with it and in fact didn't want it, you'd be on the verge of sexual harassment."

"I came here prepared to take that risk."

"It's always a question of timing."

"I agree."

"And you feel that this moment, at—what is it—eleven-fifteen on a Sunday morning, with you here on your knees and not wearing any clothes, is not the right moment for what you originally had in mind."

"I think I'm at a disadvantage, yes."

"What about me?"

"I didn't mean to suggest it has to be right for me only. It has to be right for both of us."

"It's important for you to get *buy-in* from me."

"I wouldn't put it that way, but, yes, it is."

"So, if you'd decided that this is it, i.e., this is the day..."

"Wait a minute."

"What?"

"Please, don't say *i.e.*, okay? It drives me up the wall. It's a term you'd use in an essay, not in conversation."

"It bothers you that much?"

"A lot, yes."

"You think I should say..."

"Whenever you want to say *i.e.*, just say *that is* instead."

"Well. Listen, I think we'd better have that brunch." She turned. "I thought we'd eat in the breakfast nook."

"Look, I'm sorry..."

She was already in the kitchen.

Weeks later, Wally wished there could've been more to his dalliance with Erica Mead. There wasn't. Just those restaurant meals and her rather tasty brunch—mac-and-cheese pancakes she'd taken out of a New York eatery's special cookbook and her own variation on eggs Benedict. She busied herself with serving and eating and clearing up and drying his clothes. She was cool to all his attempts to discuss anything of consequence. It was probably for the best that they didn't see each other again, and they could blame it on the Winnipeg weather.

He did have a dream about her, a couple of weeks after their brunch. Given the chaste nature of their relationship, the dream was surprisingly erotic: they were naked on his bed, and she was straddling him, head thrown back, losing herself in the pleasure, and, at its height, she cried out, *"I-I-I-eeee!"*

4.

LIGHTENING UP

His outings with Erica were the closest Wally had come to a relationship since his fling with Joyce. In the summer of 1993, shortly after his divorce had become final, his colleague Linda Friesen had asked him if he'd like to meet her friend.

"Joyce is divorced, too," Linda said over coffee in the Faculty Club, "but hers was *messy*. Hal was such an arrogant chauvinistic bastard, she needs to meet someone like you to restore her faith in men."

Linda said she and her husband, Emil, were taking Joyce on a cruise up the Red River. She suggested that Wally meet them on board. Wally was lukewarm to the idea, not at all sure that he wanted to meet anybody just yet, but it was summer, and he hadn't been on the Lord Selkirk for years. A local writers' group was sponsoring the cruise, inviting people to meet the Manitoba authors who were on board. Emil, Linda's high-school guidance-counsellor husband, had written a long novel called *The Elegant Bully* and hoped meeting authors would help him find a publisher.

"This guy is the most gentle man I know," Linda said when she introduced Wally to Joyce.

Wally wondered about Linda's comment—whether it cast him in a favourable light—but he liked Joyce's looks: her highlighted dark-blonde hair, the absence of makeup except for maybe a touch of lip gloss, pretty eyes that seemed to show both friendliness and confidence.

"There's the guy I wanted to see," Emil said, and he headed over to a bearded fellow who was standing at the railing.

Linda followed Emil, leaving Wally and Joyce only seconds after Linda had mentioned that Joyce ran a computer store. Wally asked her about word processors. He felt it was time he mastered an IBM-PC or an Apple. As the evening progressed, they became so engrossed in each other, they practically ignored the Friesens, to say nothing of the Manitoba authors. This led to a meeting in Joyce's store, a couple of product demonstrations, Wally's purchase of a Mac, dinner to celebrate the purchase, a bottle of Cristal champagne in Joyce's comfortable River Heights condo, a feverish embrace, a shucking-off of clothes, and a tumble into the satin pillows and stuffed animals that were heaped on Joyce's bed.

It wasn't until later, when he lay wide awake in his own bed, that he marvelled at what had happened. But everything had gone too fast. He'd had no time to feast his eyes on her or enjoy the feel of her or sense what moves she'd like; he'd been too busy trying to keep up with her.

Her heated rush to intimacy overwhelmed him. Now, in reflection, he had to believe that she liked him. This surely called for flowers. It must after all be the beginning of something meaningful and beautiful and long-lasting.

The next day, Wally sent Joyce a dozen roses, and he phoned her to tell her what a fabulous time he'd had. She said that was good but she didn't say what a good time *she'd* had, and she didn't mention the flowers. He asked her out for dinner the following Saturday, but she said she was busy. He asked her if she wanted to see the latest touring production of *Cats*, but she said she already had tickets.

Wally began to wonder what that great night together had meant to her. For all he knew, she always boffed her customers as a sort of one-time bonus.

He invited her out for dinner again, and she accepted. He took her a little gift—Red perfume—and she thanked him. When he called for her, he looked around her place for signs of the roses but didn't see any; of course, by this time, they would've died (that was the trouble with flowers). They went to Tiffany's restaurant, and they talked about their school days, avoiding anything to do with spouses. She said when he took her home that he hoped he wouldn't mind if she didn't ask him in; she said she was tired and she had to get an early start the next day. He noticed she'd been yawning, and he worried that his conversation skills were failing him. But he tried not to look disappointed; he didn't want her to think he was interested only in her body.

He asked her out to movies, to late-night snacks, to football games, to outdoor theatre; sometimes she went with him and sometimes she declined. Sometimes they went to bed and sometimes they didn't; when they did go to bed, she took the lead, moving them through the manoeuvres quickly as if foreplay was a highly overrated tactic that just delayed the good stuff. She often worked evenings, and she was never free on weekends. She'd go to the lake with friends on Friday nights, and was learning how to windsurf. She seemed to have no intention of introducing him to the friends; for all he knew, she was seeing other men. He'd spend the weekend thinking about her, staring at the snapshot he'd taken of her.

One Sunday night, he'd been thinking about her so much, he called her and, when she didn't answer, he left a message. He lay awake all night hoping she would call no matter what the time was. She didn't. He thought she could've been in a traffic accident and he listened to the news to find out if there'd been any fatal crashes on the highways. When the phone rang Monday morning, he grabbed it.

"Wally. Sorry I didn't call. I was beat when I got in."

"I was worried sick about you."

"Wally, you've really got to lighten up, you know?"

"Surely you realize how much you mean to me, how I think about you day and night, how important you are to me…"

"Wally, did you hear me? Would you please try to *lighten up?*"

Joyce called him the following Thursday.

"How'd you like to go to the lake on Saturday?" she

40

asked. "My friends have lent me their place at Clearwater Bay."

It was mid-September, and the weekend was going to be unusually warm. He was delighted that she wanted to give him a glimpse of her other world.

"I'll pick you up," she said. "I've rented a Jet Ski and I'll be hauling that."

Oh. He thought of protesting, not only because he wanted to be the gallant one and use his car and do the driving, but also because he was dead against the likes of power boats and skidoos—those adult toys that made a helluva lot of noise, aimlessly used up a non-renewable resource, and polluted the atmosphere. But she wanted him to *lighten up*, and this was no time to get heavy about the environment.

Wally waited on the steps of his apartment building in jeans, sneakers, and a New York tee-shirt that showed a King-Kong sized Kliban cat climbing the Empire State Building. In his married days, he would've brought a suitcase for a junket like this. Today he had only a Labatt's sport bag that contained little more than jockey shorts, a toothbrush, and some deodorant. He was wearing his bathing trunks under his jeans.

At precisely eight a.m., Joyce wheeled up in her Oldsmobile Cutlass, pulling a trailer that carried the Jet Ski—a sleek white machine with red and aquamarine rally stripes. She jumped out and went back to check the straps that held the Jet Ski in place. She was wearing a rather shapeless baby-blue tracksuit and no makeup, but her movements—assured, authoritative, and graceful—wrenched his heart.

He got into the passenger seat, and, when she got back in beside him, he said,

"You're a Greek goddess."

"Wally," she said, as she did a shoulder check and pulled out into traffic, "that'll be enough of that."

Just outside of town they stopped at a Salisbury House and picked up large coffees and a six-pack of doughnuts. They were quiet as they drove eastward toward Ontario, and Joyce played some Harry Chapin and George Michael. Maybe it was his Saturday morning blahs, or maybe it was because Joyce was in such control of everything, but Wally felt insignificant. He felt this great need to talk about their relationship, what it meant to her, where the hell it was going, but he couldn't. She wouldn't let him.

He started to sing "On the Road Again." She hummed along, decidedly off-key.

She changed in a back bedroom while he looked around the log cabin—the stone fireplace, the framed photo of somebody's golden lab, the row of old hardback books, the open chess board. When Joyce appeared in an orange and black one-piece, the word that occurred to him was *business-like*. She was curvaceous and well-proportioned and tanned, but she looked ready to *do* something. He thought they might fool around a little or have a bit of lunch, but no, they were going out. He pulled off his tee-shirt and stepped out of his jeans.

He grabbed the towel she'd put out for him and jogged out ahead of her. The cottage lot ran right down to the water, and there was a place where you could launch a boat. She'd backed the trailer down the runway so that its wheels were nearly submerged. He ran down to the sand and did a belly flop into the water. Joyce headed straight for the Jet Ski.

"Hey, I'll give you a hand with that," he called.

She unhooked the straps and started to lift the Jet Ski off the trailer into the water. She didn't look that muscular, but she obviously had good strength, and she knew what to do with leverage. Before he could scramble out of the water, she had the machine off its perch. She steadied the handlebars and held the Jet Ski so that it wouldn't list over onto its side.

"You sure are capable," he said.

"Hold this like this for a minute, would you?" She had him keep the Jet Ski upright while she went back and put on a life jacket.

He found the machine heavy and tippy, and it was all he could do to keep it from flopping over onto him. His admiration for her was growing by the minute.

"I'll take it for a spin, and then it'll be your turn," she said.

"No, no, it's okay, I'll just watch you." He wouldn't be caught dead on one of these things.

She had him hold the machine while she mounted it and knelt on it, placing her hands on the handlebars, which you could move up and down as well as sideways. He managed to stand clear when she gunned it; it rose out of the water, and she took off across the bay. There were no boats around, and the surface was relatively calm, so she churned up her own waves and made troughs that she could dive into. She resembled a rodeo rider. She waved to him and shot away from him over toward some docks and cottages way off on the other side of the bay. He enjoyed the sight of her enjoying herself, and, maybe for the first time, he thought it was wrong to try to "win her" or "make her his." It was essential that she be a free spirit.

"Your turn," she said when she came back, bringing the Jet Ski to a submerged stop right beside him.

"No, no, it's okay," he said.

"Come on, you have to."

"I hate things like motorcycles and skidoos. It's okay, I like watching you."

"It's all right to watch, but it's a lot more fun to do it yourself. Like most things in life."

She took off the life jacket and handed it to him. He took it, sure that she'd only be happy if he tried. She watched while he put the jacket on and did up the buckles. Using her strength and the buoyancy of the water, she held the Jet Ski more or less upright while he knelt on it the way she had.

"You steer it like a bike," she said, "and you'll see that your turns have to be really gradual. Press the green button to start it, the red to stop. Keep your right thumb on the throttle. The key to getting started is to give it lots of gas; that keeps you upright. Remember: *lots of gas*. If you fall off, don't worry, it'll come back to you like a boomerang, and you can pull yourself back on with the handlebars."

Joyce was earnest in her instructions and he thought he'd absorbed them, but there was a part of him that resisted.

"One ... two ... three, go!" she said, and he gave it gas.

The jet shot water out between his legs. He moved forward but only a few feet. The machine listed to the right. He and the Jet Ski sank into a few feet of water.

"You didn't give it nearly enough gas," she said.

"I'm not meant for this kind of sport," he puffed.

"You didn't give it enough gas."

"I thought I did."

"You didn't. Come on, you're going to master this."

Wally wondered why he had to. What did it matter? He'd tried, hadn't he?

She got him into position and sent him off and again he went a few feet and foundered. By now a few people had come out to swim a couple of cottages away, and they were watching. She kept on him about the gas. She made it sound so simple. He felt exhausted. She insisted he try again. So he did. This time he noticed how the gas affected the balance. He was moving ahead. She yelled at him to give it more gas. *More.* That was it! He felt the power lift him and the machine out of the water. He steered out into the bay. He was positioned a little too far back; he felt sort of splayed on the Jet Ski; it was dragging him. With an effort, he was able to pull himself farther forward and steer and stay upright. It was all in the amount of gas you gave it. She was right! He leaned a little to the left and he realized that he could start to move into a wide arc. He skimmed across the water, the wind and the spray feeling wonderful on his face. He aimed at a boathouse on the far bank. As he got closer, he leaned again and turned the Jet Ski in another direction.

Wally felt in no danger of falling now, as long as he kept on the gas and steered cautiously. He wasn't going to attempt Joyce's acrobatics, but he loved the feeling of independence out in the open water. He had one big toe sort of bent too much, but it didn't bother him. He headed back. Joyce was just a speck on the shore. He aimed toward her and poured on the power.

As he got within a hundred yards or so, his toe was starting to ache and he thought he should go in. Joyce held up her hand, probably meaning that he should cut the gas. He leaned. The toe didn't feel *that* bad. He was going to go back out again. He understood now what people saw in these damned things, the sheer hedonistic pleasure of them. He leaned more daringly than before. This enabled him to turn away from her at just the right moment. He took one hand off the handlebar long enough to wave. She waved back. He was pretty sure she was smiling. He soared across the water like a pelican. No, something lighter. A seagull? No, lighter still.

5.

UNCLE NATE'S

Wally couldn't concentrate on the papers he was marking. It was October 8, 1996, three years since Joyce had moved to Vancouver. Sometimes he wondered if that summer had ever happened, and he'd go to his filing cabinet and pull out the photos she'd given him—the two that she said had been taken by a professional photographer when she was thinking she might be a model. In one, she was modelling a dress, but in the other she was looking at the camera with pouty lips and a suggestive expression, and she was holding what might have been a man's shirt partly open to show off the upper curves of her bare breasts. She'd given him the photos the day she announced she was moving. She'd landed a good job in Vancouver, a place she said she'd always wanted to live. She was going to be manager of a computer store, with a chance of eventually becoming part-owner.

There he'd been, that afternoon at the log cabin, smugly

believing that his mastery of the Jet Ski had clinched their relationship. But it meant nothing to her; all she'd done was prove to him that he was capable of a lot more than he thought. She saw it as a lesson learned, a good note to leave on. He thought about her incessantly for months, tried phoning her several times, did speak with her once and suggested he'd like to fly out there to see her, only to be told that she was too busy and it'd be too awkward. He gradually got over her or thought he had until the next time he felt lonely and pulled the photos out again.

He wasn't going to do that tonight. To hell with marking; he'd head downtown to the bar his colleague Ross Flanagan always talked about. Ross might even be there.

The place was a spacious basement lounge called Uncle Nate's. It seemed busy for a cool mid-week night. He didn't see any sign of Ross; perhaps if he sat up at the bar, Ross might spot him. There were empty stools at the bar, and Wally took one of them, recognizing the bartender as the guy Ross had described. He wore a straw boater, a red bow tie, and a blue-striped shirt with red arm bands. He looked as if he was part of a vintage barbershop quartet. What Wally could see of his hair was ginger coloured, and he had a ginger Chaplinesque moustache.

Wally ordered a Heineken.

"One Heinie coming up," the bartender said, tossing a rolled-up towel into his sink as if he were executing a basketball shot from outside the key.

When the bartender delivered the beer, Wally said, "Has Ross been in tonight?"

"Ross?"

"Ross Flanagan."

"Don't know him. What's he look like?"

"Oh … about my height, a little more hair than I have, gun-metal grey, nicely trimmed beard, John Lennon glasses, a ready smile. Good-looking guy about my age…"

"Sounds like Wally. Yeah, Wally. Baxter, I think he said his last name was. I haven't…"

"Wait, *I'm* Wally Baxter."

"Then I guess there's two of you."

Shaken by this, Wally wondered who was playing games, the bartender or Ross. "Did … did you see that name on his credit card?"

"Always pays cash."

The bartender, whose name tag read *Harvey*, turned to take an order from one of the servers. He opened fridge doors, uncapped bottles, pulled levers for draft beer, selected glasses, cut limes, distributed ice cubes, poured liquor, all in a certain rhythm. Miffed as he was, Wally found Harvey's modulated moves fascinating; he had turned his chores into an art.

"Ross, eh?" Harvey said, as he poured another beer for Wally. "Naw. Seems more like a Wally to me." He chuckled.

"I wish he'd come in right now," Wally said. "I'd love to hear his explanation."

As Harvey returned to his ballet, he looked off into a crowded part of the lounge, staring for a few moments, filling an order, looking there again as his hands did their thing. He leaned over to Wally.

"You got a few fans over there," he said.

"I have?"

"Table in the corner. The four chicks."

Wally saw them. They were grouped around one of the

tables, and at least one of them was facing in his direction. There was an opening—a path—through all the drinkers, from Wally to the women. He had a good view of the one who was facing him, and she seemed to stare at him for a short time and then look down at her table and then look at him again. The other women were chatting, looking over at him only occasionally, and, though there was a cacophony of chatter in the place, he could identify each outburst of laughter that came from their group. Now one of the other women looked at Wally, and, as she glanced down at something on the table, he thought he heard her cry out, "That's *good!*"

If Wally wasn't mistaken, he thought the woman facing him was holding a pencil. Was she writing something? One of the women picked up a sheet of paper off the table and looked at it and looked at him and back at it. At the same time that it struck him what the woman facing him must be doing, Harvey said, "By god, I think she's *drawing* you."

"You think…?" Wally blushed.

"Want me to go and tell her she can't do that in here, or are you goin' over to demand a modelling fee?"

The idea of going over there hadn't occurred to Wally, but why not? Especially with a couple of beers in him and Harvey cheering him on. Wally winked at the bartender— the kind of thing he *never* did—and stood up from his bar stool and walked toward the women. They seemed surprised, apprehensive. One smirked. He approached the artist, as best he could with other people and their chairs in the way. He held out his hand to her.

"Hi," he said. "I'm Wally Baxter. The bartender thinks you might be doing a sketch of … of me."

"Hello," she said. She looked embarrassed, but she smiled and shook his hand. "I'm Carolyn. I thought I could do this—you know—inconspicuously. I hope you don't mind. I come to a place like this, I have to..."

"Show it to him," said one of the others.

"Oh, yes, sorry." Carolyn held it up for him. "It's not quite..."

"It's good, isn't it?" said the one closest to Carolyn. "Looks just like you."

"Oh, Wally," said Carolyn, "this is Freya—and Anita—and that's Trish."

"Hi there, hi," he said. "You're right, Freya, it is good. I mean, I think it's flattering."

"Do you want to join us?" Freya asked. She gave him a smile that he could only call *aggressive*.

"Oh, no, it's all right," Wally said. "Thank you anyway." He didn't say what he thought: The group of you together is a little overwhelming.

Just as Trish or Anita was saying, "Aww, come on, we won't bite," Carolyn said, "Do you mind if I join *you?*"

The others looked astounded. Wally, just as surprised, said, "Well, yes, I mean, *no*, if you'd like to, please do."

The three friends groaned and objected as Carolyn packed up her things. People at adjacent tables were looking now. Carolyn gave her friends a little wave as she accompanied Wally back to the bar. He carried her beer. As she sat down on the stool beside his, Harvey gave Wally a signal that said Aww-right!

"That ... that isn't a bit like me," said Carolyn, red-faced. "Being impulsive like that, I mean. You see, they've been hounding me to go out with them for weeks. They think I stay home too much and I should get out and see people. They tell me I'm too *good* as if *good* is the *worst* thing you could be. I think I just wanted to shock them a little.... Oh, but I've *used* you, haven't I? I'm sorry if you think I've used you."

"Not at all. You've livened up my evening. First, to draw me, and then..."

"It was Freya's idea, her way of getting me to come along. She knows I like to sketch people from life, and she thought a bar was a great place to see all kinds. I like to relax in a crowd and just start drawing anyone at random."

"Oh, so it wasn't my distinguished features that..."

"Sorry, I don't mean to say ... oh, I always put my foot in it. Really, something about you *did* catch my eye; I mean, I could've started with him or *him* or..."

"I was just joking. I'm flattered. And you have done a good sketch. Do you do a lot of drawing?"

"I've sold the odd sketch and a few paintings, but I'm a graphic designer by trade. Work for a small design boutique run by some very creative young men."

"I'll buy that sketch you did tonight."

"Oh. It isn't finished."

"I'd still like it."

"I'll *give* it to you."

"I definitely want to pay you, and I'd like you to sign it."

Carolyn took two sips of her beer, looking at Wally over the rim of her glass. It seemed as if it was finally dawning on her that she was sitting with him, a total stranger, in Uncle Nate's, a place notorious for pickups. He wondered if it was fear he saw in her eyes, or was she assessing him, or assessing the *risk?*

"Would you like another beer?" he asked.

"No … no, thank you. Maybe I should go back to the girls…"

"Hey, I thought you wanted to shock them. Why don't we go someplace for coffee?" The suggestion slid so easily out of Wally's mouth, even *he* was surprised. At the same time, he was wondering what Erica would think. Am I being pushy? Am I ignoring her signals?

Carolyn squirmed, and she glanced over at Freya and Trish and Anita. "I … I don't … it's not … you're married, aren't you."

"Why do you say that?"

"Freya said every man that comes in here looking for women is married."

"I'm afraid that Freya is wrong. I'm not married; I'm divorced. Have been for a fairly long time now. What about you?"

"I … I'm a widow."

"Oh, I'm sorry."

"It's okay … he's been gone for … for quite a few years. Like I told you, the girls have been bugging me to go out with them. Tonight, I just thought it was time."

"I'm a history prof. I never do this kind of thing—go to bars. I got fed up with marking papers tonight and decided to give myself a break. A colleague of mine talks about this place all the time, and I thought I might see him here."

"And you didn't."

"No."

"For some reason … I believe you. And I'm glad we met."

He looked at her; she was smiling at him. She was

attractive in a quiet sort of way. She was wearing clothes that he thought were old-fashioned; a loose shirt buttoned to the neck, shapeless khaki pants, a green cloth jacket draped over her shoulders. Her brunette hair was medium length and unruly, as if she might consider any kind of hairdo unnatural. Her face, still rather flushed, was pretty, but the look on it was apprehensive.

"There's a Salisbury House not far from here," Wally said. "Let's go there for coffee and really flabbergast your friends."

"I ... can't ... I mean, I can't believe I'm saying this, but ... I'd *like* to leave here with you. That is ... if you don't mind driving me home. I came in Anita's car."

My god, she isn't feeling harassed! "I'll be glad to take you home," he said.

"You do remember where your car is?" She laughed. "I'm sorry, I'm being silly.... Freya was telling us about the last time she was here. She met a man—she's married and so was he, but that doesn't stop Freya—oh, aren't I awful? Well, they agreed to leave separately and meet at his car, and he told her what level of the parkade it was on, and she went there and waited and waited. You know how awful it is to be alone in a concrete parkade, just standing there. He never did show up. She was sure he must've got the level wrong, but she didn't look on any of the others. She was mad. They never saw each other again."

Wally chuckled. "We don't have to leave separately, do we?"

"No, no, of course not."

"Are you ready to go, then?"

"I think so. Yes, I am. I'd better tell them what I'm doing. I don't want to be *completely* rude."

Carolyn finished off her beer, and, while she went over to speak to her friends, Wally summoned Harvey, paid his bill, and arranged to pay Carolyn's.

Harvey said, "Found a live one, did you?"

"Oh, I don't know…"

"If the other Wally Baxter shows up, I'll tell him you got lucky."

"You do that."

As Wally and Carolyn headed for the exit, she said, "You should've heard them." She imitated each of their voices: "'You've hardly said two words to him.' 'He could be an ax-murderer.' 'That's the last time we invite *you* out.'" She laughed.

When they settled into Salisbury House booths with doughnuts and decaf, Wally asked her about her work. She told him she'd most recently designed a corporate-identity package for a local cheese company. He recognized the brand. As she spoke, he watched her, wondering why a designer wouldn't be dressed more stylishly. Perhaps the frumpy clothes were intended to discourage men; he instantly scolded himself for such a thought. Hadn't he learned *anything* from Erica Mead?

She wanted to know about *his* work, what levels he taught, what he thought of today's students. He found himself telling her about some specific undergraduates, how they sat in the lecture hall, what they wore, what questions they asked. He exaggerated some descriptions because he wanted to make her laugh. He loved her laugh. He assumed that she hadn't laughed a lot in recent years, and he wanted to encourage it.

A server came to offer them refills.

"Oh, … oh, no, thanks," Carolyn said, "I really must be going."

"Okay, none for me, either, thanks. Let's not forget the sketch."

"Are you sure you…"

"I'm sure." He pulled out his wallet and, as discreetly as he could, tucked a folded pair of twenties under her plate.

She was taking the drawing out of her satchel when she saw his gesture. "Please. I want to give it to you."

"Just sign it and it'll be worth far more."

"Oh…" She signed her name on the right side, close to what was a good reproduction of his shirt collar. He saw that her last name was *Webb*. "Thank you," she said, passing the drawing over to him. "You're much too generous. You should've at least let me buy the coffee."

On the way to her place, he noticed that she sat rigidly against the passenger door. She directed him to a Munroe Avenue address in East Kildonan. He talked about the times he used to drive to EK for Dutch Maid ice cream. He mentioned a party he'd been invited to on Watt Street and he fell into a version of the old Abbott and Costello routine: "'He lived on what street?' 'That's correct.'" Carolyn didn't laugh. Wally wondered if he was trying too hard. Or was she worried that he might turn into an ax-murderer after all?

In front of her bungalow, he stopped the car, and, before he could put the gear into park and turn off the ignition, she said, "You don't need to get out. I'll be fine. Thank you for everything."

"You do believe I'm an unmarried history professor who lives alone, don't you?"

"Yes, ... yes! I'm just feeling a little embarrassed right now. Or maybe not embarrassed. I just don't go out much. Well, I told you that..."

"Carolyn. I'd like to see you again. Maybe I could call you at work—after you've had a chance to check up on me?"

She looked at him, smiled self-consciously, and leaned over and kissed him on the mouth.

"I take it that's a yes," he said.

Without speaking, she gathered up her satchel, hurried out of the car, and almost ran up her sidewalk. He waited until she was inside, and then he drove away.

"Carolyn Webb speaking."

"Carolyn. Wally Baxter."

"Well, hello. *The* Wally Baxter—history professor, specialist in Canadian studies, advocate of Canadian culture and the arts."

"You checked."

"No, Freya did. She knows one of your former students."

"So. After last night, she's still speaking to you."

Carolyn laughed—that melodious laugh. "Oh, yes. She's too inquisitive to be offended."

"That's good. Well ... um ... do you think you might like to go out for dinner on Friday night?"

"Wally, I'd like to see you on Friday night ... but, Wally, *I'm making you dinner.*"

6.

CLASS DISMISSED

The polar bear stretched to its great height and sat back on its haunches as if it were a catcher ready to receive a pitch from Geordie.

"He's smiling at you," said Wally.

"Don't you think they could open the space up more?" said Geordie. "Be more creative with the rock formations?"

Wally nodded. It was late Thursday afternoon, and he'd picked up his son from school for their weekly outing. Geordie at sixteen was as tall as Wally—around six feet—and lean, with a pleasant face; everybody said he was lucky to have Marjorie's nose. Today, despite the cold, they'd chosen the Winnipeg Zoo because Geordie liked to check up on the polar bears. He'd always been a fan of bears; in fact, he and Wally talked about taking the train up to Churchill to see these majestic animals in their natural habitat. There was talk about cutting the rail service, and Wally wanted to plan a trip before that happened.

Geordie's concern for the bears was part of a greater concern for the environment. Geordie was critical of Bill Horton for throwing milk cartons and soft drink cans into the main garbage instead of the blue box—pretty weird behaviour for a social worker. Wally thought that the few days with Geordie on a trip to Churchill would be a great bonding opportunity. But there was always something else that one of them had to do.

"If I get to be a lawyer," said Geordie, "maybe I can do something for polar bears. Maybe I can run for political office and make it part of my platform."

"No need to wait. Start your own club. Special-interest groups get most of the attention these days. Start up the Polar Bear Party—has a certain ring to it."

"You could help me."

"I'll get out on the lecture circuit. We could have tee-shirts made..."

"Dad. Why do you turn everything into a joke? I'm serious."

The polar bear moved out of its squat and strolled off to another part of the compound, its white fur coat loose on its body, as if there wasn't a bear inside at all but two short men, one behind the other.

"You've decided, then, have you? On law? You were all for medicine last week."

"No, I haven't decided."

"As long as it isn't social work."

"*Dad.*"

"Geordie, how are things on the girlfriend front? You are going out a bit, aren't you, getting away from the computer screen once in a while?"

"There's a girl in my class who beats me in the Indy 500. It's scary."

Wally grunted. He'd crashed his car every time he'd played Geordie's video game. Sometimes he worried about his reflexes.

"So, Dad, are *you* seeing someone?"

"I'll bet your mother told you to ask me that."

"No, I thought it up all by myself."

"As a matter of fact, I'm seeing someone Friday night. She's an artist—a pretty good one."

"An art professor."

"No, no. She works for a graphic design outfit. Look, it's not serious. Especially since I'm going away for a couple of months."

"You are?"

"End of January. I'm taking a sabbatical. I'll be a visiting fellow at a university in Australia."

"Wow. Wait till Mum hears this."

"Yes, you can tell her, if you like."

Friday, Wally stewed about his impending dinner date as he headed for his first class of the day. He had thought about Carolyn for most of the previous night; he didn't want to mess up by being too serious or too forward, but he did feel he'd like to get to know her. If only he could avoid looking desperate and be natural, whatever the hell *natural* was.

This was an introductory course, taught to a theatre full of first-year kids who didn't know the Quebec Act from the Magna Carta. The accepted practice for groups this size—a hundred and fifty in the theatre and seventy-five more watching on closed-circuit TV—was to lecture. Wally agreed with present-day purists that lecturing was a lousy teaching technique, at least for some people. For him, most of the time it was a performance, an art form. He believed that the best prof he'd had in his undergraduate days was old Anthony Burton. It was Burtie's orating ability that had influenced Wally more than any other single factor; it not only sparked his interest in history, but it also ignited a passion within him, a passion to be a professor, and a bloody good one. He saved his best performances for the first-years. Whether they'd learned anything in high school or not, he was going to bring history to life for them, and he had every lecture planned and outlined and rehearsed, each one in its own file folder.

"Hey," said Alicia Thornton (or was it Silverthorne?) as she walked past him.

"Hey, Doc," said a young man entering the theatre beside him.

The last few stragglers made their way to their seats.

Wally set his books and his file on the podium and looked up at the throng. His heartbeat accelerated. It always did accelerate a few moments before a lecture, but today it seemed faster, its thumping almost audible. Most of the young bodies were settled, facing him. Some in the back looked bored, some stoned. Some seemed ready to laugh at his opening remark, sure it was going to be funny. Many of the young women had those odd side curtains of hair framing their faces like alcoves. Most of the young men wore tee-shirts with slogans or logos on them. One in the back read:

Eat me

Lick me

Suck me

Do me

Wally couldn't read the next line because another guy's ball-capped head was in the way. Several young women sat in the front row in skirts, one of them daring him like Sharon Stone in *Basic Instinct*. A few chatted, a kid half way back was punching his buddy, but most of them were attentive. He gave them his patented pause, letting their outside worlds fade.

He opened today's file.

"You'll recall the other day we were talking about..."

He stared at the first page in the file, the review of the last class in point form and the anecdote he'd tell to reinforce the main message. It looked familiar. Too familiar.

"We..."

Some students frowned. Some began to giggle.

He suspected what was wrong. He *knew* what was wrong.

He'd brought the wrong file. He'd brought the one for the previous class.

When he was younger, if he'd brought the wrong notes, he would've faked it, proving what a pro he was by fabricating every sentence as he went along because he was so steeped in the knowledge of his subject. Once, when he was inebriated from a liquid lunch to celebrate a colleague's new book, he'd gone to class without a file and given the best lecture of his life. He'd tried that only once more: the time he stood with his right foot hooked around his left ankle, started to lean sideways and couldn't unhook the foot. He crashed to the floor. Despite his quick recovery, jumping up and blurting out some quotation about the "fall of man," he vowed never again to lecture when he was shit-faced.

These days, he always brought the right file. But today he hadn't.

Goddamn middle-aged infatuation. He'd let it mess with his head. Had he learned nothing from Joyce about lightening up?

"You know, there are times," he said in his strongest unwavering voice—he might've told them he'd made a mistake and had to go back to his office for the correct file, but instead—"times when the most effective way to use an hour is to take a spontaneous break. That's it for today."

The students cheered. They weren't going to question him or hang around to see if he was serious. They vacated the theatre before you could say John A. Macdonald.

Wally's office phone rang.

"Hello?"

"Wally?"

"Marjorie."

"Is this a good time to talk?"

"Sure."

"Geordie tells me you are going to Australia."

"Correct."

"When?"

"Not until February. I told Geordie that."

"He said it was the end of January."

"I leave on February the tenth."

"And you're going for how long?"

"Eight weeks."

"Two months, Wally? Aren't you forgetting something?"

"What?"

"Your weekly obligation. To Geordie. You're his father, Wally. He needs you in his life. Once a week, we expect you to go out with him, have a nice meal with him, discuss *masculine issues* with him. You can't expect *Bill* to be your surrogate."

"I *don't* expect Bill … Marjorie, it's a sabbatical."

"You should've cleared this with me."

"All right. You're right. I should've."

"Who's going with you?"

"Nobody."

"You're going alone?"

"Yes."

"Wally, I'm surprised. Have you not considered taking Geordie with you?"

"He's in school."

"Come on, Wally. You *know* how bright he is. The school would let him go in a heartbeat. The enriching experience would be invaluable to a boy his age."

"Have you asked him? What does *he* think?"

"Oh, Wally, you know he'd love it. Why don't you discuss it with him the next time you meet?"

Wally found the house on Munroe. It looked more cheerful than he remembered—the white stucco with the green trim—but perhaps his mood was affecting what he saw. He took the bottle of Wolf Blass Yellow Label pinot noir in its gift bag and stepped out of his car. He wondered if the red-and-gold bag wasn't too Christmassy. Wait. Why had he brought Australian wine? He didn't want to mention his sabbatical yet, did he?

He walked up the sidewalk to the front door and rang the bell. He expected to hear a dog bark—he wasn't sure why—but he didn't. He heard only a gust of wind in the fir tree nearby, until Carolyn came to the door. There was some fumbling with a latch. The door opened.

"Good evening, Wally," she said. She may have been nervous—her face flushed—or maybe she wore more makeup. She was dressed in a black shirt and black pants. "Oh, thank you! You didn't have to, but thank you, that's nice of you."

She took the bottle, and Wally stepped inside. He detected an unmistakable aroma: roast beef.

"Smells awfully good in here," he said.

"Oh, good. You like beef. I should've asked you, but something told me you wouldn't be a vegetarian. It's just a little roast; how do you like it?"

"Any way you want to serve it."

"Speaking of that, I'd better check it. There's a hanger."

She went into the kitchen while he took off his leather jacket and hung it up. As he went in, he noticed how immaculate everything looked. It was an older home, but it had a spruced-up appearance—no cracks in the walls, recently painted. He found the kitchen.

"I was going to serve it medium rare," she said. "We have maybe ten more minutes. Go in there to the living room; would you like a drink?"

"Please. What do you have?"

"Scotch?"

"Excellent."

"Will Glenfiddich be all right?"

"Oh, yes!"

Wally went into the modestly furnished living room and noticed that the table in the adjacent dining room was set. He couldn't help feeling smug. This attractive woman, whom he'd met only by chance, had cooked his favourite dinner and was about to bring him his favourite pre-dinner drink. He looked around for signs of her husband—perhaps a wedding photo—but he saw none. There were a few framed paintings and drawings that likely were hers, most of them realistic pastoral scenes. He wished he had put her drawing of him in a frame instead of shoving it into a dresser drawer.

"There you go," Carolyn said, handing him the drink.

"Oh, thank you. Aren't you having one?"

"Not if you want your beef just right. Please, sit down."

"I was admiring your pictures. All yours?"

"Yes, I'm afraid so."

"They're all very good. I especially like…"

"Sorry, I've got to get back; everything's nearly ready. Do sit."

Wally took a closer look at one drawing that must be the pavilion at Assiniboine Park. He took a sip of his drink, with one ice cube—just the way he liked it. As he sat down on the chesterfield, Carolyn appeared in the dining room.

"Everything is ready," she said. "Would you sit over here, Wally?"

Wally moved to the dining room. Carolyn opened the pinot and set it near Wally. She then brought out the dinner—roast beef, green peas, mashed potatoes, red pepper—already served in generous portions. She pointed to the gravy and the horseradish and told him to help himself. He poured the wine.

After he had complimented her on the meal and thanked her profusely, he asked her about her friends, the ones she'd been with the night he met her. Carolyn admitted that, for some time now, she had been living vicariously through Freya and her colourful escapades. Wally told her about Ross Flanagan, how that very morning he had told Ross he'd been to Uncle Nate's and pretended he was Ross. "Your name worked wonders,' I told him. 'It helped me pick up a very attractive woman.' And he believed me, that's how much of an egotist he is." Carolyn laughed her lovely laugh. Wally felt encouraged to tell her about taking the wrong file to class, and so he did, embellishing it with exaggerations. Carolyn listened and stared at him, awe-struck.

"You dismissed four hundred students?" she gasped.

Moved perhaps by the wine and the scotch, he felt compelled to say, "All because of you."

They sat and talked at the dining room table long after they were finished the strawberry-and-ice-cream dessert and decaf coffee. Carolyn laughed at virtually everything Wally said. He was enchanted.

It was nearly ten o'clock when he helped her clear the table. He offered to help with whatever needed to be done in the kitchen.

"No, no," she said, "I'll just load up the dishwasher and leave everything else until tomorrow. There really isn't much to do."

"Should we watch a little TV?"

"You know, Wally, … I've had a heck of a week at work. I … I'm pretty weary. I'm sorry to be a party-pooper, but…"

Wally felt crushed but tried not to show it. "I completely understand," he said, even though he didn't.

"Are you sure you don't mind? I'm sorry, honestly. I'm even getting a little woozy. It happens to me; I get to a point where I just have to crash."

"No need to apologize, Carolyn. I've been jabbering away—"

"No, no, Wally, I've enjoyed every minute tonight, honestly. I've just hit a wall."

She did look tired. He headed for the closet by the door and took out his jacket.

"Carolyn, I truly haven't had such a delicious dinner for a long while." He zipped up his jacket. "Can I call you, and maybe we can see each other again next week?"

"Oh, Wally, of course you can, of course we can. It's been fun."

He looked at her. He reached for her, took her into his arms and wanted to kiss her, but she kissed his cheek and pushed him away.

"Good night, Wally," she said.

7.

THE SIGNAL

Wally lay awake, wondering why they had stayed at the table so long and what he'd done to make Carolyn just about throw him out of the house at ten o'clock. He replayed the evening over and over in his head and then cursed himself for getting hung up on her, especially when he should be concentrating on his upcoming sabbatical.

He fell asleep around three thirty and woke up at eight. He showered, ate breakfast, and walked back and forth in his apartment. It was Saturday, and he resisted calling Carolyn until almost nine thirty.

"Hello?" Her voice was sleepy.

"Oh, damn—I'm so sorry—I've awakened you, haven't I?"

"Is that you, Wally?"

"Yes. Forgive me for calling so early. I'll call you back later..."

"I'm awake now, Wally."

"Carolyn, I had to tell you what a wonderful time I had last night."

"That's nice."

"I talked too much."

"No, you didn't, Wally. I'm still laughing about you dismissing that class."

"Could we see each other again?"

"If you don't mind me passing out on you at ten o'clock."

"Tonight?"

"Could we make it sometime next week? Tonight I'm expected over at my parents."

Monday afternoon, Wally sat in his car outside Marjorie and Bill Horton's house in St. Vital, the house that used to be *his* and Marjorie's. He thought he knew when Geordie would be arriving home from school, and he wanted to talk to him face to face rather than deal with this over the telephone. When Geordie didn't appear at the expected time—or even in the next fifteen minutes—Wally stepped out of his car. He approached the two-storey home with its attached garage and the basketball hoop that Geordie might've used once or twice. Wally went up the front steps and rang the bell.

He waited. No one answered.

He rang the bell again and listened for the ring inside. He heard nothing. One of the qualities Marjorie had claimed she wanted in a husband was the ability to fix little things that went on the fritz. Had Bill Horton failed the test?

Wally knocked.

No answer. He was considering going back to his car

to write a note when he saw Bill Horton walking up the street.

"Hello!" Wally called.

"Oh, hello, Wally. Is there something I can help you with?" Bill Horton was a tall man, with blond hair turning grey, and puffy features that suggested acne problems in his youth. He wore a beige overcoat and was carrying a satchel with its strap over his shoulder.

"I was looking for Geordie."

"And he's not home."

"No. I thought this was about the time he'd be here."

"Well, that's right, Wally, but sometimes he doesn't come straight home, you know; he can get involved in other things, like so many kids today—well, you know that better than I do."

"Do you know when I might be able to catch him?"

"Well, I don't, do I? I mean, I'm just coming home myself, and Marjorie's into a new venture; did you know that?"

"No. What is she doing?"

"Well, she's helping her friend Dodie—well, you know Dodie, or maybe you don't—helping her with a party-planning business, arranging the decorations and what have you. They've got a success on their hands, if you ask me. They're off doing a party this afternoon."

"Good for Marjorie."

"You're probably wondering why I'm walking. Well, Marjorie needs a car for the parties. We sold hers. I'd just as soon take the bus and walk. Well, we took the proceeds from the car and a couple of other things we sold and put them into a mutual fund, and I must say it's not doing badly. Fun, you know, watching the prices every day, going up and down, well, mostly up, you know; well, I'm sure you do know. Well, look here, Wally, is there anything I can do? I'd be happy to pass along a message to Geordie."

"I suppose you know that I'm going to Australia on a sabbatical."

"Well, yes, I do know that, Wally. Marjorie was a mite upset—not that she begrudges your going, you understand, but she thought you might've discussed it with her—well, not your going, per se, but how it will affect Geordie."

"She thinks I should take Geordie with me."

"Well, yes, she did mention that."

"So I've come over to talk to him about it. I guess I should've phoned."

"Well, let's not worry about the old *coulda-shoulda*, eh, Wally? Geordie should be along any time now. Do you want to come in for a minute?"

"No, no, I can wait in the car."

"Nonsense, Wally. I might be able to scare up … I don't know, I think I have a bottle of J & B."

"That sounds good, but, really, Bill…"

"Come on in. I believe I even have a snack or two."

They went inside. The first thing Wally saw was a reminder of Marjorie: an empty pink trash can on the stairs waiting for someone to take it up to the bathroom. Bill Horton excused himself and disappeared somewhere, leaving Wally in the vestibule. Wally heard him talking.

"Look who I found," Bill Horton said, reappearing with Geordie beside him.

"Geordie," said Wally. "I rang the bell."

"I'm afraid it doesn't work, Wally," said Bill Horton. "I've been meaning to…"

"I knocked."

"Geordie, he knocked. Didn't you hear him?"

"No."

"Look," said Bill Horton, "why don't you two go into the living room while I get those drinks. What'll it be, Geordie?"

"Nothing."

Bill Horton went to the kitchen, and Wally moved toward the living room, but Geordie didn't budge.

"Geord, I wanted to talk with you about Australia. I apologize for not suggesting this on Thursday, but you are welcome to come with me. We could talk to your principal, and I'm sure he'll agree that the trip would be far more educational than what you'll be doing in school."

"This is Mum's idea."

"All right, but it's a good one. It could be fun."

"No."

"Come in here, and let's at least talk about it."

"Dad. I don't want to go."

Bill Horton appeared again. "Come on, you two. Take a load off your feet and relax a little; what do you say?"

Wally and Carolyn went out for dinner on Wednesday, the only weekday night that she didn't have to work late. They went to The Round Table on Pembina Highway, Carolyn admitting that she liked roast beef just as much as he did. They talked about all kinds of things—the latest corporate identity she was working on, the Selkirk Settlers, the latest news—and, at times when she laughed, she'd reach over and touch his hand. That proved to be her most intimate gesture; when he took her home, she didn't invite him in, and, when he tried to hug her at the door, she seemed to stiffen up. And, when he tried to kiss her, he missed her lips, and she burst into laughter and turned away as if that was the last thing she wanted.

That weekend, they went skating at a community club and saw a movie, and, afterward over decafs, he said, "I'm just so out of practice when it comes to dating," and she said, "*You're* out of practice?" And again at her door she slipped out of his grasp with a "Night, night." He kept patient and reminded himself that at least he was correctly reading her signals. About three weeks after they'd met, she did ask him in and they sat together on the chester-field, and she surprised him by kissing him, really kissing him, and he ran his hand up her thigh. She turned away from him, saying, "Wally, I like you, surely you know that, and I think you like me, but we don't know each other very well, do we? If you knew me, Wally, you'd know I've come a long way in these last few days, one *hell* of a long way, Wally." He said, "I know," and she said, "No, you *don't* know. We've known each other what, two weeks?"

"More like three."

"Three frigging weeks. Whoop de doo! Wally, maybe we shouldn't see each other for a while, give me a chance to catch my breath."

He protested and said he wanted to keep seeing her as often as he could, and why didn't they just let nature take its course. The next time he saw her, he thought they were both more relaxed. They went inside to kiss good night but she still wouldn't let him stay.

One Saturday, they went to Freya's house for a party. Freya's husband, Kel, was a little more dorky than Wally expected but pleasant; there were three other couples, and Kel had them playing games like Match the Celebrities. But Freya still found an opportunity to speak privately to Wally, saying, "I hope you're not going to hurt that girl; she's one in a million, you know."

They saw each other about twice a week after that, and only once did he have an inkling that he should try to seduce her; that was the night he took her to see his apartment. He'd now had her drawing of him framed and hanging in the kitchen. He swore she was wearing mascara for the first time and a deeper shade of red lipstick and a shorter skirt and higher heels. Positively provocative, he thought. He got it into his head that she *wanted* to make love in his suite, that the real problem had been *the place*; it freaked her out to think of having sex where the ghost of her husband still lingered. But when he held her and told her he loved her and gestured toward the bedroom, she pushed him away and said, "Damn it, Wally, I *told* you. I'll let you know. I'll give you a *signal.*" He didn't say it, but he thought the makeup and the clothes *were* the signal. He realized he hadn't learned as much from Erica Mead as he'd thought. He was the absolute shits at reading signs.

It was two days before Christmas. The term was over, and Wally had spent some time in his office cleaning his desk, sorting files, and making a plan for January when his only duties would be advising two students about their theses and doing some research for papers he intended to write. He left the office late, had a beer and some chicken fingers at Applebee's, and headed home. He wasn't seeing Carolyn until the next night—Christmas Eve.

There was a post-it note stuck to his door. It was from Miles:

> Wal.
> Knock.
> A surprise.
> M.

Wally knocked on his neighbour's door.

"Hey, buddy!" cried Miles, almost before he had the door open. "Come in and see who's here."

Miles stepped back to let Wally in. Sitting on a stool at the wet bar Miles had recently installed was Marjorie.

She wore an indigo tracksuit Wally had never seen before. She looked years older than anyone in Miles's usual harem, but she had her hair done differently and was wearing the perfume Wally used to say was his favourite—Shalimar—and she seemed trimmer. She had a drink in front of her.

"So I come home, eh?" said Miles. "And look who's sitting on the stairs. I say to myself, Santa's come a little early, but then I put two and two together, eh, and I say, 'Aren't you Wally's ex?'"

"I've only been here five minutes," said Marjorie, as if to remind Wally that she knew Miles's reputation, which was pretty obvious from the surroundings: a pepper mill shaped like a phallus, a framed shot from *Hustler*, a wall hanging with fifty-seven copulation positions embroidered on it, and a framed bumper sticker that read, 2-4-6-8, now it's time to fornicate!

"Ho, ho!" said Miles. "It must be at least *ten* minutes."

"Wally," Marjorie said, "I need to talk with you."

"If this is about…"

"Could we go to your place?"

"Hey," said Miles, "you two stay right here. Sounds like you may need a referee."

"Marjorie," said Wally, "what've you been telling this guy?"

"Wait a minute," said Miles, "I'm not just any guy. This is Mr. Sensitive here."

"Oh, my god."

"Wally, I've told Miles nothing. He was nice enough to take me in while I waited."

"There, see?" said Miles. "Pour you a beer, Wal?"

Wally did not like the idea of being alone with Marjorie, but discuss Geordie or Australia in front of Miles?

"Thank you, no, Miles," he said. "We'll adjourn across the hall." He picked up his briefcase and his cloth bag of books and papers, and headed out.

Marjorie stood up and took her coat from a kitchen chair.

"Aww," said Miles. "Listen, if things get ugly, you know who to call. Marj, you can take the drink with you."

"What is it," said Wally, "pure vodka?"

"*Soda water*," Marjorie said. "Thank you, Miles."

Wally led the way to his apartment. As he opened the door, he tried to remember how he'd left the place. He was relieved to see it looking orderly, and he was proud of the little Christmas tree on top of his TV. He was sure there were no traces anywhere of Carolyn, but why the hell would he want to hide them if there were?

"Okay," he said, closing the door. "I tried to interest Geordie in going away with me. He barely spoke, Marjorie. But he did make it clear that he has no interest in going to Australia. I don't know what his problem is, but I'm not going to force him. As far as I'm concerned, this is settled. If you need a few more dollars to entertain him on the days when I would normally take him for dinner, fine. But *I* am going."

"Could we go in and sit down?"

"I don't ... all right. Let me throw this stuff in the den."

When he returned to hang up his coat, she was hanging up her own. She seemed subdued.

Maybe he was being harsh. He could at least be civil.

"Could I have something stronger than this?" she said.

"Sure. Scotch?"

"Rum and diet Coke, if you have it."

"Yes, I do. I think I'll have the same."

He went to the kitchen and made the drinks. He took them into the living room and found her sitting, perched on his hassock.

"It's a while since you've been here," he said, handing her the drink.

"Ta. Maybe two and a half years?"

"All of that, I guess." He sat on his old chesterfield, the first one they'd had at the house. "Well. Merry Christmas to you." He raised his glass.

"Yes, cheers," she said. She took a sip and then another. "That's nice, Wally."

"Marjorie, what is it you want to talk to me about?"

She took another sip. She looked at the drink and smiled. He hadn't seen her like this in years—soft-spoken, gentle, almost diffident.

"I think we made a mistake," she said.

"We probably did. Yeah, we probably should've insisted he do some sports, get out more, get more friends. We…"

"No, I'm not talking about Geordie. We made a mistake about *us*. We should not have split up."

"Wait a minute, Marjorie. We agonized over this. We talked about it and talked about it. We split and then kept seeing each other. We knew exactly what we were doing when we split for the final time. We analyzed every possible way and we both came to the same conclusion. We are better off apart. And you've found yourself another husband. And a pretty nice guy, too."

"All right, if you won't admit it was a mistake, I will. I gave this relationship with Bill a good shot, but, Wally, I don't love him."

"Oh, no."

"Wally, take me with you to Australia. We'll have a second honeymoon. We'll…"

The telephone rang.

"Please don't answer that," Marjorie said, standing.

"I'll … um … no, I'd better."

He went to the phone, which was on the kitchen pass-through. He turned to see Marjorie walking slowly toward him and he put up his hand as if to tell her to stay where she was, to come no further.

He picked up the phone and said, "Hello?"

At that moment, Marjorie lifted her top and showed him her familiar and beautiful breasts, showed them to him now in all their unrestrained glory, just as a familiar, slightly quivering, yet urgent voice said into his ear: "Please come now. *I want you.*"

8.

NOW, YOU

That's ... um ... very good."
      "Wally? Is someone there?"
   "Yes, but it's all right. I'll be leaving shortly."
   "Please hurry ... please, before I lose my nerve!"
   "Yes. I'll be right there."
   Wally hung up the phone. Marjorie had pulled her top
back down. She frowned, looking embarrassed.
   "Who was that?" she asked.
   "A friend."
   "Your artist friend."
   "My...? Oh. Geordie told you."
   "You told *him* it wasn't serious."
   "Marjorie, I had no idea you were coming here tonight."
   "You have to leave."
   "Yes."
   "And make me feel like an utter fool."

"I'm sorry about you and Bill, but you can't blame me for getting on with my life."

"I need to talk to you, Wally! You used to be such a good listener."

"We *will* talk. God, Marjorie, it's Christmas. Does Bill know how you feel?"

"He probably suspects. I didn't lie about where I was going. But if you can't spare a few minutes, I'll see what your neighbour's doing. *He's* hospitable."

"Marjorie, the man's a predator!"

She laughed a sarcastic laugh as she took her coat to the door. Wally watched her, for a moment wanted to save her from Miles, then grabbed his own coat and bolted past her and down the stairs. Maybe she'd close his door and maybe she wouldn't. Maybe she'd go back into his apartment and snoop around. He couldn't worry about that right now. When he got to his car, still hearing Carolyn's urgent voice even as he tried to forget Marjorie's breasts, he suddenly thought he'd better get to a drugstore. The condom he'd taken to Erica's was still in his wallet, but it was well past its best-by date.

The pharmacy he chose wasn't one he'd ever been in before, but he believed drugstores were all more or less the same. He should be able to find what he wanted right away. Whenever he went in for dental floss or vitamins or artificial tears or one kind of painkiller or another, the rack of colourful condom packages jumped right out at him. They had traded places with cigarettes, which were now behind the counter where condoms used to be. In his anxious state—knowing what Carolyn wanted him for and not wanting to keep her waiting—he hurried up and down the aisles, past everything from plastic toys and echinacea and huge plastic bottles of Coke to hair colouring and greeting cards and baby wipes, but the condom display was not jumping out. He looked for a clerk. The first one he found was a lovely blonde woman with a mischievous smile.

He said, "Can you please tell me where the ... the *condoms* are?"

"I *can*," she said, beaming. She led him to a display rack under a sign that read Family Planning. "*Voilà!*"

He had no idea how he could've missed it. "Thank you," he said, trying not to sound too eager. He looked at the many brands and the package illustrations of couples beside moonlit beaches.

"Would you like some help?" the young woman said, lingering.

Wally wasn't sure what she meant. He saw a twelve-pack he thought he recognized, took it off the hook, fumbled, dropped it. She picked it up and handed it to him.

"Thank you."

"No problem," she said, cheerily. "Any time!"

He headed for the check-out counter. He didn't feel right about making the condoms his only purchase, so he grabbed a package of five-flavours Life Savers and the latest *New Yorker*. At the cash desk was a red-faced man who picked up the condoms and eyed Wally's coat as if he might be hiding more. He put the items into a plastic bag so slowly that Wally wanted to scream. Wally paid him cash and headed for the exit. The young woman who'd helped him stood near the door.

"Merry Christmas!" she said.

"Same to you!" he said.

Once he thought he was out of her sight, he ran. At his car, he felt in his coat pocket for his key, and it wasn't there. Panicking, he thought he must have dropped it in the pharmacy; he checked his trouser pockets and found it in his back pocket where he usually kept his change. What was it doing there? He told himself to focus on the task at hand—to reach her house without an accident—and he thanked the Lord when his car started, even though there was no reason why it shouldn't. He started to back out of his parking spot and checked his rear-view mirror just in time to see a red half-ton truck flash past him. *Jesus!* Didn't anybody wait to let you back out of your spot anymore? He looked at his side mirrors and out all of his windows. He slowly backed up. Nobody hit him, and he proceeded forward, slowly. He glanced at his watch. How long had it been since she phoned? Half an hour? She wouldn't have been counting on his having to stop at a drug store, and she very well might be losing her nerve.

It was dark, after eight o'clock, and it was starting to snow. Once he had pulled out onto the street, he tried to keep concentrating on his driving, stay at the speed limit, and obey the lights. This was no time to be pulled over by a cop. The Disraeli Bridge seemed longer than usual—interminable. He had to stop for a red light at Hespeler, and it stayed red for so long, he thought there must be something wrong with it. When it did change, a car coming off the Redwood Bridge ran the light, causing Wally to jam on the brakes. "Fucking asshole!" Wally cried aloud, and he braced himself for the impact of the car behind him hitting him. It didn't. He started up again, looking both ways even though he had the right of way. The snow came down a little more heavily. Washington. Ottawa. Winterton. At last, Munroe. He made the turn too quickly, and his car skidded, reminding him that he was driving in winter conditions and he'd better try to think only about that and not about what was awaiting him, but it was difficult.

There was an outside light on at her house, one he didn't remember. He thought he saw someone looking through the venetian blinds. The front door opened before he rang the bell.

"What kept you? I was really worried," Carolyn said. She looked frantic, even scared, or annoyed. She wore a black shirt and black jeans, and she'd changed her hair somehow; it looked soft and pretty around her face. "Come in, come in."

"I'm sorry. When you called, my neighbour was there. I couldn't get rid of him." Damned if he was going to mention his *ex-wife*.

"Give me that and take off your coat." She pointed to the bag he was clutching.

"Life Savers," he said, taking the roll of candy out of the bag.

"And a magazine. In case we get bored?"

"And, ... ta-daaaa!" He pulled out the box of condoms as if this were a conjuring trick.

"Oh, Wally." She blushed and took his coat.

There was music playing. It sounded like *Bolero*. And the perfume—Opium?

He inhaled deeply of her fragrance. "Lovely."

"Come in. Let's try to relax for a few minutes. I'll pour the wine."

She had a bottle of red opened on the dining table. He noticed that her hand shook a little as she poured. He took off his shoes and entered the room, tossing the *New Yorker* onto a side table and tucking the other two purchases into his pants pocket. Trying to appear jaunty, he did a little dance step to the music.

Carolyn brought his glass of wine to him and raised her own. "I thought we should drink a toast to … to…"

"A beautiful evening?"

"Yes, oh, yes, I hope it will be…"

"Of course it will." He clinked her glass with his, and they sipped. He tried to gaze into her eyes, but she was avoiding direct eye contact.

She said, "I can't believe I'm so…"

He reached for her glass.

"What?" she said, as he put both glasses on the coffee table.

He said nothing and reached out for her.

"Oh!" she said.

She let him kiss her, gently but full on the lips. He'd lost his own nervousness in light of hers. He felt her shudder and, a moment later, push herself closer to him.

"May I undress you?" he whispered. "Please."

"Not here…"

She broke away and took him by the hand, leading him down a short hall to a small guest bedroom. There was a scent—perhaps the same perfume she was wearing—and a low-lit table lamp on a dresser, giving the room a rosy hue. A wave of warmth rolled through him when he saw that the bedclothes were turned down. Above the bed was a painting of a naked couple in an embrace; it might be one of her own works. She stood in front of him beside the bed, looking shy and awkward.

"You go first," he said, somehow feeling both calm and giddy.

She took the bottom of his sweater and lifted it, and he raised his arms to let her pull it up and off. She ran one hand over his shoulder; the hand felt cold. He took both her hands between his to warm them. She kissed the back of his hand.

"Now, you," she whispered.

He was enjoying the slowness of their moves, the suspense. He slowly unbuttoned her shirt and folded the two front halves to the side. Her lacy bra gave her breasts a prominence normally hidden by her conservative clothes.

He stared. "You are beautiful," he said.

He took off her shirt and hung it over a chair.

"My turn," she said.

She looked into his eyes as she undid the buttons of his shirt. It was the first time she'd looked directly at him for more than a second. She freed his shirttails from his trousers. She touched her lips to the centre of his bare chest.

"You smell so *good*," she said.

She tossed his shirt onto the chair beside hers.

He undid her jeans and eased the zipper down. He slid them off her hips and saw she was wearing lace-trimmed bikini panties.

"My goodness," he gasped, stepping around her to look at her from many angles. Her ass curved more than he had imagined—another surprise. Her clothes had muted all these lovely contours.

"I'm enjoying this," she said, stepping out of her jeans

and pushing them aside with her foot. "I'm ... I'm glad you weren't in a big hurry." She undid his belt. "I ... I thought I would need a ... a glass of wine..." She slid his zipper down. "I thought I might need the whole *bottle*..." She undid the button at the top of his trousers. "Thank you ... thank you for not rushing me..." She kept looking into his eyes as she let his trousers drop to his feet.

He stepped out of his trousers. He slipped her bra off one shoulder and then the other, and, standing behind her, managed to undo it without touching her. Tossing the bra onto the chair, he stepped in front of her again.

"You're incredibly lovely," he said.

"No, I'm not," she said, and she instinctively covered her chest with her arms.

"Hey," he said, "no time to be shy." With a delicate touch, he took her arms and moved them aside.

She inhaled, pretending to be the opposite of shy. Sweet Jesus! He wanted to bury his face in her bosom ... but he restrained himself.

"My turn," she whispered.

She looped two fingers of each hand over his waistband on either side, and inched his shorts down with excruciating slowness, down ... down ...

"It's so *long* ... ," she said, "so long since I've done anything like this..."

9.

BODIES

Wally had no idea what time it was when they made love for the second time. He lay on the double bed, on his back, with Carolyn cuddled up beside him, her head on his chest, the covers pulled up over their hips. He glowed with post-coital contentment.

The first time had been a near disaster. Her burst of nervous laughter at a crucial time made *him* laugh, and that was only the beginning; he got back in the mood pretty quickly when she lay down for his removal of her last item of clothing. He slid her panties slowly down the length of her legs, past her ankles and over her pedicured toes. He moved to lie down beside her, but she sat up and said she had another turn, and she pointed to his socks. They laughed about that.

To divert her attention from his feet, he sat up, remembering the condom. He got up, found the package in his pants, and started out of the room.

"Where are you going?" she said.

"The bathroom," he said.

"But, can't I watch?"

"I'm not entirely sure what to do."

He heard her groan, so he didn't go all the way to the bathroom but stood in the hall with his back to the bedroom. He tore open the box and cursed under his breath when he had to rip open the little package and found it was a lubricated kind; he didn't recall ever handling one of these slippery things, and he had some trouble getting it on, especially since all this commotion had had a negative effect on his readiness. However, as soon as he went back into the bedroom and saw the naked Carolyn, the readiness returned. When he lay down beside her, she turned to him, and their arms seemed to get in the way—he felt as if he and she were octopuses—and he felt so anxious and greedy that he immediately placed himself above her. She seemed suddenly reluctant and tense.

"Be careful," she said. "Please don't hurt me."

He assured her he'd be gentle and keep his weight off her, and she cried out and seemed to be bracing herself for something terrible when he had to tell her it was over. For a second he thought this relationship was probably a mistake; in the next second he reminded himself how out of practice he was, and a few seconds later he kissed a sweet spot between her breasts and told himself how lucky he was to have discovered Carolyn at this stage of his life. He was sure that the next time would be better.

And it was.

They lay quietly side by side for a while.

"I was in too much of a hurry," Wally said.

"It's okay."

He got rid of the condom and climbed back into bed. She raised herself up to kiss him—as warm and complete a kiss as she'd ever given him—and he kissed her neck and her face. And he caressed her body and she uttered sounds like "ohh!" and "mmm" and "ooh," and when he fondled her she said, "Oh, no" and "Oh, *yes!*" And when he whispered, "Just a minute," and moved to leave the bed, she pulled him down to her, and they made love again.

As they lay there afterward, both breathing heavily, their hearts pounding away, Wally's mind was leaping ahead: Carolyn is amazing. I want to see her again and again. I don't want to mess this up. I know it's nuts to think this when we've known each other for such a short time, but I think I'm falling in love with her. I can't leave her. I won't go to Australia. She doesn't even know about Australia, and now she doesn't need to know because I can cancel my plans. But the more he thought about it, as he felt her warmth beside him and heard her breathing become regular, the more he thought that maybe he didn't have to cancel his trip. Wouldn't it be fun to take her with me? Is there any chance that she could take time off work to go with me?

"Carolyn?"

"Mmm."

"There … um … there's something I need to tell you."

"Oh, no."

"What?"

"It can't be anything good. Tell me after Christmas."

"No, listen. I have a sabbatical coming up. I'm going away at the end of January."

"Oh, Jeez, is that all?" She leaned up to him and playfully chewed on his lower lip. "When do you come back?"

"April."

"So, two months. I should be able to cope." She placed her head back down on his shoulder.

"Don't you want to know where I'm going?"

"Not particularly. I'm only interested in where you are right now."

Wally had to admit that where he was right now was the best place he'd been in years. *This* was a good argument for cancelling his plans. But how *cool* it would be if the two of them could...

"Have you ever been to Australia?" he asked.

"No. Is that where you're going?"

"Yes."

"To study?"

"I'll be what they call a *visiting fellow*. I'll have some obligations, but there will be lots of time to see the country. Carolyn, why don't you come with me?"

"Oh, Wally, I couldn't."

"Do you have any vacation time coming to you?"

"Well, actually, I've got nearly eight weeks I haven't taken. We were short a couple of people last year, and this year there's been so much work..."

"Then the length of time isn't a problem."

"No, not really, but the guys would freak out if I wanted that kind of time off." She teased his earlobe with her mouth. "Besides that, going away with you ... the two of us ... that far ... what would my mother think?"

"Your *mother?*"

"All right, then, not just my mother." She ran her hand

over his chest, playing with tufts of hair. "My father, my aunt, my friends, and Dobber and Karnak and Orde and..."

"*Who?*"

"The guys I work with? They wouldn't let me go on a trip like that without meeting you first..."

"What are you saying? You'd need their approval of me?"

Her hand moved over his abdomen as she pushed herself against him. "Wally, you've been in my life for what? Eight, ten weeks?"

"I know, but listen. We have more than a month before I have to leave. Lots of time for me to meet your family and your..."

She was touching his cock.

"Wally, it *is* tempting..."

She gently encircled it with her hand.

"Carolyn..."

She started to move her hand up and down. He lay back, setting aside all the crazy thoughts swirling around in his head, losing himself to the experience.

On his way home, he composed a letter in his head, the letter he'd have to send to Dr. Lockridge: "Please forgive me, but there is a change in my plans. I will not be alone after all. I will be accompanied by my new friend." ... No.... "I am happy to be able to tell you that I will be accompanied by ... by ... by my new paramour." ... Yes! ... "I'm bringing my luscious new paramour.... Yeah, Doc, you won't believe this, but I've met the hottest babe this side of the

International Date Line, and you'd better make sure that bed you've got for us is fucking earthquake-proof."

It was after three in the morning when he parked his car in the fenced lot behind his apartment building. A siren sounded in the winter air, and, as he walked to the River Avenue entrance, he caught a glimpse of an ambulance speeding past on Osborne Street. Wally thought briefly of the poor soul who was heading to a hospital so close to Christmas. He still couldn't quite believe his own good fortune, and he felt warm all over as he went up in the elevator.

At his apartment door, he glanced at his neighbour's, wondering for the first time since he'd left if Marjorie had gone back into Miles's. At least she had closed Wally's door.

He quietly unlocked it. As soon as he opened it, he detected the familiar Shalimar scent. He was amazed that it was still lingering; maybe she had angrily blasted a few squirts into the apartment before she left. Then he saw the body curled up on his chesterfield, and he nearly cried out with fright. It was covered by one of his favourite blankets.

10.

BACON AND EGGS

It took a few moments for the truth to register: this was neither a dead body nor an anonymous intruder; this was Marjorie, fast asleep. Wally went through a crazy series of emotions: relief that it was a live person he knew, confusion about why she was there, anger that he had to deal with her at such an outrageous time of night, a vague sense of guilt given where he'd spent the last few hours, and a feeling of bravado for the same reason.

He *had* to wake Marjorie. He was amazed that the noise of unlocking and opening the door and the sudden light from the hall hadn't wakened her. He closed the door, allowing the latch to click loudly, yet still she didn't stir. He wondered if she was faking sleep, but he didn't know why she would, and he recalled that, when they were together for all those years, she'd been a pretty sound sleeper. He resented her being there, spoiling what had been a glorious night. What had she told Bill Horton? Did he and

Geordie know where she was? Wally found himself feeling sorry for Bill Horton; he was a nice enough guy, mild mannered and inoffensive ... just the kind of guy who might lose it completely and barge into Wally's apartment at any minute with a gun!

As these thoughts rattled through his brain, Wally ran water, turned on his bedroom lamp, opened the fridge, poured a glass of milk, closed the fridge, shut a door, and opened and shut a drawer, and, when Marjorie still didn't stir, he checked to be sure she was breathing. She was.

At last, he decided he would go to bed. He'd rather deal with her in the morning. He made sure the deadbolt was in its slot, and he went to his bedroom. It felt strange to undress while his ex-wife was in the living room. He found he had put his shorts on backwards; he'd been *that* distracted when he was leaving Carolyn's. Ah, Carolyn. Would he be able to tell her what he'd come home to? The thought made him angry at Marjorie all over again for putting him in this situation. In his pyjamas, he decided he would not brush his teeth; he'd stay in his room. He turned out his lamp and opened his door, leaving it slightly ajar. He got into bed and lay there on his back, sure that he'd never be able to sleep.

The apartment was quiet now. He couldn't hear anyone in the building. Street noise was minimal. He lay still, daring to think again about Carolyn, her body, her heat...

"Wally?"

Marjorie's sleepy voice made him jump.

"Wally, are you there?"

It seemed absurd to answer her from his bedroom, but he did: "Yes, Marjorie. I hope I didn't wake you."

"You didn't."

He wondered if she meant she'd been awake the whole time, but, no, she wouldn't have waited until now to speak to him. Oh, why was she here?

All was quiet again. He heard something, perhaps her turning over, rearranging herself on the chesterfield ... or was she coming into his room?

Wally sat up and stared at the space he'd left between the door and the jamb. Was she there looking in on him? He thought if she was there her silhouette would be darker than the darkness behind her. He heard nothing more. He lay down again. He'd try to get to sleep.

"Wally? Do you want to talk?"

The prospect of talking—about her wanting to leave Bill Horton, if in fact she hadn't already left him, or about taking her to Australia, or about taking both her and Geordie to Australia, or about how serious his relationship was with *his artist*—the prospect of talking about *any* subject in the middle of the night made him alarmingly weary.

"Let's try to get some sleep," he said. "We'll talk in the morning."

"All right," she answered.

He was surprised that she agreed, but he was grateful. He thought that if he tried hard to think of nothing, he might be able to drift off. He turned over, away from the door.

Someone closed a door somewhere in the block, too loudly. He heard muffled voices and some laughter.

Quiet returned.

"Wally?"

"Yes?"

"Did you have a nice time tonight?"

Oh, God. "Yes, very nice."

"That's nice."

"Good night, Marjorie."

"Good night."

Wally woke to the smell of coffee. Morning sun seeped through his venetian blinds, and his bedside clock told him it was nine-thirty-five. He heard muffled kitchen sounds and remembered that Marjorie was in his apartment. His ex-wife had quietly risen and made coffee. She was being ridiculously pleasant, and he kind of liked it. Certainly beat a shouting match. They had known each other for more than half their lives; why not be civil? He got up, put on his dressing gown and slippers, and headed for the kitchen. Marjorie was in last night's clothes—the clothes she'd slept in—looking into his fridge.

"Good morning," he said.

"Oh, hi!"

"Thanks for making this." He took a mug she'd bought him in Dallas, Texas, and filled it. She already had one on the go.

"I see you have eggs," she said. "Shall I fry some up?"

Wally thought it was a lovely idea, but he said, "Marjorie. Sit down for a minute."

She closed the fridge door and sat at the tiny kitchen table. She took a sip of her coffee while he pulled out the other chair and sat.

"Please tell me, what does Bill think is going on?" Wally said. "Where does Geordie think you spent the night? I'm picturing Geordie and Bill in your kitchen this morning—right now..."

Marjorie shrugged. "They aren't there, Wally. Geordie has school, at least till noon. Bill has work."

"But where do they think you are?"

"I told you last night that Bill knew I was coming here. He knew I wanted to talk with you—we didn't get into why—he isn't nosy that way. I called him to tell him you'd gone out and I was going to wait for you."

"But I came home last night, and you're still here in the morning."

"He knows I don't like driving late at night, and he doesn't need the car this morning—he takes the bus."

"Oh, oh. Where are you parked? You might have a ticket by now; you could've been towed away..."

"Wally, I don't *care*. Listen, I know Geordie told you he doesn't want to go to Australia, but *I do*. And if you and I both go, I'm sure he'll come with us, and we'll be a family again, in a whole different place. We'll have a chance to start again away from anybody we know."

"Marjorie, if there was even a shred of a chance that the three of us could go—which you and I know is a preposterous idea—it wouldn't work because the accommodation they have for me won't take three people. There's one bedroom in the principal's basement."

"We can improvise."

"Marjorie, where is this coming from? Are you jealous because I'm going to an exotic place and you aren't? Is that what this is all about?"

She turned away from him and took a sip of her coffee and turned back.

"I'll forgive that remark," she said, keeping her composure better than he'd ever seen before. "If you're trying to pull my chain, it isn't going to work. You know we belong together, and I'm telling you I've finally seen the light, and I'm asking you to take me back." She reached over and touched his hand. "I haven't stopped loving you, Wally."

He knew she expected him to embrace her. He even wanted to, even though he suspected that she was manipulating him. The tender, non-combative Marjorie had appealed to him from the first time he met her. As he fought any impulse to comfort her and remembered where he'd been only a few hours ago, he said: "I've asked Carolyn to go to Australia with me."

"Carolyn." Marjorie pulled her hand back from his.

"Yes."

"The artist."

"The graphic designer, yes."

"You've had sex with her and now you feel obligated."

"Marjorie…"

"Has she accepted?"

Wally hesitated. "I don't have to discuss this with you. I don't *want* to discuss this with you."

"Kind of makes you more interesting, you know? You having another woman after all this time."

"We get along well…"

"She's younger than you. How much younger?"

"Five years."

"Divorced?"

"Widowed."

"Mmm. And she hasn't said if she can go with you."

"I didn't say…"

"Why don't I fry those eggs?"

There was a pause, and then he said, "All right."

"Is that a picture of you?" She pointed to the framed drawing on the wall.

"Yes."

"By your artist."

"Yes."

"Not bad. She didn't get your eyes quite right, though, or your mouth."

"She was sitting a long way away."

And so they settled into a re-enactment of those countless domestic scenes that had characterized their marriage: Marjorie frying the bacon and the eggs, Wally pouring the orange juice, refreshing the coffee, toasting the multi-grain bread, and setting out a dish of strawberry jam. And when they sat down to eat, they conversed, as they always had. Wally complimented Marjorie on the eggs and bacon as if they were works of culinary art prepared by a master chef. Marjorie asked him what a visiting fellow did and how he'd learned of such a gig and where exactly the college was. They even discussed Geordie, how he was doing at school and whether the phase he was going through was natural or troublesome. They avoided the elephant in the room. "Some elephant!" Wally might've said, referring to his thrashing about with a love-starved young widow just a few hours earlier. Oh, but there was another elephant, and Wally, once he'd swallowed his last morsel, turned his attention to it.

"Now, Marjorie. It's Christmas."

"And you're still coming over on Christmas Day."

"Just a minute. What I mean is—what you were saying about Bill. He has no inkling of the way you feel."

"He … he *must*."

"It's *Christmas*. Please don't spring anything on Bill—or Geordie, for that matter—in this holiday time."

"You want me to pretend. It's all right, I'm good at pretending."

"And how will you explain being here overnight?"

"We had to discuss Geordie, and you had to go out, and it was getting late, so I stayed over. I already told him that. I'll play this little charade, Wally, if you agree to chat in the new year. And think about what I said."

He had to agree to that. She hadn't raised her voice. As much as he believed her calmness was part of a ruse, it intrigued him.

"Okay," he said. "And right now, you'd better get moving. I'll do the dishes. In fact, I'd better go with you and see if your car is still there."

"Oh, yes." She gave him a quick kiss on the cheek. "Thanks, Wally."

They put on their coats, and, when they left the apartment, Miles appeared at his door.

"Well, hel-lo, you two!" he said, with his best leer. "How was your night?"

Wally started to say something like "It isn't what you think," but Marjorie handled the encounter, beaming and saying with emphasis, "*Wunn*-derful!"

11.

STEPHEN

That was one terrible day to get through," said Carolyn. "I kept forgetting things, making mistakes. I should've hung around to do some corrections, but the guys kicked me out. I'm a basket case."

"I apologize for staying so late last night," Wally said.

"It was *my* fault. I wouldn't let you go. It was like I was on a *drug* or something."

"We were both enjoying ourselves; you have to admit that."

"Wally, that wasn't *me*. When I woke up this morning, I thought about last night, and it *scared* me. I turned into a *crazy* woman. I don't even know what we talked about. I don't even know *if* we talked."

It was six-thirty, and they were downtown in Old Bailey's, not far from Dobber Design, where Carolyn worked. They'd agreed to meet at the restaurant to save her going home first. Wally was sipping a glass of sauvignon blanc, while Carolyn drank water, fearing that liquor would make her instantly drunk or put her to sleep. Wally hoped that what she was saying was a result of her fatigue; he adored the way she'd behaved last night and was hoping for more of the same—tomorrow, if not tonight.

"You were *horny*, that's all," he said.

"God, would you keep your voice down, please! Or do you want the whole place to ... you *do!* You want the whole restaurant to know you've found a *live one*."

"Carolyn ... I didn't..."

"Wally, I don't even like that word you just used. You know what it does? It turns me into an animal. I picture a ... a *goat*."

"But a beautiful goat..."

"I'm worried, Wally. That wasn't me last night. Really, I don't know what got into me.... Oh, God. Could we get the waiter? Or maybe we should just leave."

Carolyn found a facial tissue and dabbed at her eyes.

Wally said, "Hey. Let's relax, shall we? Let's just take it easy and try to have a nice, relaxing dinner."

He waved the waiter over, and they both ordered the salmon. She let him take her hand and gently hold it. He asked her about the work she'd been doing—sketches and typography selections for a corporate identity that a bustling new software company wanted early in the new year. At first, she didn't want to elaborate on anything, but she gradually gave him a few details, and he was glad to find that he was capable of calming her down.

Their dinners arrived, and, after taking her first bite, Carolyn said, "There's something else bothering me."

"Do you want to talk about it?"

"It … it's part of the whole last-night thing. This time of year … Christmas … was always special. Stephen loved it."

"Stephen. Your … husband."

"Of course, my husband! Who…"

"You've never mentioned his name before."

"I must've."

"Whether you have or haven't, I respect your feelings about him. I know you had a good marriage."

"Okay, I don't want to cry. I don't want to get all maudlin. I just know he's going to be on my mind tomorrow and the next day, and I don't want to ruin everything for you."

"If you're saying we should cool it over Christmas…"

"I … I don't know *what* I'm saying…"

"I was hoping we could talk about Australia."

"Aus … Australia?"

"Where I'm going on my sabbatical."

"Wait. Last night. Did you mention Australia last night?"

Wally checked himself before he blurted out something hurtful; he could see what a fragile state she was in. Another part of him marvelled at the apparent fact that she really had been *so into it* last night, she couldn't remember what had been said. He needed to cherish that, encourage it, preserve it. *If he could.*

"Well," he said and paused. "I mentioned I was going away in February … and I thought it'd be fun if you could go, too, and you kind of liked the idea, at least I think you did, but you weren't sure if you could get off work, even though you have a lot of time saved up."

"Wait. It's coming back. You said you were going to Australia."

"Yes."

"So I didn't dream it."

"Carolyn, you … you were distracted. Distracted in a beautiful way. It probably wasn't the best time to talk about planning a trip."

"Oh, Wally, I don't know. I can't think about it now, either."

She took out a tissue and blew her nose. She took a deep breath and then another. She avoided looking at him. With her fork, she picked up a portion of her half-finished dinner, looked at it, and put it back on her plate.

"Wally, could we leave?"

"Don't you want to finish your dinner?"

"I can't…"

Wally judged that it was not a time for coaxing. Carolyn went to the washroom while he dealt with the waiter, explaining that their sudden departure had nothing to do with the food or the service. As they left, Wally offered to take her home and come back downtown by cab to pick up her car. She was so relieved and so amazed at his generosity, she wept. She apologized for spoiling the evening and she hoped he still wanted to see her on Christmas Day. She directed him to a surface lot on Market Street, and they drove there so that he'd know where to go later. They hardly spoke on the way to her place; he commented on a few of the decorations they passed, and she answered, "Mmm," or "Mmhmm." He insisted on tucking her into bed, and, once the cab arrived, he took her house key as well as her car key so that he could look in on her when he returned.

He went back downtown with a tough-looking older

cabbie in a Winnipeg Jets jersey. The NHL Jets had been moved to Phoenix the previous spring.

"I guess you miss the Jets, eh?" Wally said.

"Huh?" the cabbie answered. "Those overpaid namby-pambies? Don't get me started. You take a good look at this shirt—number 14 on the old WHA Jets, Ulf Nilsson. I kid you not, that team we had back in the seventies was the best friggin' hockey team you ever seen. Nilsson, Hull, and Hedberg—sweetest friggin' line ever. Drove the other teams nuts the way they'd skate circles around 'em. Ulf, the quiet one; could he lay down a pass? I tell ya. And those two other guys? The way they shot the puck? Made ya forget Rocket Richard, you know what I mean?"

He talked and talked and nearly drove past their destination.

Wally retrieved the car and drove back to Carolyn's. His plan was to enter the house as quietly as he could, listen at her bedroom door, leave the keys on the dining-room table, and make sure the outside door was locked when he left. He parked the car and let himself into the house. She had left a lamp on in the living room, and the house was quiet and still. He stood there until he thought he heard her breathing. It gave him a warm feeling to know she was sleeping. With slow, silent steps, he headed for the outside door.

"Wally?"

A shiver invaded his warmth. It was barely eighteen hours since another woman had called out his name when he thought she was sleeping. For a moment, he had this whacky notion that Marjorie was in Carolyn's bedroom.

"Yes?" he answered.

In a subdued voice, Carolyn said, "It's nice of you to want to take me to Australia."

"We can talk about it some other time."

"Wally, could we go to my parents' place tomorrow? I have to go there anyway, and I want them to meet you."

"Sure. Good idea, sure."

"Maybe on the way we could talk about Australia."

"Great idea. Carolyn, are you okay?"

"I'm not feeling all that well, but I'll be okay. Wally, thank you for being so considerate."

"I'd better go."

"Yes. Wally, I promise I'll be back to normal tomorrow."

"Good night. Pleasant dreams."

"Good night, Wally."

It was just past nine when he left Carolyn's—so much earlier than he'd expected to. As he drove home, he contented himself with thoughts of the previous evening. He tried to recall everything they did, from the moment they began undressing each other. He thought how right she'd been to take it easy on this next night, to abstain, to avoid trying to re-enact their wonderful initiation. Her fatigue and her feeling unwell were natural signals to take a time out, to reflect on how marvellous it was that they had found each other and how perfectly they *fit* together.

He entered his apartment to a ringing telephone. He thought it might be Carolyn. She might be lying there having the same recollections. She might even want him to come back.

"Hello?"

"Wally! How the hell are you?"

"Who is this?"

"A former good friend of yours, i.e., someone you should remember."

"Erica?"

"Yes, Wally, I'll jump right to the point. I'm having a li'l old *soirée* over here on New Year's Eve. Want to join us?"

"Oh, Erica, I think I'm going to have other plans."

"You *think?* You mean you have a new squeeze and she hasn't told you what you're doing yet?"

"Something like that."

"Bring her here!"

"Sorry, Erica. Thanks, anyway. Merry Christmas."

"Merry fuckin' Christmas to you, too."

12.

HOCKEY IN THE AFTERNOON

Christmas morning.

Wally arrived at Marjorie's with his wrapped gifts—CDs and a watch for Geordie, a gift certificate for a spa (hidden in a large box) for Marjorie, and a book on the Middle East for Bill Horton; and it was Bill Horton who answered the door.

"Merry Christmas, Wally!" he said. He shook Wally's hand and patted him on the shoulder. "Well, now, it looks like you've outdone yourself in the gift department again this year. How can we possibly compete? Here, let me take those from you, and do come in."

"Merry Christmas, Wally!" Marjorie came out of the kitchen and through the living room toward him.

It was an awkward moment in what was surely going to be a series of awkward moments. Wally panicked, hoping the panic didn't show, as he tried to remember how he'd greeted Marjorie on previous Christmas Days since the divorce. He did not want to appear to be any more friendly than normal, not because he was afraid of arousing Bill Horton's suspicions, but because he didn't want Marjorie to think he was warming to her plan to dump Bill Horton and run off to Australia. And, of course, being less friendly might be interpreted by her as a cover for the same thing. As it turned out, Bill Horton had his back to them while he placed Wally's gifts under the tree, and Marjorie gave Wally an enthusiastic hug and kissed him near, but not *on*, the mouth. She gave him a quick wink—so quick, he wasn't sure that it was a wink and not a nervous tic. Wink or tic, it troubled him, surely meaning, You see, I'm going along with your little game and not spoiling Bill's Christmas.

"And here's our little gift for you, Wally," Bill Horton said, handing Wally a handsomely wrapped box.

"We're going to open ours, aren't we?" said Marjorie.

"I hope so," said Bill Horton. "Do sit down, both of you, and I'll fetch us some mimosas. That sound all right, Wally?"

"Sounds terrific," Wally said. "And, thank you, Bill, and Marjorie, for this."

"Oh, and Geordie has something to tell you," Marjorie said. "Where is he?"

"I'll get him," Bill Horton said.

Wally worried about what Marjorie might do with Bill Horton out of the room. He was relieved but perhaps a little disappointed when she did nothing but retrieve the gifts he'd brought and go to the chesterfield and sit down with them.

Geordie and Bill Horton came into the room carrying four fizzing flute glasses.

"Merry Christmas, Dad," Geordie said, handing a glass to Wally.

"Thank you. Same to you, m'boy." *M'boy?* Wally never called Geordie M'boy.

"Geordie...?" said Marjorie.

"Dad ... I ... I'm sorry about the way I acted about the Australia thing."

"It's okay. Don't even—"

"Dad, I've been thinking about it, looking at maps and stuff. It'd be cool to go that far away. Dad, I'd like to go with you."

Wally looked at Marjorie, who was smiling as if in triumph. Wally wanted to object, but it was *he* who'd asked *her* to keep the peace through Christmas. For Geordie's sake, he had to seem pleased, even as he recalled Carolyn's sleepy voice from the night before: Nice of you to want to take me to Australia. He reached for his son's hand.

"That ... that *is* good news," Wally said. "What triggered your change of heart?"

Geordie looked at his mother as he said, "You know Mom's all for it, but Bill and I had a talk about it. Bill helped me see how cool the whole idea is."

Wally was already composing a new letter to Dr. Lockridge—"Besides my new woman friend, I'll be accompanied by my teen-aged son, and I'm wondering if there's space for a cot in my study"—while remembering that this was only the first stage in Marjorie's plan, and *she* wanted to go, too ...

He was missing what Bill Horton was saying: "Didn't mean to interfere, Wally, but gosh, I just think it's a wonderful opportunity for a young man as bright as Geordie obviously is. As you know, Wally, Geordie's principal, Harry Allardyce, is a buddy of mine—Harry and I go way back—and I know that Harry would encourage this every step of the way; in fact, Harry would no doubt take it upon himself to work on a plan with the teachers so that Geordie could be free to make the trip without having to worry about a whole lot of extra work..."

On the way to Carolyn's parents' house, Carolyn said, "I'm warming up to the idea of Australia. I'd sort of like to tell them we're thinking about it, see what they say."

By now, Wally regarded going away with Carolyn as a premature idea, especially given what had transpired at Marjorie's.

"Maybe we shouldn't mention it until you and I have discussed it a lot more," said Wally.

"I love surprising them. It'll be fun."

When they pulled up to the split-level house on Baldry Bay, Carolyn told Wally to turn in to the driveway. There was a late-model Toyota Camry in the carport. A slender grey-haired woman stood in the centre of the picture window watching them. Beside her was what appeared to be an artificial Christmas tree; all its lights were white, and they were on. Carolyn waved from the car.

"That's Mom," said Carolyn. "We won't say anything about Australia for a while. Maybe the best time will be when we sit down to brunch. Don't you worry about it; I'll bring it up. You just be your scintillating self."

"All right," said Wally.

"Wait. Where did we meet?"

"In a bar?"

"No, no, I mean where will we *tell them* we met? We can't say we met in a bar."

"We should've talked about this before—"

"Come on, think of something—"

"I know. You're considering taking a history course and you came to me to—"

"That's nuts."

"Is it?"

"Come on, we have to go in; she'll think we're arguing."

"We *are*."

"Let's go. *I'll* think of something."

It was eleven o'clock. Though Wally felt rather odd in this role of a suitor going to meet his girlfriend's parents for the first time, he was hoping it would take his mind off the Marjorie situation. When he'd left her place, all three— Marjorie, Geordie, and Bill Horton—looked immensely pleased with themselves, and Wally felt sick. Not only had Marjorie complied with his suggestion that she put on hold anything that would spoil Bill Horton's Christmas, she'd talked Bill Horton into having a serious chat with Geordie, and now that Geordie wanted to go to Australia, she'd be planning the next move that would enable her to go too. Worst of all, Carolyn knew nothing of Marjorie's recent shenanigans, and here was Wally, expected to be "scintillating" for Carolyn's parents while Carolyn picked the right time to tell them she was going to Australia with him. Trying to look cheerful as they approached the front door, Wally composed another letter: "Dr. Lockridge, you'll never guess what's happened..."

Carolyn's mother opened the door.

"Carolyn," she said, "you look *tired*."

"Oh, Mother. Mum, I'd like you to meet Wally Baxter."

"Hello, Mr. Baxter. Don't you think she looks tired? She works too hard; I've told her and told her."

"Please, call me Wally … Mrs… "

"*Laidlaw*," Carolyn said.

Had Carolyn ever told Wally her maiden name? He didn't think so.

"Mother, where's Dad?"

"Oh, you know him and his game. He's off playing it in the den; imagine, even on Christmas Day. Louis! Your daughter is here!"

Wally busied himself with taking off his gloves, leather jacket, scarf, and shoes, all of which Carolyn deposited in the closet next to the door. She had slipped out of her own outerwear as she was entering, giving Wally no chance to appear gallant.

"Look at the two of you," said Mrs. Laidlaw. "Twins."

They both wore red sweaters and jeans, though the shades of red differed.

"Louis!" Mrs. Laidlaw called again.

"Send them up here!" a man's voice replied.

"That means he's in the middle of a game. Carolyn, take Wally up there and tell your father he's being rude."

"Come on," said Carolyn, taking Wally's hand. "You'll get a kick out of this."

She led Wally up a half-flight of stairs, past a bedroom to a small den where a big-shouldered bald man sat at a desk rolling dice. He let the dice go and, when they came to rest on the desk, glanced at them and said, "He scores!"

"Hi, Dad. If you can take a minute away from that, I'd like you to meet Wally Baxter."

"Caught me in the act," said Mr. Laidlaw, and he gave a chuckle not unlike Carolyn's. He stood up—he was taller than Wally—and he shook Wally's hand. "Pleased to meet you, Wally. Merry Christmas."

"Merry Christmas to you, sir."

"Can you leave this, Daddy? Mum wants us…"

"Aww … just one total to go. Either a goal or a penalty or an injury will do it. Let me finish."

"Okay if I watch?" said Wally.

"Damn right. You can be one of the teams. Which one do you want, Stony Mountain Convicts or Winnipeg Beach Combers?"

"All right, I'll leave you both to it," said Carolyn. "I'll see if Mum needs help."

She left, giving Wally a look that seemed to say, *Congratulations! Not everybody gets to play Dad's game.*

"Uh—I'll be Winnipeg Beach," Wally said.

"Fine. Sorry you're losing 6 to 1. But here, this is the team lineup. You'll see that the Beach Boys—as the media affectionately call them—have a first line of Rip Tushreds, Matthew Marklukenjon and Lanny Prochaine. I won't get into explaining the names of all twenty-four guys on the roster but … oh, see that picture on the wall? That's Marklukenjon. Bit of a heartthrob."

"You drew him?"

"Yup."

"I see where Carolyn gets her talent."

"I guess. Well, I won't show you the pictures of all the players in the league—about eight hundred—we'll finish up here so Carolyn's mother doesn't have a bird. These are the rules—sort of like a board game." He pointed to a tattered sheet that appeared to be two loose-leaf pages taped together. There were many columns drawn on the pages, each broken into many boxes. In each box something was printed in black, red, blue, green, or orange. "Red's a goal, blue's a penalty—I won't explain too much— you'll see what happens as we go. Stony Mountain just scored, so it's your puck and we start here in the *Face-Off* column. You want the Tushreds line out there?"

"Uh ... sure."

"Okay. I'll put out *my* best line—Hal Zapoppin, Ray Furarside, and Russell Upsumgrub. Oh, by the way, your starting goaltender was yanked, so Croesus Toobig is in your net. Convicts have old Phil Inn between the pipes. Okay, roll."

Wally shook the dice and dropped them onto the open scribbler beside the rules. Mr. Laidlaw was apparently keeping a written record of the game.

"Bad luck ... seven," he said. He reached for the dice.

"Seven isn't lucky?" Wally asked.

"If you're on a power play, it's a goal. Off the faceoff, seven means you lose the draw. My puck."

He shook the dice over his head as if he were in Las Vegas playing craps. He threw the dice onto the desk, and both rolled off onto the floor.

"Puck goes into the crowd," he said.

"My puck, then?"

"No, I roll again. Mind bending down there and getting 'em for me? Damned arthritis is acting up."

Wally had to get down on all fours, but he was enjoying this; meeting the parents wasn't so bad.

"Thanks," said Mr. Laidlaw. "Okay, now."

He shook the dice less vigorously and threw them onto the scribbler. Eleven. "He scores!" he cried.

"Wow!"

"I have to roll again to see *who* scored … okay, Furarside from Hiccup—that's the defenceman Wild Bill Hiccup—and Zapoppin. Game over. Convicts win it, 7 to 1. Hey, that gets them out of the Canadian Division cellar." He recorded the goal in his scribbler. "Another big win for Phil Inn."

On another day, Wally might've thought Louis Laidlaw was nuts. But meeting Carolyn's father had turned out to be so unlike what he'd imagined that he saw the man's devotion to his fantasy game as a loveable eccentricity.

"Uh … how many teams do you have," he asked, "and what league are they in?"

"Sixteen. Eight originally, but there have been two expansions. They're in the Tundra Taiga Hockey League. Camby—that's my good friend Campbell Harringdotter—has a rival league he calls the United Inter-Continental Inter-Racial Bilingual Hockey League—the UICIRBHL for short. We have four interlocking games in our regular sixty-four-game season. And our champions meet in the World Series." He pointed to a trophy on top of a filing cabinet. "My Olyutorsk Oxen won the series last year."

"How long have you…"

"Camby and I dreamed this thing up in high school. When he moved back here after we both retired, we started playing again. We send each other game write-ups and statistics; beats exercise or poker." He chuckled.

"It's fascinating."

"Stephen—Carolyn's husband?—he used to tell us we should patent the game. He looked into it, found out there were more hockey board games than McDonald's has big macs, but he thought ours was different enough; he liked all the players' names and the variety of things that can happen. He was going to find us a niche ... until he ... well, the poor guy."

"Yes," said Wally. Carolyn had never talked about how her husband died. "Um ... could we play another game?"

"You want to?"

"Hey, you two." Carolyn appeared in the den doorway. "Mum wants us at the table."

"Wally here is hooked on my hockey league."

"I'm not surprised," Carolyn said, winking at Wally. "Did you tell him about the scandal?"

"Well, no, we didn't get that far..."

"One of Dad's best players—Len Meyereres..."

"Plays on a line with Franz Romanzan and Con Trymen—you know, Franz Romanzan Con Trymen Len Meyereres?"

"Left his wife for the coach's daughter."

"What?"

"Oh, yes, we're talking the complete package here; gets into the players' private lives, what they have for breakfast..."

"Okay, okay," Mr. Laidlaw said. "Let's have that brunch."

He led the way down the stairs, through the living room, and past the tree, to the dining room.

"Oh, good, you're here," said Mrs. Laidlaw. "Wally, you're over there. Carolyn, you'll help me bring everything in?"

Mr. Laidlaw sat down at the end on Wally's right, his back to the window that looked out on a rambling, snow-covered back yard. Mrs. Laidlaw and Carolyn both wore oven mitts to bring in plates that had been heated up. On each plate was what Mrs. Laidlaw described as a mushroom-and-spinach omelette.

"You can help yourselves to bacon ... here ... ham, hash browns, tomatoes, rye toast, strawberry jam; oh, and there's orange juice," she said. "And Louis—the champagne?"

"Damn, yes!" He took a bottle from an ice-filled bucket and expertly removed the cork. Pop!

Wally helped himself to a little of everything, saying, "This is a *feast*."

They took turns pouring juice into their glasses, and Mr. Laidlaw poured the champagne.

"*Bon appétit,*" he said.

"And Merry Christmas," said Carolyn, holding up her glass in a toast.

Once everyone had begun eating, Mrs. Laidlaw said, "Wally, did Louis bore you to tears with his hockey game?"

"He was transfixed," Mr. Laidlaw said.

"Indeed I was," said Wally. "I'd love to see more of it. I'd like to play a whole game."

"Did you tell him what Stephen said about it?"

"Mother..."

"Carolyn, I am not going to pretend that Stephen never existed. I think about him a lot, especially at this time of year. Wally, Stephen was a lovely young man. Our family thought the world of him."

Carolyn looked pained and seemed on the verge of bolting from the room or screaming, when Mr. Laidlaw, in an assertive voice, said, "Yes, Margaret, I did tell Wally what Stephen said about the game."

Wally thought he'd better say something. He said, "Everything I've heard about Stephen tells me he was a terrific guy. I wish I'd known him."

Carolyn seemed anxious to compose herself, determined not to burst into tears.

Mrs. Laidlaw said, "Yes. Well. You've seen what keeps my husband occupied in his retirement. Now, Wally, Carolyn tells me you are a history professor."

Before Wally could answer, Carolyn said, "And guess where we met."

Wally looked at her. He was quite ready to go over his curriculum vitae for the parents, and she had leaped into a topic he thought she'd wanted to avoid.

Mrs. Laidlaw was about to speak, when Carolyn said, "Uncle Nate's."

"The basement bar downtown?" said Mr. Laidlaw.

Wally was aghast.

"How do you know about a place like that?" Mrs. Laidlaw said to her husband.

"Let's just say it has a certain reputation," he said.

No one looked comfortable.

"It's a nice enough bar, as bars go," said Carolyn. "And I was there with Freya and Trish and Anita, sort of a girls' night out. And I took out a sketch pad and started to draw some of the people, and one of them was Wally. He noticed me sketching him and came over to our table."

"How romantic," said Mrs. Laidlaw.

Wally couldn't tell whether or not she was being sarcastic.

"Not half as romantic as the announcement I have to make," said Carolyn.

Mrs. Laidlaw, looking alarmed, stared at her daughter, and even checked her left hand for a ring. Wally couldn't believe how quickly all this was unfolding. It occurred to him that this might be a tactic Carolyn was using to deflect the conversation away from Stephen.

"Wally is going to Australia in February," said Carolyn, "and he wants me to go with him. If I can arrange it at work, I think I'm going to go."

Wally was stunned, but he tried to keep a benign smile on his face.

"This is all pretty sudden, isn't it?" said Mr. Laidlaw.

He and Carolyn and Wally all looked at Mrs. Laidlaw, who seemed shocked, and then, as if she remembered that these were different times now and people did these kinds of things spontaneously, or as if she wished she'd had a chance to do something similar, she smiled—perhaps for the first time all day.

"Carolyn, I think that's *lovely*," said Mrs. Laidlaw.

Carolyn jumped up and went to her mother and hugged her.

They settled into an animated discussion of what Wally would be doing in Australia, and that led to more details of his work. When they cleared the table, Wally offered to help in the kitchen, but both Laidlaws encouraged him to go back into the den with Louis. Wally looked forward to a quick and mindless game of hockey. Mr. Laidlaw closed the den door.

"Sit down, Wally," he said. "Not sure when you might get back this way, so I thought it best I make a point here. You're divorced, and I'm not sure what that says about your ability to commit yourself."

"Sir, I…"

"Let me finish here. When Stephen died, of an aggressive form of pancreatic cancer, there were three hearts broken in this family, not just one. And it's pained Carolyn's mother and me to see that girl suffer. And now it looks like she has another chance at happiness. You know why Margaret didn't throw a fit over this Australia thing? Because she can see that the light is back in her daughter's eyes. I just thought that needed to be said. We don't give a crap if you take her to *Antarctica* if it makes her happy. We're counting on you."

On their way to her place, Carolyn said, "I'm sorry about all that talk about Stephen."

"I was glad your mother mentioned him. Your dad, too. It's healthier to talk about him, don't you think?"

"I was never sure…. You never talk about your wife."

"You're right."

"Well, we cleared the air on one thing—they're fine with Australia."

"And you told the truth about how we met."

"I could tell they both liked you. Dad's never talked so much to *anybody* about his game since…"

"Since Stephen."

"Right."

They rode along in silence for a while. Carolyn encircled Wally's right arm with both her arms. Wally knew it was time.

"About my wife," he said.

"Your ex-wife."

"Yes."

"Do we have to talk about her right now?"

"No, but..."

"I'd rather not, if that's okay. Not now."

She kept her arms around his arm and didn't speak. As much as he wanted to discuss his predicament, he did not want to interfere with this quiet time Carolyn seemed to need. She was likely reminiscing about past Christmases.

Once they were inside her place, Carolyn took him into her arms and held him tightly. She said, "I want to make love, not crazily and wildly the way it was the other night, but gently and slowly and quietly."

"Are you sure?" he whispered.

After the previous night, he'd been afraid they'd go back to a more or less platonic relationship for the duration of the holiday season. He'd resigned himself to it and thought it would be a good time to deal with what he hadn't yet told her. But...

"That's what I *want*, Wally, desperately, but, Wally ... I can't. You can leave if you want to, or leave after we open the presents, and I won't be at all offended. But Wally, it would mean a lot to me if you would stay, and I'll make you something, and we'll have a quiet night, and maybe I'll show you a few photo albums."

He so badly wanted the wild and crazy lovemaking of the other night, but he said, "Whatever you want to do, Carolyn, is fine by me. I completely understand."

13.

AT DOBBER'S

Dobber Dreger's house was an old two-and-a-half storey with a screened-in verandah that let snow in to pile up on the summer toys and garden furniture that were stored there. The screen door was propped open by an old *Queenston St.* sign. Taped to the main door was a message in what Carolyn identified as Dobber's favourite typeface, Baskerville bold: **Walk in at your own risk.**

Wally pushed open the oak door, narrowly missing a fellow who was quick to get out of the way. People filled the vestibule, there were closely packed conversation groups in the hall beyond, and young men and women sat in no particular pattern all the way up the stairs. The noise of many voices all but blocked out what didn't sound like holiday music. Laughing and shouting seemed to come from every part of the house, and nothing was comprehensible until a young woman noticed Carolyn.

"*Here she is!*" the young woman shrieked.

"Carolyn! You devil!" cried the fellow Wally had almost hit.

"*Dobber! They're here!*" someone else yelled.

A young man in a black muscle shirt that showed off his tattooed arms broke through the crowd to hug Carolyn before she'd had a chance to take off her coat. A woman whose frizzy hair smelled of pot squeezed past Wally to hug one of Carolyn's arms.

"So *this* is the guy," someone else said.

Wally saw everyone turning and ceasing conversation to look at Carolyn and at him. He knew the Dobber Design staff numbered no more than twelve or thirteen, so this crowd likely included spouses and dates, and friends and clients, and clients' spouses and dates. It occurred to him, as he felt everyone's scrutiny, that Dobber must've given Carolyn a nine-thirty time for this party and all other guests eight or eight-thirty so that her arrival—with her new boyfriend—could be heralded in this way: a kind of grand entrance. Guys took turns hugging her and kissing her—not only on the cheek but also on the lips and the neck—and women hugged her and kissed her too. Wally wasn't sure how she felt about all the attention; one guy took off her coat, and a woman took her scarf and gloves and handbag. Her new peacock-blue dress—more form fitting than anything he'd ever seen her in—was being pawed and grabbed from every angle. Wally was forced away from her side by the crush of people. The tattooed guy grabbed Wally's hand and shook it, someone else began to pull off his coat, and a young woman in a red tank top kissed his mouth with wet lips that tasted of Kahlua.

A bespectacled fellow who looked like photos Wally had seen of Buddy Holly stepped out of the throng and said, "Hey, come on, you guys, back off, would you?" This must be Dobber, the host. He didn't look like the kind of boss who, according to Carolyn, expected his graphic designers to keep a rolled-up sleeping bag in their cubicles for jobs that required all-nighters. "Come *on*. Hey, Carolyn, look at you! You look *great!*" He kissed her quickly on one cheek and gave Wally a look that seemed to deliver an instant evaluation: Wally was too old, too professorial, too drab. The look flashed disappointment, perhaps even horror or anger, that such a guy was sleeping with the darling of Dobber Design. But wait, wasn't this whole reception just a tad overwhelming? "All right," Dobber said, "into the living room!"

He took Carolyn by the hand and, like Moses did, he parted the sea of people between the front door and the far wall of the living room, where there was a log-burning fire. Carolyn glanced at Wally as she took *his* hand, and he followed her, tripping on someone's foot, spilling someone's drink. He offered apologies as he went, all the while feeling as if he'd been captured by aliens.

"*Okay!*" Dobber said. "Can everybody hear me—up the stairs and in the kitchen and wherever the hell else you are—*can you hear me?*"

Lots of people yelled back "*YES!*" and a male voice from somewhere above, maybe the attic, called down, "*Loud and clear!*"

"Okay, right. Okay. I am not going to say anybody in the company is inferior, so I am not going to say Carolyn here is *the best designer* on our staff, but I think you know she

131

has a special place in all our hearts. And when it comes to Carolyn, you gotta believe we get a little *protective*. So when she tells me she's seeing a guy, I tell 'er we gotta meet him. He's gotta understand that going out with Carolyn is like going out with *Dobber Design*. So, Carolyn, without further ado, let's hear who the hell this guy *is*."

People laughed and clapped and hooted throughout Dobber's spiel, but rather than make Wally feel silly, all the attention had the opposite effect. Wally felt pumped, as if he'd won a lottery. Of all the eligible guys out there—and presumably there were some here tonight—Carolyn had chosen *him*.

She let go of Wally's hand just when he thought she might need it for support. Somebody gave her a glass nearly full of something, and she surprised Wally by taking two hefty swigs. He thought she must be nervous, even frantic, but she lifted her head, stood taller and straighter, and cleared her throat.

"Thanks, Dobber," she began. "I am so pleased and happy to introduce Wally Baxter—*Doctor* Wally Baxter to you academic types—professor of history at the University of Manitoba, specialist in Canadian studies, and most important, a good man. I'm going to embarrass Wally only a little bit by telling you how we met."

Wally might have cringed, thinking "Oh, no!" had he not become galvanized by the command Carolyn had taken of the audience. He reminded himself that she must be good at presentations to clients, and this was just another client.

"I took Wally to meet my parents on Christmas Day, and at first I thought we were going to have to *lie* about how we met. Even at my age, how do you tell your parents you met at Uncle Nate's?"

The place erupted in laughter, much of it the nervous kind coming from the married folks who'd likely done some serious trolling at Uncle Nate's at one time or another.

"Wally and I went into my parents' house not sure what we'd say when the subject came up, but once we were inside and they were hitting it off with Wally, I thought, What the heck, go for it!"

"You mean, *What the fuck!*" someone shouted, drawing snickers.

"You said it!" Carolyn retorted, and everyone laughed. "So this is what I told them. True story: One night in October, three of my friends talked me into going to Uncle Nate's to hang out and people-watch."

"Oh, *sure*. We *know* your friends," someone blurted.

"Can we let Carolyn *speak?*" Dobber yelled.

"It's okay, Dobber. The fact is, we not only went to watch people, I went to *draw* people. It was the only way the girls could get me to go with them—let me take my sketch pad. So we settled into a typical girls' night out, except I had to have a good view of everybody without being too obvious about it. And I saw this *face* that intrigued me."

Wally blushed as people turned to look at his face. Oh, yeah! he imagined them saying as they whipped out their own sketch pads. Or more likely, That face? Are you kidding me?

Carolyn went on to tell how the evening unfolded, with Wally going over to see what she was drawing.

"Wait, Carolyn," someone called. "What did you *say?*" Someone else shouted, "What did *he* say?"

"Oh, God," Carolyn said, "I don't remember. The girls welcomed him and made me show him the sketch. I was embarrassed—hard to believe that was two and a half months ago—but, hey, listen to this: If I can talk Dobber into letting me use up some of my vacation, Wally has asked me to go with him to Australia."

Wally had to force a broad smile onto his face to hide the feeling of nausea a mention of *Australia* could bring on. It reminded him that he had told Carolyn nothing about the visit he'd had from Marjorie, her request that they get back together, her sleeping at his place, her making breakfast for him, Geordie's change of heart, and Marjorie's strong desire to make it a threesome. Christmas Day was the last time they'd been together, and it just didn't seem the right time to talk about *the Marjorie problem* when Carolyn was feeling so melancholy and reflective. She'd spent the whole time after they'd opened their presents (he'd given her a gold bracelet that she was wearing tonight; she'd given him a blue sweater that didn't quite fit) looking at year-books and photo albums that documented her childhood, her teen years and then her wedding to Stephen (who had curly blond hair but wasn't as handsome as Wally had expected), their honeymoon in Niagara Falls, their first apartment and their Munroe Avenue house, and parties with some of her friends and their spouses. It was now Saturday, December 28, and he was beginning to believe that it really wasn't necessary to talk about *the Marjorie problem* with Carolyn, that it was his problem to solve; he further rationalized that he should let tranquility prevail in Bill Horton's life and at least wait until New Year's Eve had passed. At the same time, he dreaded the next phone call that might come from Marjorie, telling him she'd told Bill Horton to get the hell out of her house.

Many who'd been sitting were standing now, applauding, looking at Wally, expecting him to say something.

He spoke: "I want to thank everybody for your warm welcome. Needless to say, I'm so glad Carolyn picked me to draw. I look forward to meeting every single one of you."

And then he gave Carolyn a brief hug before those people closest came up to shake his hand and to introduce themselves. Wally felt as if this were a wedding—he expected somebody to throw confetti.

Dobber appeared in front of him, shaking his hand and patting his shoulder. "You're being a good sport, God damn you," Dobber said. "What can I get you to drink?"

"Any kind of beer would be great," Wally said. "Dobber, Carolyn hasn't really decided if she's going away, especially at what must be a busy time..."

"Christ, Carolyn's going away will *cripple* us—but it's about *time* she buzzed off. She's *too* dedicated. You get her the hell out of here, and so far away that we can't go begging her to come back in and help us out for a day. Hey, you're not taking her away just yet—not till February, right?"

"So you didn't just find out tonight..."

"Jesus, no. She talked to me about it yesterday. Hey, I'll get you that beer."

It was two in the morning when Wally, who had cut himself off at two beers, drove a contented, slightly drunk Carolyn home. Wally felt a little unnerved by an encounter he'd had with a tough-looking guy named Karnak, one of Dobber's computer technicians. Wally came out of the upstairs bathroom and was confronted by him. Karnak, a tall guy with a shaved head and married eyebrows, gave Wally a nice enough smile, meeting him for the first time, but he gestured to Wally to step into one of the bedrooms. There were coats piled on the beds but no one else was in the room. Karnak closed the door. The only light came from a street light outside.

"You and I have a mutual acquaintance," Karnak said.

"Really?" said Wally. "Well, it *is* Winnipeg, isn't it? Not many degrees of separation." Wally knew he sounded too jaunty. "Who is it?"

"Your neighbour."

"Miles?"

"Pretty good friend, I understand."

"Well, we do see each other in the hall..."

"I'll cut through the crap. Miles tells me you are still pretty sweet on your ex-wife."

Wally felt himself sinking into some sort of purgatory, as if he were being cornered by thugs in a downtown back lane. Yet all Karnak had done was quote Miles.

"We ... we still communicate, if that's what you mean," Wally said. "We have a teen-aged son; she's married again..."

"Miles tells me she was at your place the other night. Alone."

"Look ... if you're..."

"Wally. I don't give a fuck about your ex-wife. I *do* give a fuck about Carolyn. She had a straight shooter of a husband, and she went through hell when Stephen got sick. She obviously thinks you're a straight shooter. You'd better be. The crew at Dobber's is counting on it. That's all I've got to say, Wally. Carolyn deserves an honest, straight-shooting guy, and we hope like hell she's found one."

Carolyn rested her head on Wally's shoulder as they drove down Main Street and over the Disraeli Bridge. She was at peace; maybe she was snoozing. She trusted him. Knowing nothing about his upstairs encounter with Karnak, she couldn't detect Wally's turmoil. He had waited too long to tell her about *the Marjorie problem.* Much as he told himself that he had initiated none of it, he still believed he should have told Carolyn what Marjorie had been up to. Now, if he told Carolyn tonight, he'd have to tell her that Karnak knew—and God knows how many others—and she'd think he was telling her not because he was *a straight shooter* but because he'd been threatened. No matter how angry or disappointed she might be, however, he had to tell her as soon as possible. He'd let her rest on the way home and once they got there, he'd insist on her hearing him out.

When they reached her house, he parked the car and walked her up the sidewalk. She staggered and slipped and she chuckled as he caught her and kept her from falling. She was tipsy.

"That was *such* a good evening," she sighed. She giggled as she fumbled with her key.

"It was," he said, taking the key from her hand and unlocking the door. "You were *magnificent.*"

"Come o-o-o-on in."

"Carolyn, if you don't mind, I really have to discuss something with you."

She shut the door, and they took off their coats. "Jesus, you're always saying that at the craziest times."

She hugged him. She kissed him.

"I'm serious," he said. "Could we turn on the lights and maybe pour a glass of milk or something, and sit down at the kitchen table..."

"Oh, sure," she said, kissing his face. "Sure, sure, sure."

"I mean it, Carolyn, we need to talk about ... *Carolyn*..."

She whispered into his ear, "I was so proud of you tonight, Wally, I could hardly wait to get you home." And he knew that all his determination was lost when she unzipped his trousers and dropped to her knees in front of him.

14.

CALL WAITING

Sunday morning, after lying awake in his bed, going over and over what he would say to Marjorie, Wally got up and phoned her. It was nearly always she who answered, and he'd tell her they had to meet somewhere today. They could not wait a day longer. It was fairly early—nine-thirty—but not too early. He was sure she would be there, sipping her second cup of coffee, catching up on the Saturday *Free Press*.

"Hello?"

It was Bill Horton, who never answered when Marjorie was at home. What could Wally possibly say to Bill Horton?

"Bill, it's Wally. Could I please speak with Marjorie?"

"Well, I wish you could, Wally, but she isn't home right now. She and Dodie—well, you know this party-planning business of theirs—they've got a client who lives in one of those castle-like houses on Wellington Crescent. They think they've hit the jackpot with this one, Wally, doing all the decorations and what-have-you for a New Year's Eve party at the client's home. I believe Marjorie said there are seventy to one hundred invited guests, and she and Dodie are arranging everything, even the catering. I don't know which house it is, but can you imagine one hundred people sitting down to dinner? It boggles the mind. Well, maybe they aren't all sitting down, maybe ... well, I'm glad I don't have to worry about it. Marjorie and Dodie are really quite amazing, I must say—well, but they've had to bring in one or two of their friends—do you remember Kristy?"

Wally was becoming more and more anxious. "Yes, Kristy Elliott, but..."

"That's her. Lovely person, really, and Marjorie says she has a real knack for decorating, so she'll be a real..."

"*Bill?*"

"...help in what they're doing today. Marjorie says Kristy is one of those people who get right to it—she'll be doing the job while others are standing there trying to visualize what..."

"*Bill?*"

"...exactly they want to ... oh, sorry, you were..."

"Is there any way that I can contact Marjorie?"

"Well, she doesn't like anyone to call her at a client's house, and I guess I don't blame her—nothing more annoying for the client, I would think, having to field other people's calls; and Marjorie wants to stay on the good side of this client, who could bring them—Marjorie and Dodie, I mean—a lot of business. But, Wally, she did say she'd call here when she goes on her lunch break. If she does, should I tell her to call you?"

"Would you please?"

"I certainly will, Wally. I think she likely wants to talk with you anyway, to tell you our news."

"Your *news?*"

"Yes, I think you'd call it news. I can't tell you any more than that, Wally. I know she wants to tell you herself. I'm a little surprised she hasn't told you already, but she's been so busy, she…"

"Bill, Bill. I really have to go. Please tell her to call me."

"Yes, all right, I will. As I say, she said she would call me on her lunch break, and I can't be sure when that would be, because she has to—well, they both have to pick their spots—when…"

"Thank you, Bill."

"Oh. Right. Oh, don't mention it, Wally. It was good speaking with you."

Wally hung up and was now rattled even more. *News.* News? Bill Horton was a complacent fellow, but even he wouldn't sound that cheerful if Marjorie had told him she wanted to leave him. What news? Maybe she was going to head over to Wally's to tell him, once she'd got this party-planning business with the Wellington Crescent folks out of the way—if there really was a party being planned, that is. That could be a lie. She could be on her way over to Wally's right now to throw herself on his mercy, if not on his bed. And there was Carolyn, over on Munroe, sleeping in, completely oblivious to *the Marjorie problem.*

Now he couldn't go out. He wanted to go for a long walk in the cold winter air, along River Avenue, past Osborne Street, all the way to where Wellington Crescent began, and walk and walk because he was so anxious, so hyper, so riddled with guilt about telling Carolyn nothing, so consumed by worry about Marjorie's scheming and about Karnak's threats. He wanted to walk and walk along Wellington, looking for Bill Horton's car in a driveway, unsure if he'd be able to recognize the car, worried about screwing up Marjorie and Dodie's job by suddenly appearing at the client's house, alternating between not giving a fuck about what the client thought and not wanting to create yet another problem. He cursed himself for being so selfish he'd given in to Carolyn in her kitchen (but, oh God, it was marvellous!) and not told her about his worries. He cursed the sabbatical and considered faxing another letter ("Dear Dr. Lockridge: I regret to say that I am incapable of sorting out who should accompany me to your college and therefore must inform you that I will not be able to fulfill my obligation as visiting fellow in the coming academic term"), but how could he leave Lockridge in the lurch less than two months before he was due to arrive? Wally paced back and forth in his apartment, checking the telephone a hundred times to be sure it was not off the hook, drank one beer and then another, stared out his window at the bleak sky, and paced some more. He checked his microwave clock, his bedside clock, and his watch every few minutes, appalled at how long it took for the digital numbers on the clocks to change, for the hands on his watch to move. As noon approached, he thought, What if Marjorie was too busy to go to lunch? What if she went for lunch and didn't bother to call Bill Horton? What if she went for lunch, called Bill Horton, was told Wally wanted her to call him, and told Bill Horton she would and decided to hell with it, let Wally stew?

The phone rang. He leaped for it.

"Hello?"

"Wally?" It was Carolyn.

"Hi." He was sure she'd hear the disappointment in his voice.

"Are you all right?"

"Yes, yes…"

"I thought you might've called."

"I didn't want to wake you; I thought you'd want to sleep in…"

"Didn't you like…"

"The party at Dobber's?" He was rushing his words. "Of course I did; I liked meeting all your workmates."

"No, no, I mean *after*."

"Oh, my god, yes; it was *amazing*. But, Carolyn?"

"What's wrong?"

"Can I call you back? I'm expecting a call, and it's…"

"Don't you have call waiting?"

"I don't know…"

"You don't *know*? Wally, you *must* have it. You'll hear a couple of quick beeps and you just tell me to hold on for a minute and you push the Flash button…"

"What Flash button?"

"There on your receiver."

"Carolyn, if it's okay, I'll call you back just as soon as I've heard from…"

"Who?"

"Uh … my ex-wife."

"Oh…"

"You know all those times I've told you I have to talk

with you about something? Well, as soon as I hear from her, I hope to resolve a few things, and..."

"Like what?"

"Carolyn, I can't get into it now—I'll explain—but she might be trying to call me right this minute."

"I don't understand."

"It's nothing to worry about."

"Now I *am* worried."

"I've got it under control; it's nothing I can't handle."

"Oh, dear!"

"Are you going to be there?"

"I think so—"

"I'll call you back just as soon as I can."

He wasn't sure if she'd hung up first or he did. Now she was probably angry with him, or disappointed, and worried. He should've insisted on telling her everything before this, but he thought he could still save the day by talking with Marjorie, if only she would call.

The phone rang. He grabbed it.

"Hello!"

A male voice chuckled. "Baxter, you bastard. How the hell *are* you? A belated Merry Christmas, you old fart."

"Who—who—?"

"What, you've turned into an owl?"

"Is that Verne? Verne Lovett?"

"I know it's been ages, but, shit, you could call *me* once in a while, you know."

"Verne—"

"I was just saying to Lois over breakfast, did that son of a bitch send us a Christmas card this year? We got one from Marjorie, but nothing from you, so Lois says, 'Why don't you call him and tell him it's time he came out here to visit us.' What is it, three years? Cripes, you're like family, you know; you don't need a freakin' gold-plated invitation."

"Verne—"

"Know what I said to Lois? I said the reason he isn't keeping in touch is he probably has a new lady friend who has him wrapped around her little pinkie. Am I right, Casanova?"

"Verne, could I call you back? I'm expecting a call."

"Don't you have call waiting?"

"I—no, I don't."

"Jesus."

"Okay if I call you back?"

"Suit yourself, old buddy. Or wait another three or six years. Jeez, there was something I wanted to ask you—what—oh, yeah, remember that..."

"I'll call you back."

Wally hung up, wondering if Verne would ever speak to him again. His worries were multiplying. He wanted to call Carolyn to apologize and suggest they go somewhere for dinner, and he could tell her all the nutty things that had been—

The phone rang. He'd never had this many calls in—

"Hello?"

"Wally. I've been trying to get you."

"Sorry, Marjorie. Other people have been calling."

"Don't you have call waiting?"

"I don't think so."

"Well, you'd know if you did. Look, I'm just about out of time, and I'm tying up Dodie's cell phone—"

"Bill said you had news."

"Yes. Wally, you'll be glad to know I got over that little bit of insanity—and now that you're taking Geordie to Australia with you, Bill and I have decided to go on a long trip ourselves. Sort of a second honeymoon, if you like. I've always wanted to go on a safari, so we'll be going to Africa and then India and—"

"Wait. Marjorie, I'm glad you aren't talking about leaving Bill anymore, but Marjorie, I don't know if I can take Geordie. You know that when I said I would it was all part of not wanting to upset anybody during the holiday season."

"I'm sorry, Wally. Geordie is counting on the trip. And Bill and I have made plans."

"That fast? You couldn't have."

"Wally, I have a New Year's Eve set-up I have to get back to."

"Marjorie, there isn't enough room—"

"For you and him and your artist? That's *your* problem."

"I don't think I—"

"You are morally obligated. Even legally."

"Marjorie—"

She hung up.

15.

BAGGAGE

Wally drove down the newly plowed street, hoping that Geordie would be watching for him. He did not want to have to get out of his car, go to the door and ring the bell, or knock, if Bill Horton hadn't fixed it.

It was the day Geordie was going to meet Carolyn—Saturday, January 4.

Wally had not seen Carolyn since they'd met for coffee on Sunday, December 29, at a Starbucks; it was the afternoon after Dobber's party.

"I knew this time of year was going to be tough," she had said. "Not just the memories, but the rituals. Twice a year—on Stephen's birthday and on New Year's—I spend a couple of days with his folks. They live in Brandon. Lovely people. I'll leave work early on Tuesday, New Year's Eve, and drive out there, spend the evening and all the next day, and drive in first thing Thursday."

Here he'd been looking forward to ringing in the New Year with sex and champagne. Wasn't she carrying her grieving way too far?

"I'm sorry," she said. "But just think of all the time we'll have in Australia."

Who said they'd have any time alone in Australia, now that … Wait a minute. Was she saying she was definitely going? It was time to unload everything on her.

"Please don't look so sad, Wally."

"Carolyn. You know there are some things I've been wanting to tell you." Here goes. At last.

"You mentioned that this morning. You had to talk to Marjorie. Did you?"

"Yes. And this is about her and my son."

"I don't know if I'm ready to hear it—sounds serious."

"I can't put it off any longer."

"Oh, dear. All right. I guess it's only fair; you've been putting up with a lot of stuff about Stephen." She looked nervous. "Can I get another coffee?"

They fetched new cups of coffee, and Wally told all, beginning with the night he'd received Carolyn's call ("Please come now. I want you"). He told her that it was Marjorie who was there at the time, not his neighbour; that he'd left Marjorie in the hallway and was so anxious to get to Carolyn's that he hadn't shut his door and she must have gone back into his apartment; that he'd absolutely forgotten all about Marjorie during those ensuing hours of rapture; that Marjorie was there in his apartment when he got back; that he felt the only decent thing to do was let her stay until morning, and she did—on the chesterfield; that she had made their breakfast; that she told him she thought it would be a great experience for their son if Wally took him to Australia; that Geordie had shown no interest in the idea at first but had changed his mind; that Marjorie had decided to go on a lengthy vacation with her husband, putting responsibility for Geordie squarely on Wally; and that Wally had faxed Dr. Lockridge at Jane Franklin College to ask if there could be accommodation for three. What Wally did not mention was Marjorie's short-lived plea for Wally to take her back; it seemed unnecessary to mention it now, but of course it was the main reason she had shown up at his place that night.

And, wouldn't you know it? As Carolyn sat there looking by turns stunned and angry and upset, what was the first comment she made? "I don't get it. Why did she have to show up at your place and spend the night just to discuss your son?"

"She ... she does these irrational things sometimes..."

"You mean she's dropped in before and stayed the night?"

"Well, no..."

"Where is her husband in all this?"

"Bill Horton is a pretty laid-back guy, and sometimes she takes advantage of that ... Okay, she came over, and she waited because right out of the blue she'd got this crazy notion that she and I should..."

"Should *what?*"

"Get back together."

"Oh, God, Wally..." There were tears in her eyes. "Why are you even telling me this?"

"I thought you should know everything."

She jumped up and headed for the door. The few other customers watched him hurry after her. She was wearing her coat; he had to go back to the table for his. He ran out to the parking lot, hoping she wasn't dashing off down the street. He saw her at the car, and he hurried to unlock the doors; he thanked the Lord when she got in.

As soon as he was inside with her, she said, "I gave you everything that night, Wally, *everything*—my body, my *soul*—and what do you do? You go home and spend the rest of the night with your fucking *wife*..."

"My *ex*-wife..."

"Oh, excuse me, your fucking *ex*-wife. And what did you do in the morning, fuck her before the two of you ate your bacon and eggs?"

"Carolyn, she dropped in, and I left, and I never dreamed she'd be there when I got back. I gave her no encouragement..."

"You should've kicked her out!"

"You know what I think? I told her this. I think she was jealous of me going to Australia. That's all it was. Now, she's talked Bill Horton into an exotic trip, and she's unloaded Geordie, and she's happy again. I think it's that simple."

"I can't get involved with this shit, Wally. I have enough to sort out and think about, getting ready to go to the other side of the world with a guy I've known for barely five minutes. I thought you were a solid guy, but now I'm not so sure. And this whole thing about your son going with us, a kid I've never met..."

"I want you to meet him. Maybe when you get back from Brandon, we could…"

"You know what? I worried about this Brandon thing, but now I'm *glad* I'm going. And I'm going to think hard about whether I even do want to go to Australia. Right now, it seems like utter madness. I'll call you when I get back. Thursday. And if I decide I'm going, we'll meet with your kid."

"Geordie," Wally said. "His name is Geordie."

And he drove her home without another word.

On New Year's Eve, he worried about Carolyn driving the two hundred kilometres to Brandon. The weather was blustery, and he wished he had asked her to call him when she got there. To distract himself, he decided to tackle the reference letter he'd been putting off writing for a graduate student. He sat in his kitchen, trying to compose a first sentence that would grab the reader's attention. So far, he'd written "If," as in "If you are looking for a truly dynamic young historian, look no further," and he told himself that starting anything with *if* placed doubt in the reader's mind. He kept looking at the clock on his microwave oven. He wondered if Carolyn and her in-laws were watching the countdown on TV or if they'd already gone to bed. He was sure they'd spent the evening sharing anecdotes about Stephen, while Carolyn recalled lovely memories of embracing Stephen at midnight. Goddamn Stephen. Wally thought of all the New Year's Eves he'd spent with Marjorie: the noisemakers, and "Auld Lang Syne," and kissing other people's wives and girlfriends. He remembered his pre-puberty years at home when, at the stroke of twelve, he ran to first one bathroom and then the other to flush the toilet. Back then, he felt he had to do *something* to celebrate. Now he watched the microwave clock change to 12:00 and 12:01 and 12:02 without a sound. The new year arrived without the pop of a cork in one of the neighbouring suites, without any cheers, without a cry from one of Miles's girlfriends rejoicing in her first orgasm of 1997. Miles was in Mexico.

Wally's phone rang. It wasn't a long-distance ring, so he considered not answering it. Then he thought, What the hell.

"Happy New Year!" he said instead of "Hello."

"You're home."

"Hi, Erica."

"Are you alone?"

"Um … I … yes, I am."

"You told me you had a date."

"Well, … it didn't work out."

"Why am I not surprised? You know, I had … what, this sixth sense? … that you'd be there all by yourself. That's why I thought I'd call, just to see if I was right."

"And you are."

"You're a sad case, you know?"

"Okay, okay. How's your party going?"

"Pretty damn slow. You know you can do yourself a favour and me too, i e., you can get your ass over here right now."

"I'm sorry, Erica. I'm just not a party animal these days."

"No kidding. That's why I'm insisting you get over here. Loosen you up a little."

"I think I'm content to hang out here, pour myself a glass of milk, and hit the sack."

"For Christ's sake, Wally, Sheena wants her New Year's hug."

"She ... oh, the iguana. Sorry, Erica. I'm going to bed."

"Fuckin' party pooper."

Carolyn called him on Thursday, from work.

"Well, listen to this, Wally," she said. "Stephen's mum and dad said you must be pretty special to let me visit them on New Year's. I told them all about you, and they were happy for me. Oh, sure, we had our good cry, and we talked a lot about the old days. But they said I was still young and I should be getting on with my life. They said they really appreciated me keeping in touch with them, and I told them that wouldn't change, but they said it could be any old time, it didn't have to be on an *occasion*. They said they'd like to meet you, but I don't know if I could ever handle *that*. Anyway, I've gotta get back to work, but, if you still want me to, I'm going to Australia. Can I meet Geordie soon, whenever it makes sense to you both?"

And now here was Geordie, coming out to meet Wally just as he'd hoped. It was eleven thirty, and they were picking up Carolyn at noon and going for lunch.

"Morning, Geord."

Geordie got in and slammed the door.

"Oh, oh," said Wally as he pulled away. "What's up?"

"Nothing." He was scowling.

"Come on. We'd better talk about it before we get to Carolyn's."

"Mum's being a total jerk."

"Really?"

"Setting curfews, telling me where I can't go. Dad, I'm going into grade twelve next year. I'm not a kid."

"What caused…"

"I stayed out on New Year's. She used to get mad when I *didn't* go out."

"How long did you stay out?"

"I was at a party … until, I don't know, five or six. It was *New Year's.*"

"Where were you?"

"I told you—at a party. Now you're sounding like Mum."

"Okay, we'd better cool it for now."

"I don't know if I can do this, Dad. Meet your *girlfriend.* It's surreal."

"Geordie, we said we'd do this today. The three of us are going away together in five weeks."

"Yeah, well … I don't know about that anymore."

"All right, one thing *I* know for sure: you're going to like Carolyn." Wally realized as he said it that he didn't know that at all.

They didn't talk the rest of the way to Munroe Avenue. Carolyn was waiting outside, dressed in a parka and suede snow boots. Her cheeks were rosy, and she had a shy smile on her face. He pulled up beside her. She was standing on the passenger side, and Geordie, suddenly animated, jumped out.

"I'll get in the back," he said, holding the door open for her.

"No, no," she said. "You stay up front with your dad. Hi, I'm Carolyn."

She shook his hand, and her smile widened.

"Sorry, yeah, I'm Geordie, but are you sure you..."

"Positive." Carolyn opened the back door and jumped in. "Greetings!" She gave Wally's shoulder a quick squeeze.

"Weren't you freezing out there?" Wally asked.

"Naw. I love the crisp air. Great skiing weather."

They headed for the Salisbury House on Ellice, the one out by the airport. Carolyn led the conversation, drawing from Geordie that he'd played hockey as a kid in elementary school. She talked about her work, mentioning clients whose ads Geordie might've seen, and, when he recognized one brand and said he liked their ads, she asked him what he liked about them. Wally barely spoke. He was awed by the way Carolyn was carrying this off.

All three of them had Mr. Big platters for lunch; they were at ease with each other, Geordie blushing only once or twice—when Wally and Carolyn touched hands. Geordie seemed to be enjoying himself. Carolyn had taken his mind off whatever he'd been going through with Marjorie; not only was she discussing things with him as if he and she were equals, but she also had the knack of choosing topics that appealed to him. On top of that, she looked smashing in her soft red sweater. Wally saw real eye contact between the two of them and rejoiced. He began to believe the three of them *could* get along fine together in Australia. (He had received a rather cool reply to his latest fax. Dr. Lockridge wrote: "It is entirely possible that our housekeeping staff will be able to locate a cot that could be placed in the visiting fellow's study.") The conversation came around to board games; Wally mentioned that Geordie was unbeatable at chess.

Carolyn's eyes sparkled as she said, "Geordie, you would *love* my dad's fantasy hockey game. Wouldn't he, Wally?"

"You know, I think you would, Geord. It's tremendously realistic."

Geordie said, "You don't mean the table-top game where you move the players with rods…"

"No!" said Carolyn. "It's played with dice. Really complex rules. My dad makes up the players' names—for instance, there's a goalie called Arthur Puxbehimi—and he has a whole league: sixteen teams, a sixty-four-game schedule. You've got to see it to believe it."

"Sounds kind of weird…"

"I've played it," Wally said. "Not just goals and assists, but passing plays and penalties and injuries…"

"I know," said Carolyn. "Why don't the three of us drop over to my parents' place right now? My dad always likes to show off his game."

Before either Wally or Geordie could comment, Carolyn took her cell phone from her parka pocket and went off to the washroom area to call her dad.

If Mrs. Laidlaw was unhappy about the short notice, she didn't show it. When they arrived, she seemed thrilled to meet Geordie, perhaps because she seldom had young people in her house, or perhaps because this sudden visit had nicely shattered the boredom of yet another day with her husband off in his room rolling dice, even though the game was the reason for the visit. Wally thought his son looked apprehensive, even flustered, maybe wondering what the fuck he was doing here meeting a couple of old folks and likely feeling he was being forced to take an interest in a senior citizen's pastime, like lawn bowling or whist. But Laidlaw had used the time between his daughter's call and the threesome's arrival to prepare an impressive introduction to the game. He had a card table set up with three chairs around it. At each of two places was a printed lineup with player pictures, and the rules were in the middle facing the third place, where a real microphone lay. Laidlaw was going to let Wally and Geordie play the next game in his regular schedule, and he would do a play-by-play broadcast while he kept a record of what happened. By the time the game ended, Geordie was so hooked, he was talking about starting up his own league.

After they had dropped Carolyn off at home, Carolyn giving Wally a chaste kiss on the cheek and agreeing they'd talk later, Geordie reverted to his earlier mood, almost as if he'd been faking his excitement all afternoon

"Well, *that* was fun," Wally said, trying to imply that Geordie had no right to get sullen again after such a remarkably pleasant afternoon.

"Dad."

Wally didn't like the tone Geordie gave that one word. He expected Geordie's next words to be *Do I have to go home? Can't I move in with you?*

Instead, Geordie said, "I don't want to go to Australia."

This floored Wally. He made a left turn off Henderson and parked in a lot next to the Roxy Bowling Lanes.

"Okay," Wally said in his calmest voice. "You gotta be kidding. You and Carolyn seem to have hit it off big time."

"Carolyn's great, Dad. But you're my *dad*. And she's your girlfriend. I'll just be this kid—this third wheel—getting in the way."

"The three of us will have *fun*, just the way we did today."

"The whole thing is, Mum is using me to screw things up for you…"

"Oh, I don't…"

"And to keep me away from Michelle."

"Michelle."

"*My* girlfriend, Dad. I told you about her."

"The girl who beats you in your video game…"

"I really like her. We saw each other a lot over Christmas. *Too* much, Mum thinks. It's *unhealthy*, Mum says. What kind of garbage is that?"

So that's what all this was about. Geordie had the hots for a girl. Like father, like son. And good old Marjorie was trying to make life miserable for both her son and her ex.

"Geordie, your mum thinks you want to go to Australia with me. We both think it'd be a great experience for you to see another country. Bill Horton is even making sure your school is on side. And we won't be away *that* long."

"I don't want to go, Dad."

"If you don't, where will you stay?"

"I can stay home alone! I'm *sixteen*."

"Your mother will never agree to that."

"I could stay at Trevor's. Or I'll bet Michelle's family would let me stay there…"

"Whoa! Look, why don't you think about this a little more, and I will, too. We don't need this sabbatical of mine to make life miserable for everybody."

That evening, Wally and Carolyn had a leisurely dinner at Basil's in Osborne Village. Carolyn was excited about a call she'd received an hour earlier from Dobber, congratulating her because her ad designs had clinched the landing of a new account—an upscale restaurant that was opening in the Exchange District. This news reminded Wally that Carolyn's work was a big part of her life. He would love to have kept talking about what made a restaurant *upscale*, what kinds of people the owners wanted to attract, and where Dobber would place the ads to get at those people, but eventually Carolyn mentioned Geordie. She laughed about how the game had captivated him. As they sipped wine and waited for dessert, she said that she could see the three of them getting along fine in Australia; they could take turns suggesting places they wanted to visit, and, when they weren't sightseeing, they could play her dad's hockey game. All they had to do was get Laidlaw to give them a copy of his rules.

Wally, hating to destroy her bantering mood, said, "Geordie doesn't want to go now."

"What? How ... did I ..."

"You were terrific, and so were your parents. It's just that he's suddenly got a girlfriend he thinks he's crazy about."

"Did he just tell you this?"

"On the way home after we dropped you off."

"But you said he couldn't stay at home because..."

"His mother and her husband are going off on a trip of their own."

"There's nowhere else he could stay?"

"He thinks his girlfriend's family might..."

"Ah, bad idea."

As the server placed wedges of banana cream pie in front of them, Carolyn's expression went from a troubled frown to the elation that had accompanied her story about the new client.

She said, "Why don't we ask Mum and Dad if he can stay there?"

"What?"

"He made a big hit with them. Let me at least ask; I'll call them tomorrow."

"What?" Wally said again. Did she not see how absolutely outlandish that idea was?

Later, in the car outside Carolyn's, Wally said, "Can I come in?"

"Oh, Wally, not tonight, okay? Let's get your frigging family problems out of the way. I honestly didn't think when I fell for you that you came with so much *baggage…*"

Carolyn called him on Tuesday to tell him that her parents loved the idea of Geordie moving in with them. She said her mother would like to meet with Geordie a few more times, but she was already preparing the guest room and wanted a list of his favourite meals.

Wally couldn't comprehend Geordie thinking this was a good idea, and he grappled with how he'd deal with it. He lay awake Tuesday night worrying about the situation and what Marjorie's reaction was going to be. He decided there was no point discussing it with Geordie;

he'd better go straight to Marjorie and get that over with.

Before he had figured out when to call her and what exactly to say, she called him. It was nine-fifteen Wednesday morning, after Geordie had gone to school.

"Our son finally got over his snit and actually talked to me," she said. "Last night. Took me a while to get it out of him. I gather he told you he didn't want to go to Australia."

"He told me that, yes."

"And he told you why?"

"There's a girl … Michelle…"

"And they are having lots of sex."

"They aren't!" Given Wally's meagre record of lovemaking in the last three-plus years, this was not something he wanted to hear about his teen-aged son.

"Oh, yeah. They can't get enough of each other. I'm trying to cut down on their opportunities, and I hope you will back me up. When he's gone for the two months, she'll chase somebody else and maybe he'll get over her."

"Marjorie, we can't *force* him to go."

"Well, he can't stay here, can he? Didn't you make that clear?"

"I found a good place for him to stay."

When he explained where, Marjorie blew up. She threw every curse word in her considerable vocabulary at him and said he was insane if he thought she would let her son stay one minute with his fucking artist's old man and old lady, and she hung up. She called right back to threaten Wally: she'd sue him, she'd sic a hit man on him, she'd string him up by the balls, she'd tell the University he was unfit to teach, she'd smear his name so badly in Australia, he'd be picked up by cops at the Sydney Airport. If he didn't take his son to Australia and leave the fucking artist at home, she'd make sure he never saw Geordie again.

That afternoon, Wally sat in his office, staring at the wall. *The Marjorie problem* was worse than ever, so there was no point in even calling Carolyn. The trip to Australia was a disaster. Best thing he could do now was cancel the three tickets he'd bought—he'd used up a huge chunk of his savings—and maybe he could get most of the money back.

There was a tap on his open office door. It startled him, and, when he turned to see who it was, that startled him even more.

"Joyce!"

She wore a caramel-coloured suede coat that was open, showing a brown sweater and skirt, a bright green silk scarf, and a hint of her memorable figure.

"Hey, Wally," she said, plopping her brown leather handbag onto his side table. "I was down the hall talking with Linda, and I wondered if you'd be in. She said she thought you were."

He jumped up and gave her a hug. Her scent took him back the few years to what seemed in retrospect like a simpler, happier time.

He said, "Linda just told me the other day you were still in Vancouver. What brings you here?"

"Ohh, I can tell you about that … but I thought you might be close to leaving for the day. Maybe we could go for a drink?"

He glanced at his messy desk. He'd intended to do a few things today, but he'd accomplished nothing.

"Fantastic idea!" he said, clapping his hands.

"And then do you think you could give me a lift? I'm staying downtown."

They went to the bar in the Holiday Inn. When she took off her coat and scarf, his mind flashed back to that evening after he'd bought a computer from her, when she took him home and she was feeling so amorous that she doffed all her clothes, and, delightfully surprised, he followed her lead, and they tumbled onto her bed for a most amazing time. As he clinked his beer glass with Joyce's Caesar, he had a fleeting thought of Carolyn working late at Dobber Design, but it was instantly replaced by the reality of Joyce's relaxed and pretty presence.

"So, with the business going well," she was saying, "and having two extremely capable assistants, I figured it was time I went back to school. I want to do a master's in computer science before I get old and grey. I love Vancouver, but I thought, since I've got some time and some flexibility, why not have a look at programs in a few different universities. So this week I'm checking out Manitoba."

Joyce sat there, sipping her drink, content, a seemingly beautiful picture of sanity and serenity.

"You've got the world by the tail," Wally said, trying to hide his envy.

"But so have you! Linda tells me you're going on sabbatical to Australia."

"Well, yes, but it's not a scholarship or anything. It's costing me an arm and a leg."

"I'd *love* to go to Australia!"

"You know, I keep saying I'm going to Australia, but really I'm spending most of the time in Tasmania. It's supposed to have all the dramatic scenery of Canada condensed into a pretty small space. They say the western half is mostly wild and uninhabitable."

"Tasmania! I'm envious!"

He could see she was interested, and he rambled on about the pristine beaches and the mountainous wilderness and a charismatic character named Anthony Fenn Kemp and the shipping of convicts from England.

After their third drink, Joyce said, "Are you as hungry as I am?"

"Now that you mention it, yes. Should we order some pretzels or…"

"Do you have time for dinner?"

"Why not!"

"My treat."

They went to the Round Table, and Wally was happy to settle into one of the alcoves—less likely to be seen. But hell, what would it matter if he *was* seen?

"Do you remember the day you taught me to Jet Ski?"

"Of course I do."

"You kept telling me to give it more gas. 'Give it more gas!'"

"And you did. Have you kept up with your Jet Skiing?"

"You've got to be kidding."

"Oh, Wally, you should've."

They got back to talking about Tasmania, and Joyce asked questions that tested Wally's book knowledge.

"You know," she said, after finishing off her roast beef and her second glass of wine, "right now would be the perfect time for me to go there. I don't expect to start my studies until fall, wherever I decide to go."

Wally tried not to think about taking her to Australia instead of anyone else ("Dear Dr. Lockridge: This is gonna knock your mother-fuckin' Tasmanian socks off…"); he knew he wasn't thinking clearly. He tried to see this evening as a little bit of serendipity and nothing more. He had a couple of cups of coffee, knowing he still had to take her to wherever she was staying.

In the car, she made an elaborate gesture of looking in her handbag for her key and told him she was staying at the Fort Garry Hotel.

"Joyce," he said, before shifting into Drive, "I have to tell you, you are even more gorgeous than I remember you, possibly the most beautiful creature on the planet."

"Oh, Wally, thank you; your compliments always were pretty exaggerated, but hey, I'm not complaining." She giggled.

He tried to drive carefully, and, when they reached the Fort Garry in what seemed like no time at all, he pulled up to the carpeted steps of the front entrance.

"The night's young," she said. "Come on in for a nightcap."

He knew he shouldn't, but why not? This was the best time he'd had in a while. They had a valet park the car, and they went into the main-floor lounge. As they talked and laughed about the time when he mastered the Jet Ski, he had difficulty keeping his eyes off her bosom. It seemed almost inevitable that, after they had finished off their glasses of Cointreau on ice, she placed her hand on his, looked him in the eye and softly said, "Want to go upstairs?"

And he knew what he should answer, but his boggled mind made him hesitate—Isn't this just what I need to tide me over?

16.

CAROLYN'S JOURNAL I

Monday, February 10, 1997
I'm going to Australia! I finally convinced myself that I should go, and I promised myself I'd keep a journal on this trip. I have to. It's the longest trip I've ever been on. So here goes!

I've always wanted to keep a journal. I've started them before. But I just get so busy. Well, I'm not going to be busy now, am I?

Dobber was the last familiar face we saw in Winnipeg. He caught us just before we went through security. A set of proofs he wanted me to see! I signed off on them. He gave me a hug and told me to forget the shop. Yeah, right!

We left on time. We're going business class all the way! So much for Calgary. I snoozed in the lounge while

Wally browsed in the airport bookstore. I've started worrying about what I packed. I can't remember!

The next stop is San Francisco. Stephen and I went there on our first anniversary. He bought me two sweaters on Fisherman's Wharf. A green one and a gold one. They were always his favourites. Mine too.

My eyes filled up when I looked down at the lights of the city and remembered how it felt with Stephen back in 1981. I slipped into a washroom and splashed cold water on my face, splashed away my tears.

Wally asked me if I was okay. He so much wants me to enjoy this trip.

On our way now. Fourteen hours to Sydney. The flight attendants handed out headsets and little kits (sleep mask, socks, toothbrush). They intend to show three movies. A few people put on their masks. They look like Lone Rangers without eyeholes.

Wally is keeping the flight attendant busy with requests for scotch and ice. He wants to hold my hand, so I'm going to stop writing. It's nice that he wants to hold my hand.

Tuesday, February 11, 1997
This day was lost in time changes. I mostly slept. Or tried to sleep. Once when I woke up I didn't know where I was. I thought for a second it was Stephen beside me.

Wednesday, February 12, 1997
They served us breakfast at six this morning. Omelette,

blueberry muffin, croissant, huge sausage, large chunks of pineapple, juice, coffee.

Wally said he hadn't slept. I told him he was crazy. He snored.

It was raining when we landed in Sydney at seven thirty a.m. Wally said it was two thirty the day before in Winnipeg. We're seventeen hours ahead. Thinking about it makes my head ache.

We're in Australia!!!

Our luggage arrived, wet. We took a taxi to our hotel in the Wooloomooloo district. Love that name! Sat in the back and tried to ignore being on the wrong side of the road. Driver said they'd had thirty-eight-degree heat over the weekend.

At the Wooloomooloo Waters Hotel, we had to sit in the lobby waiting until they had a room. And it hit me. We're going to sleep together for the first time. Literally <u>sleep</u> together. Not right away. It's morning. And we had jet lag to worry about.

At nine thirty, a bellman took us to our room. He showed us how the plastic thingy attached to the key fit into a pocket on the wall. That activates the electric power, and energy is conserved while you're out.

The room is huge! Large living area, king-size bed on a pedestal, spacious bathroom. I'm writing this in the bathroom. Wally wanted to kiss me, and I told him I had to brush my teeth first. I'm sitting on the toilet with the water running. Wondering why I came all this way with a man I hardly know.

He'll be whipping his clothes off. He'll be expecting to fool around! Why can't he be tired?

I can't fool around, I just can't. Please don't be naked, Wally!

He wasn't. He was watching TV, still dressed. He'd found a newscast. Cyclone Gillian was bearing down on Queensland. Where we're going on Friday. He went into the bathroom and closed the door.

He came out and said he needed a shave and a shower. If he'd said "a shit," I don't know what I would've done. I might've laughed. It might've been what needed to be said.

We showered, one after the other. We undressed and dressed in the bathroom, separately. Like brother and sister.

We bought umbrellas in a sleazy area close by. The King's Cross district. Strip shows, porn stores. But there was a McDonald's. I had fries and a Coke and Wally had a quarter pounder with cheese.

We followed our map and walked to the Opera House. A Japanese couple asked us to take their picture with their camera. Wally was happy to. Then they took us, our arms flung out like divas. I imagined our photo on their Tokyo refrigerator door.

After buying Olympic tee-shirts and drinking Foster's Lagers on Circular Quay, we took a bus back to the hotel and crashed. We woke up too late for dinner. We had beers and chips from the mini-bar and both felt lousy. I had wondered if he would wear pyjamas, and, sure enough, he does. He put them and went to bed while I brought this journal up to date. I pretended to write more than I actually did. Wally turned over in a noisy way, like he was angry. I sure hope he isn't.

Stephen never wore pyjamas.

Thursday, February 13, 1997
Wally woke up at three thirty a.m. I hadn't been in bed long, and I pretended to be asleep. After a while, he whispered, "I can't sleep." I didn't answer. He went into the living room and closed a door I didn't know was there.

We are so out of sync right now. I wonder if we are going to be able to stand each other for eight weeks.

He woke me around seven, which was really irritating. Surely a person should be allowed to sleep in after a million-hour trip. He was dressed. He said we should get some breakfast and do a bit of sightseeing. Why couldn't he leave me a note and go for a bite on his own? Jesus!

At breakfast, we read the local newspapers like an old married couple. I took a good look at the ads. They are really no different from ours back home.

We took a bus tour. Wildlife park in the morning. Best thing was the sheep shearing. Kangaroos, koalas, crocodiles. They were mostly asleep. I envied them. Good lunch, though: steak, salad, vegetables, three scoops of ice cream for dessert. Afternoon at Bondi (pronounced <u>bond-eye</u>) Beach, where the wind pelted us with sand.

When we got back to the hotel around six, we made the mistake of lying down. Crash!

Again we woke too late for dinner. Good old beer and chips, watching TV.

I told him I was sorry I don't feel like messing around.

"It's the jet lag," he said. "Don't worry."

Friday, February 14, 1997
I dreamed of being with Stephen in Italy. We went into a café where every server sang arias. Loudly. It was

deafening. Stephen went to complain and didn't come back.

I woke up, turned over, and bumped my head on something. A box. The box smelt chocolaty.

"Happy Valentine's Day," someone said. It was Wally. Standing there in a pair of shorts he'd bought especially for the trip.

I sat up and saw there was an envelope with my name on it. I opened it, found a card featuring Snoopy and, hand-written, "Lots of love, Wally."

"What a sweet thing to do!" I said and reached for his hand.

He said he'd brought the card and the box of chocolates from Winnipeg. He bent to give me a kiss. I turned my lips away and instantly regretted it. Wally looked so sad.

At breakfast, we got some good news: Cyclone Gillian has dissipated.

We packed for our five-day jaunt into Queensland. Felt a little weird to put his stuff with mine in my suitcase. Everything else we put in his and a garment bag and left them at the Wooloomooloo.

We took a cab to the airport. Flew to Cairns in northern Queensland. Now in the Tropics! North of the Tropic of Capricorn.

Vicki from the Silky Oaks Lodge met us at arrivals. Tall, handsome woman who tried hard to make us feel welcome.

She drove us in a luxurious sedan north on the coastal highway. At Mossman, she took us on a narrow road through fields of sugar cane. She said the dense greenery rising up the mountain ahead of us was the Daintree

Rainforest. Where Silky Oaks is located. Wally rode up front, turning to look at Vicki a lot as they talked and laughed. I was jealous, to my surprise, and vowed to try harder.

Vicki delivered us into the hands of a green-shirted guy at the main lodge. Wally gave Vicki a hug and a huge tip. I was sweating. We checked in, and another green-shirted guy took us by electric cart to Chalet #35. It's almost hidden by tropical trees and bushes. Beautifully air-conditioned, though, with a spacious bathroom and spa (Jacuzzi). One queen-size bed, depressingly smaller and lower to the floor than our bed at the Wooloomooloo.

When the guy left, Wally turned to me. Vicki had put him in a good mood. He kissed me and slid his hand over my ass.

"Is this all right?" he asked. He must've felt me tense up.

"Yes," I said. "I think so, but I need a shower."

He suggested we try the outdoor pool over by the main lodge. I agreed to that. He asked me if he could watch me change into my bathing suit. What an unbelievably stupid request!

"No," was all I said.

When I changed, by myself in the bathroom, I told myself to make an effort. Maybe my new pink bathing suit would cheer me up. I looked at myself in the mirror. Not great, but not bad either. Nice tits anyway. The thighs could use a little work. I glanced out the bathroom window.

In a cobweb outside was the ugliest and biggest insect I'd ever seen. Looked like a giant orange and black grasshopper. I called Wally to come and look.

"You look absolutely smashing!" he said.

I think he meant it. I thanked him and pointed to the insect.

He looked and said he thought the giant bug was dead. I looked in a few corners and behind furniture for other creatures. I didn't want one of those things crawling over my face in the night.

The water in the open-air pool felt so good. I began to look forward to the guest cocktail party. At six in the main lodge.

Maybe thirty people attended. We sipped complimentary drinks, got a pitch from the manager on lodge activities, met folks from Switzerland. Dinner was served in an open verandah. Sometime during the main course, disaster struck.

A power failure! The reserve generator kicked in, but it could handle only the main lodge. Power to all the chalets was off. Someone said these outages could last for days.

Most of us looked for refuge in the bar. I worried about lack of air in the chalet but liked having people to distract us. Like the handsome devil Lionel from England and his friendly wife, Marietta. When it was time to leave, Lionel got flashlights from the front desk and said he'd see us to our place. We all said good night like we'd been friends for years.

Wally said he was sorry about all this. I told him it wasn't his fault. We lay outside the covers, he in his pyjamas, I in my nightgown. We were too close together in the heat. I wanted to be naked, but I didn't want Wally to get the wrong idea.

At ten minutes before eleven, the lights came on, thank Christ. Wally got up to reset the air conditioner. He turned out the lights and came back to bed. I lay there thinking I should reach over and touch him, but I didn't.

Saturday, February 15, 1997
Busy day today. Coach to Port Douglas, catamaran to the Great Barrier Reef. We went with Lionel and Marietta. We were in the Coral Sea! From the platform where we docked, we took a submersible boat so we could look at all the different kinds of coral and fish. I snorkelled off the platform, and Wally took pictures of me.

On the coach going back to the lodge, we remarked on the black cloud that seemed to hang permanently over Silky Oaks. Lionel said it was like the Star of Bethlehem.

After a dip in our hot tub (in our bathing suits), we met Lionel and Marietta for dinner. Exhausted, I crashed at nine thirty. I wonder why I don't want to have sex with Wally. Please, God, may it be temporary.

Sunday, February 16, 1997
Did a bit of shopping in the Port Douglas market and had lunch there, coral trout in a batter with chips. In mid-afternoon, I swam in the river with Marietta. She's so thin. Her nervous energy keeps her that way, she says. She can look old and wise or girlish and fun loving, depending on how she does her long dark hair. I did a sketch of her that she loved. She told me she and Lionel have been married "forever." They have a twenty-year-old son who's studying at Cambridge. I told her Wally has a son. I didn't tell her Stephen and I had wanted children. I didn't mention Stephen.

The four of us had pre-dinner drinks and then dinner

together again. Lionel amazed us with his rendition of Allan Sherman's "Hello Muddah, Hello Fadduh." He knew all the words. After dinner, we exchanged addresses. I cried a little when we hugged them goodbye.

Monday, February 17, 1997
A young fellow, not Vicki, drove us to Cairns airport. We took a Qantas flight to Brisbane, picked up our suitcase, and headed for the car rentals.

I can barely write this. I'm still petrified!

Wally admitted he hadn't driven on the "wrong side" in years, and I never had. I did not like riding on what to me is the driver's side without a steering wheel. Before we were even out of the parking lot, I panicked, sure we were in the wrong lane. Wally kept saying out loud, "You cross the traffic when you make a right turn." We had to drive into the city to the Brisbane Sheraton. I held my breath so long, I almost passed out. It was hard not to be mad at Wally for putting me through such an ordeal. We did make it to the hotel and were happy to give the car to a valet.

Dead tired, I fell asleep in what, thank God, is a king-sized bed.

Tuesday, February 18, 1997
Took the glass elevator to the top floor, the thirtieth, to look out over the city. Then we were on our way. While I cried out at every turn, Wally found the route to the Gold Coast. I managed to forget the roads and was blown away by the sheer beauty of the seascape. Saw the nets that

protect swimmers from the box jellyfish. Its sting can stop the human heart in minutes. Yet surfers go out in great numbers, mostly young men with lean glistening bodies.

Beautiful rolling hills, flat land with scrubby forests, the sea, scary curving roads. We found a decent hotel in Port Macquarie, had beer and so-so steak sandwiches. I, still reeling from the drive, sat for a long time in a scuffed armchair, writing this, feeling lonely. I wanted Stephen, I wanted Dobber Design. Christ, I wanted my mother. And I hated myself for not enjoying this experience as much as I felt I was expected to.

Wednesday, February 19, 1997
Continental breakfast (all the rage in Australia), more Pacific Highway, more nail-biting. We stopped for lunch at a handsome new McDonald's in Raymond Terrace.

Hit Sydney's urban sprawl in mid-afternoon. Wally tried to stay in his lane and keep left. As usual, I was no help. He got into a lane that took us into a tunnel under Sydney Harbour. We hurtled with freeway-style traffic, and, by some miracle, we ended up in the Wooloomooloo district. Soon, we were driving into the car park of the Wooloomooloo Waters Hotel, which, to my surprise, felt a little bit like coming home.

Later, at the Sydney Hard Rock Café for dinner, our waitress turned out to be Canadian. She noticed our accents and introduced herself as Kate from Sydney, Nova Scotia. She and her boyfriend had lived in England before coming to Australia. He was doing well in telecommunications. She'd worked in a London Hard Rock Café and got a transfer to Sydney. I liked Kate. Though she was a lot younger than me, I tried to see her as an adventurous role model. She put me in a good mood.

As we walked back, I took Wally's hand. We took a shortcut through a park, and I stopped him. We kissed, and a beautiful kiss it was. I said I'd race him to the hotel.

In our room, we scrambled out of our clothes and onto the bed, colliding, giggling. We both wanted to get on top.

Afterward, Wally went to sleep with a smile on his face. I was glad. He deserved a pleasant companion after all that terrifying driving. I brought this journal up to date and cried a little. How on earth am I going to get through the next six weeks?

17.

LORD JOHN AND LADY JANE

It was Thursday, February 20, the day they were heading to Hobart, Tasmania, and they had just checked out of the Wooloomooloo. As Wally placed the last suitcase in the car trunk, Carolyn slid into the passenger seat.

"Wally," she said.

"What?" he said.

He saw her ashen face through the window. She pointed to the windshield. On the outside of it, straddling the wiper, was a sand-coloured hairy spider that was about the size of Wally's fist. Alarmed, Wally swung at it with a rolled-up map.

"Don't kill it!" Carolyn screamed.

"What do you want me to do?" Wally yelled back.

"I don't know, but don't kill it!"

The spider scurried to the front of the hood and disappeared. Wally rushed to the back, slammed the trunk lid, and slipped into the driver's seat. He slammed his door, hoping the creature had left the car or would fall off once they were moving.

"What was it?" Carolyn said.

"I don't know what kind it was, but I know Australia is famous for its spiders."

"Oh, dear, I'm not fussy about spiders."

"That's the first we've seen, isn't it?"

"I hope it's the last."

When Wally filled up at a nearby Shell station, he looked under the front bumper and all around the car.

"No sign of it," he said as they started out for the Sydney airport.

In the final few weeks before they left home, Wally had seen *The Marjorie Problem* fade. She knew she'd been out-manoeuvred, and that was difficult for her to accept; it was probably as simple as that. In the end, she seemed not to give a damn what Geordie did, and she and Bill Horton left on their trip earlier than they'd originally planned. Geordie moved into the Laidlaws' guest room; Mr. Laidlaw drove him to school every morning, and either Mrs. Laidlaw picked him up or his pal Trevor drove him. Wally's main worry was not whether Geordie was finding time for Michelle but whether he could tear himself away from his new hockey league long enough to maintain his A average.

Before much of that had been resolved, there was the evening with Joyce. That night in the Hotel Fort Garry bar, he watched her crossing and uncrossing her legs; watched her skirt gradually inching farther up; watched her taking a bit of lint off the front of her sweater; watched her moist lips take tiny sips of the Cointreau. He told himself that a power greater than he had brought her to him on that particular evening when his life seemed to be totally in the tank, that she was exactly what he needed right then, and, Lord God Almighty, there magically was her hand touching his, a mere touch that raged with sensuality. And then there were her eyes looking into his, promising him pleasure without commitment, and there was her breathy voice saying what he craved to hear: "Want to go upstairs?"

He hesitated. And hesitated. And then he told her about Carolyn. Not just that she existed in his life but also that they had a lot of fun together and he believed they had a future together. He told Joyce that Carolyn was a widow who'd lost her husband much too soon, that she was a talented graphic artist, and that she was going with him to Australia. He said the reason he wasn't seeing much of her these evenings was that she was working late almost every day so that she could leave Dobber Design in good shape. She was so conscientious, she wanted to leave none of her current projects unfinished, and she was working ahead on presentations and pitches that so far were mostly in Dobber's planning stage. He mentioned nothing of the coolness between them caused by *The Marjorie Problem*.

"Well," Joyce said, none-too-quickly withdrawing her hand from his, "it sounds like you are in love with her."

"I am," he admitted.

As soon as he said it, he regretted having said it. Carolyn could be aggravating. She thought about work too much. She might never get over Stephen. She was insecure about sex. Besides all that, she wasn't here, and Joyce was. Was he being an utter fool? There was no real bond between him and Carolyn. He wasn't even sure why he was taking her to Australia. Anyway, what would a little indiscretion tonight matter in the grand scheme of things?

They were finished their drinks. Joyce gathered together her coat, her scarf, and her handbag, and said, "Well, Wally, it was such fun to catch up. Thank you so much for tonight, the lift, the drinks…" And he said, "Thank you for stopping by and for dinner…" They stood up. Wally left the tip, and he imagined they must look like lovers to the waiter and the few other people in the bar as they drifted into the hotel lobby.

At the elevator, Wally told her he hoped she'd let him know which university she intended to enroll in, and he wished her luck, and, as the elevator doors opened, she hugged him and said, "You can still come up, you know. I'll never tell." Those were the most beautiful words he'd ever heard. He *had* to go with her. He wanted to go with her more than anything he'd ever wanted in his whole life. She wasn't saying it, but her expression was telling him, You still need to lighten up a little, Wally, you're still too serious, too devoted, you need to enjoy yourself, seize the moment! He opened his mouth but didn't speak. They stepped back from each other, she boarded the elevator, and she gave him a little wave. As the elevator doors closed, she smiled at him the way you might smile at a puppy you feel sorry for. Then she was gone, and boiling inside him was this terrible desire to follow her, to feel her body against him again, to inhale her scent again, to touch her hand again.

He looked at the closed elevator door as if it might open again and she'd jump out and grab his hand and lead him up to her room. A hotel employee walked by and gave him a look, and Wally thought he'd better tear himself away, even as he thought he could still go to a house phone and call her and tell her he was on his way up. He went outside, saw the valet, gave him his ticket, and, as he waited on the steps for his car, he fought the urge to run back into the hotel. Then, telling himself he was an imbecile to fight it, he ran back in, only to see the business-as-usual front desk clerk looking at him with a quizzical look, and that was enough to turn Wally around. He headed out to find the valet wondering what the fuck. Wally drove away, still telling himself it wasn't too late to go back and call her from the lobby. He told himself to drive carefully as he headed through the winter streets, and still he thought it wasn't too late to go back and call her from the lobby. He parked behind his apartment building and went inside, hoping he wouldn't run into Miles, and, when he reached his dismal, all-too-quiet and stuffy apartment, he thought he could still call her from home and tell her he hoped she wouldn't mind if he came back and he'd be there right away. And he thought of her legs crossing and uncrossing in the bar, her restless legs that he wanted so much to feel around his waist. When he couldn't stand it any longer, he picked up the phone.

After a few rings, a sleepy voice answered. "Hello?"

"Carolyn," he said.

"Wally! What is it? What time is it?"

"I just wanted to tell you I love you, that's all," he said, wondering if it was a lie.

Dear Dr. Lockridge:

Thank you so much for tolerating my uncertainty about whether I would be accompanied when I arrive in Hobart and, if I were, who that person might be. I am delighted to tell you that Ms Carolyn Webb will be with me as my sole companion....

Early in their touristy trip through eastern Australia, Wally discovered something he had either forgotten or never acknowledged in his marriage: it was one thing to know a woman carnally and quite another to live with her. Of course, his carnal knowledge of her was relatively slight— she had promised more, but her holiday-season memories, her late working hours, and *The Marjorie Problem* had led them to agree to postpone it until their sojourn abroad. Before they rediscovered the mood, though, there was the new experience of living together day after day. So many petty annoyances: her chewing gum noisily when the plane began its descent, blowing bubbles in gum that wasn't bubble gum, bubbles that immediately popped; her fixation on keeping a journal (he couldn't help but wonder what horrible things she was writing about him); her sitting up with a light on when they should both be trying to sleep; her needing the privacy of the bathroom when she changed her clothes; her preferring to keep as much distance as possible between them when they were lying in bed; the twitch of her eyebrows when she was tired or embarrassed or impatient; her frequent drifting into her thoughts, especially when something reminded her of Stephen; her seeming inability or unwillingness to adapt to new or foreign or slightly sub-standard accommodation; her mid-sleep snorting; her shrieks when he tried to concentrate on driving; her apparent intention, when they were among new acquaintances, to look less attractive than she could look, wearing clothes that hid her figure and using a minimum of makeup; her general coolness toward him most of the time. The more he tried to tolerate these annoyances and noticed new ones, the less interested he was in making love, and he was sure she was feeling the same way. Perhaps they were getting on each other's nerves because they'd lived alone too long. If they were going to settle into an amicable relationship at Jane Franklin Hall, they'd have to discuss it and make some concessions. That's the way he was thinking as they drove the last leg into Sydney.

And then, last night, the combination of returning to a familiar and comfortable hotel and relaxing with a few drinks and meeting a friendly Canadian waitress over a good meal at the Hard Rock Café mellowed both of them. But whether last night was a turn for the better or something else, he didn't know. He would at least try to improve his own behaviour.

And so, as the 767 prepared to land in Melbourne, where they'd have to switch to the smaller plane that would take them to Hobart, when Carolyn offered him some gum, for the first time, he'd accepted it. He'd match her chew for chew and pop for pop.

On the flight to Hobart, Carolyn asked, "Are we being met?"

"Dr. Lockridge's secretary sent me a fax saying our

arrival time is pretty close to the dinner hour, but he intends to be there. The first high-table dinner of the school term is tonight and he wants us to go with him. We may not have time to unpack."

"What is a high-table dinner?"

"It's an idea borrowed from English residential colleges. Kind of a formal dinner hosted by the administration, attended by some faculty and all the resident students..."

"*Formal?* I didn't bring a dress..."

"You'll be fine."

"Are you sure?"

"Absolutely sure. You're beautiful, and I'm sure it's not a prom-type formal, or we would've been given a dress code before this."

"Wow, you must be really important. A formal dinner with the head honcho."

"Let's just take everything as a new experience..."

"The way Marietta would."

"Yes. Marietta."

"And Kate."

"Kate? Oh, the young woman at the Hard Rock."

"Yes. Wally, the place is called Jane Franklin Hall. You were going to give me a crash course on the Franklins."

"Right. The place we're going to is part of the University of Tasmania. It began in 1950 as a women's college. The woman they named it after was born Jane Griffin in London, England, in 1791. Unlike most of the women in her social circle, she turned down marriage proposals and was still unmarried in her thirties. She apparently carried a torch for Peter Mark Roget, a doctor and scientist twelve years her senior. He became famous for the reference book *Roget's Thesaurus*."

"*The* Roget!"

"Yes. But let me tell you a bit about John Franklin. He served in the Royal Navy under Admiral Nelson at the famous Battle of Trafalgar, and some years later he signed up for an Arctic expedition..."

"The Franklin Expedition. I've heard of that. Didn't all of them perish trying to find the Northwest Passage?"

"That was later. He actually went on three other expeditions to the Arctic before the one that cost him his life. I think his first one was in 1818. As a lieutenant, he was in charge of one of the four ships, and his was damaged by ice in a storm. He had to go back to England. Just a year later, he returned to the Arctic, took his ship into Hudson Bay, and even did some exploring on land. On that trip, he and his entourage of nineteen men underwent incredible hardship. The winter was harsh, and most of his men died. John survived by eating the deerskin from old boots. He wrote about the ordeal in a book that was published after he was back in England. The book, *Narrative of a Journey to the Shores of the Polar Sea*, became quite popular. He headed to the Arctic again in 1825, but not before he'd married a poet named Eleanor Porden, who was a fairly good friend of Jane Griffin."

"The plot thickens."

"Yes, well ... John and Eleanor had to overcome a few obstacles. He was a thick-headed plodder, and she was imaginative and bright. He was devoutly religious, and she was not. He didn't like her wanting to be a published author. Yet they were married, in 1823. Unfortunately, she proved to be rather sickly, and, just a week after he'd set sail for his third trip to the Arctic, Eleanor died."

"How awful!"

"In those days, I guess it was impossible to change your plans once you'd embarked on a long sea voyage, and, anyway, I don't know when or how John got the news. Jane and the Griffins helped Eleanor's family organize the funeral. When Franklin came home in the fall of 1827, no more successful than he had been before, he was touted for a knighthood for his service in the Arctic. Since he came from humble beginnings—his father was a shop-keeper—this would've been the highest honour he could aspire to, and maybe it was intended to give him a message that three tries at the Northwest Passage were enough."

"But he doggedly went for a fourth."

"I don't think he intended to—at least, not right away. He got busy calling on Jane."

"If she couldn't have Roget..."

"She had turned down many suitors and often vowed she'd remain unmarried. But when Franklin showed an interest, she encouraged him. Some people said they'd begun plotting before he even left, given Eleanor's questionable health. Well, Jane was just as bright as Eleanor, and you wonder what she would see in Franklin, but it's been suggested that she believed he could be manipulated. Besides, it seemed only a matter of time until he'd be knighted, and she could become Lady Jane. They were married in November, 1828. She was not quite thirty-seven, and he was forty-two. Just six months later, John received his knighthood."

"Jane got what she wanted."

"In more ways than one. She loved to travel and, in the next few years, with John and the Royal Navy maintaining a presence in the Mediterranean, she visited with him in Malta and Corfu before venturing into North Africa and the Middle East. Over two years, she spent only three months with John—the rest of the time, she travelled, with two servants, several trunks, and her four-poster iron bedstead."

"I wish we'd done that."

"What?"

"Brought our own four-poster."

Wally laughed—a little nervously, because he had no idea what kind of sleeping accommodation awaited them in Hobart.

"Jane met a handsome missionary in Cairo and talked him into giving her lessons in Arabic ... but I really should get to the Tasmania part..."

"Did she have a fling with the missionary?"

"She might've—but they were both religious ... Anyway, a short time after John and Jane were back in England, they heard the government intended to send a new expedition to the Arctic. John wanted to lead it and Jane helped figure out what strategy they should follow to clinch the commission."

"She wanted to get rid of him again."

"Historians tell us it was more her wanting him to get something he deserved. She thought giving the expedition to anyone else would be an affront to him. But give it to someone else they did—a former subordinate of John's. To appease the Franklins, the government offered John the position of lieutenant governor of Antigua, a small island in the Caribbean. Jane considered it a further insult and started lobbying her influential friends so that another offer came quickly, to be governor of Van Diemen's Land; that's the old name for Tasmania. The salary was twice as much. The Franklins accepted and moved there in 1836. Well, they left in August 1836 and arrived there in the new year. It was a four-month trip.

"The job would prove to be no picnic, running a land populated mostly by convicts sent from England, convicts that were forced to work for rich landowners. Franklin soon showed himself to be a bumbler, completely out of his depth, and his wife did her best to help him, even editing all his official messages. She took on her own causes: trying to improve conditions for the women convicts, creating a lecture series, encouraging the visual arts. She worked on the advancement of education and started a state college. Though we look back now and see her as an assertive and intelligent woman who was far ahead of her time, she was regarded then as interfering and too much of an influence on her husband."

"So the college she started isn't the one we're going to now."

"No. She started a boys' college, but she did think there should be one for girls, so it's appropriate that the girls' college that began in 1950 took her name."

"But now it's co-ed."

"Right. And of course everything I've just told you is just the background of the name. It has nothing to do with the kind of place it's turned out to be."

18.

THE UNDERLODGE

A drizzle greeted the 737 as it touched down in Hobart. The passengers had to walk from the plane through the sprinkling rain. Wally and Carolyn entered the terminal to find a small crowd of greeters, standing back, looking expectant.

"Dr. Baxter."

Directly in front of Wally was the tanned and freckled face of the man he had met in Winnipeg all those months ago.

"Yes, hello," Wally said, taking the man's extended hand. "Dr. Lockridge. Let me introduce Carolyn Webb."

"Pleased to meet you, Carolyn. Welcome to Tasmania."

"Thank you, Dr. Lockridge…"

"Dennis, please. You had a good flight?"

"Two!" Carolyn said. "We didn't expect to stop in Melbourne."

"The majority of our flights go through Melbourne.

Now, we shall have to see about your bags. How many are there?"

"Three," Wally said. "Hope they made it."

"Bags are never lost on our domestic flights."

Lockridge no sooner said that than the conveyer started up. Wally moved toward it feeling odd after all the months of anguish, anticipation, and preparation. The visiting fellow has landed. What he felt most odd about was being accompanied by Carolyn.

"You know tonight is our high table dinner," Lockridge said. "We have them every Monday and Thursday. Tonight, the freshers will be there, and I shall introduce you to them. The lifers—that's what we call every student who is not a fresher—they don't return until the weekend. Did you bring your academic gown?"

"No, I'm afraid I didn't," Wally said.

"It's all right. You'll find one in the flat. Not your doctoral gown, though, but a simple bachelor's. And Carolyn, you of course will be joining us."

"I ... I don't have a gown, either."

"No worries. There will be one in the flat for you as well."

The two suitcases and garment bag arrived. Lockridge and Wally placed them on a cart, along with Wally's briefcase, and Lockridge wheeled the cart outside, with Wally and Carolyn a step or two behind. Setting a brisk pace, Lockridge called back to them to follow him right out to the parking lot. Carolyn half-ran, as if it were important not to fall behind.

As they drove out of the airport grounds, with one of the bags in the back seat beside Carolyn, Lockridge explained that it was fifteen kilometres into Hobart, mostly on a dual carriageway. The terrain around the airport was flat, but they soon came to hills and, in the distance, mountains. As they approached a long bridge that crossed the wide River Derwent, Lockridge pointed out that the mouth of the river provided a harbour that was so quiet and safe, it was a favourite port of call for the American navy. The premier of Tasmania was promoting the idea of making Hobart a permanent US naval base. The millions spent on supplies each time a ship stopped in gave a significant boost to the local economy.

"This bridge had to be rebuilt about fifteen years ago," said Lockridge. "A drunken sea captain rammed his ship into it and knocked it down. Lives were lost. The airport side of the river was cut off from the city for ages. Took much, much longer to go upriver to the next bridge and around."

Wally said, "The captain wasn't American, I hope."

"No, I'm afraid he was one of ours."

Lockridge drove through downtown Hobart on a wide thoroughfare called Davey Street. Population, last time Wally checked, was 180,000, making Hobart by far the largest city in Tasmania. The buildings were modest in height, and many businesses looked like those in English towns. At a narrow street called Elboden, Lockridge turned in and immediately made another turn into the college grounds. He said Jane Franklin Hall was one of two colleges not on the University of Tasmania campus. He drove up a steep hill—"A real heart-starter, that one," he said—and followed a winding road that passed several three-storey orange buildings, all of them student residences. He made a left turn behind the last of these and drove into a cobbled parking lot, pulling at last into a sheltered carport flanked by trees. Behind the trees, Wally could see a house.

"This is the principal's lodge," said Lockridge. "We shall get you settled, and then I must attend to a few things before dinner."

With all three of them carrying the bags, Lockridge led the way around one side of the house, past a gate, and down a hill to another gate.

"This is where you'll be," he said. "We call it the underlodge."

He went through the gate, along a cement path that had a fence overrun with bushes, vegetation that looked both exotic and out of control. There was fruit on some of the branches. The underlodge was part of the main house—part of the basement, it seemed—but it had its own entrance. Lockridge produced a brown envelope and handed it to Wally. It contained the key and a pamphlet entitled *Information for Guests*. Wally slid the key into the lock and opened the door.

"After you," he said to Carolyn.

He wasn't sure what she was thinking about this island, this city, this college, this *underlodge*. He glanced at her face as she preceded him through the door. She didn't look at him, was looking inside, expectantly. They stepped into a verandah with a linoleum floor and one piece of furniture—a battered patio chair. He noticed a little worm in a spot where there was a hole in the linoleum. He hoped Carolyn wouldn't expect him to do something about it but for Heaven's sake not kill it. He pretended to ignore it and went through an open doorway into the living area.

"You will find they've put in some provisions," Lockridge said, bringing the bags inside. "Let us know if you need anything. The main dining room is in the building we just drove behind, on the other side of the car park. At regular mealtimes, you can see the people in the kitchen for more bread or milk or whatever you fancy. Some visiting fellows have preferred to eat with the students. It is up to you. But tonight's dinner is obligatory. Gowns—in the closet off the study—in there. We meet in the senior common room prior to dinner. It is on the far side of the dining room; please be there at six, and I shall introduce you to the other fellows."

"Right," said Wally. "Thank you again for picking us up. For everything."

"My pleasure." At the door, Lockridge stopped. "You may wonder what that tall building is down there." Wally and Carolyn stepped outside and looked into the distance where Lockridge was pointing, what seemed to be a bay and part of the Derwent. "You see the building? That is the Wrest Point Casino. You may wish to go there one day and try your luck."

He gave Carolyn a quick salute and hurried off.

"It *is* a nice view," said Carolyn.

"Yes," Wally said. "Come on, let's see what it's like *in*side."

The pastel yellow cement-and-brick walls and the large windows gave the place a Mediterranean feel. The living area was small; its floor was linoleum on concrete, and it was furnished with a chesterfield, a TV, a wooden table, and three wooden chairs. The tiny kitchen, separated from the main room by a counter, contained a fridge, a stove, a sink, and a cupboard where there were glasses, dishes, and cutlery. As Lockridge had indicated, the fridge was stocked with milk, eggs, bread, and biscuits. At one end of the living room was a rather spartan bathroom with a modern sink and counter, an old-fashioned tub, and a relic of a shower head. Carolyn pointed to a bug on the counter and another in the window, and Wally squashed them both in a tissue with no apology. Carolyn didn't react. He supposed insects had to be of a certain size before he wasn't allowed to kill them. The toilet was separate, in a kind of closet, with a window that was permanently open for ventilation. Back near the entrance was the spacious study, a step up from the rest of the place and carpeted, with bare bookshelves, a large desk, and an upholstered chair on wheels, the kind usually used by office admin assistants. All of one wall was devoted to a storage area that had sliding doors. One of the doors was open, and hanging inside were four academic gowns. On the opposite wall was a picture window that gave the same view of the river and the casino they had seen outside.

And then there was the bedroom. Along the outside wall were French doors, and the view from them was again the one of Wrest Point. There were wall-to-wall drapes you'd have to pull across the doors for privacy. One wall was devoted to closet space and a built-in vanity. On either side of the bed was a night table and lamp. The bed itself was a double that seemed lower than normal and not nearly as inviting as the one they'd left in the Wooloomooloo Waters.

"Well, this is home for the next few weeks," Wally said, trying to sound cheerful.

"It's all right, isn't it?" said Carolyn. "I love the French doors, and the view is splendid."

Wally was so relieved, he had to fight back tears.

She likely hated the bedroom, could not see herself relaxing in it. Wally didn't want to admit that their arrival at this humble final destination felt anticlimactic.

"We'd better get ready for high table," he said.

"Do you think we'll be able to get a drink there?"

"I'm sure there will be wine."

"What are you going to wear?"

"What I have on." Wally was wearing a blazer, grey pants, white shirt, and tie. "You'll be fine in what you have on. We'll be wearing gowns, so it doesn't matter. Let's go and see how they fit."

Carolyn found one that fit well enough; she went to look at herself in the vanity mirror, gave a little twirl, and again relief wafted over Wally like a cool Winnipeg autumn breeze.

At six o'clock, Wally and Carolyn presented themselves at the senior common room. As they entered, Dr. Lockridge stepped out of a conversation group and came toward them. He was dressed in his doctoral regalia, or perhaps the trappings of his position as principal.

"Ah, Ms Webb, Dr. Baxter," he said. "Allow me to present one of our resident fellows, Beatrice Jane Higgins. B.J., this is Ms Carolyn Webb and Dr. Walter Baxter, our visiting fellow."

B.J., a young woman with short-cropped dark hair,

stepped forward and shook Carolyn's hand. As she shook Wally's, a lock of her hair fell over one eye.

"I guess we're going to be … uh … fellow fellows," Wally said.

"Yes," she said, and she gave a polite chuckle. "When did you arrive?"

"This afternoon," said Carolyn. "From Sydney."

"I understand you are both from Canada."

"Yes," said Wally. "Winnipeg, right in the middle. We left behind snowdrifts this high." He held his hand at chest level and laughed.

"B.J. is a music tutor and a brilliant pianist," said Lockridge. "May I fetch some wine for the three of you?"

"Oh, that would be lovely!" said Carolyn. "Could I please have red?"

"And I'll have white, please, Dennis," B.J. said.

"I think I'll have red," said Wally, "but why don't I help you?"

"No, no, stay right there." Lockridge hurried over to a corner of the room where a young man was pouring wine.

"So you must live here on campus," Wally said to B.J.

"Yes, with my husband," B.J. said. "Patrick is a violinist, and he's off to Canada next week to complete his master's degree. Let me introduce you to him."

She called over a handsome young man with curly black hair.

"Walter, this is Patrick," said B.J. She seemed naturally good-natured, not at all bothered by her errant lock of hair. "Walter is from Canada. And this is his … this is Carolyn."

"Please call me Wally. Hi, Patrick." The violinist's

handshake was unexpectedly firm, if not crunching. "B.J. tells us you're off to Canada next week."

Patrick's eyes widened as if he was surprised that B.J. would divulge such a thing so quickly. "I have to do a six-week residency at McGill in Montreal," he said. "Do you know it?"

"One of our best universities," Wally said.

"You shall be treated to a concert before Patrick leaves," said Lockridge, stepping into their midst with the wine. "Patrick accompanied by Beatrice Jane. This coming Monday." He went off to greet someone new, one of the official fellows.

"Your first time in Australia, Carolyn?" said Patrick.

"Yes," Carolyn said, and blushed, perhaps because Patrick was staring at her so intensely. B.J. didn't notice. She was busy beckoning to a smiley young man with receding red hair and a stern-looking woman of matronly stature.

"Regina, Tyler, this is our new visiting fellow," said B.J. "Dr. Wally Baxter. Regina Dales, our dean of studies, and Tyler Chipman, the senior tutor."

"And I'm Carolyn Webb, the visiting fellow's roommate."

"Ahh!" said Tyler, with a grin and raised eyebrows.

Regina examined Wally through her thick glasses and offered him a limp handshake. "So glad to meet you," she said, in a tone that suggested the opposite.

"The capital city of the province I was born in is called Regina," Wally said and immediately wished he hadn't. It sounded inane.

"I don't know if anyone has told you," said Tyler, "but we'd like you to give an informal talk some evening."

"Oh?" said Wally. "What would you like me to speak on?"

"Canadian literature, perhaps? Say, have you met Peter?"

"I don't believe I have…"

"Peter! A moment. I'd like you to meet our new visiting fellow."

Tyler took the arm of a barrel-chested man who held his head high as if he were straining to be taller. His name was Peter Russell.

"What is your specialty?" he asked Wally, though his gaze fell on Carolyn.

"History and Canadian studies," Wally answered. "Oh, Peter, may I present Carolyn Webb."

"Good evening," Peter said, but now his eyes were turned to a young woman who was grappling with a bottle of wine. "Here, allow me."

She was attempting to open the bottle with one of those corkscrews that depend on leverage. "No, no, I have it," she said, and she did.

"Dr. Baxter, this is Rebecca Bonner," Peter said.

"The new visiting fellow," Wally said. "Hello."

"Hello!" Rebecca was tall, with long blonde hair and lovely blue eyes. "Oh, sorry, my hands are full…"

"Rebecca is a lifer," Peter said. "Do you know what a lifer is?"

"Yes. Dr. Lockridge explained. And he said the lifers weren't due to return until the weekend."

"Quite. But Rebecca is here tonight as a member of the Student Committee."

Rebecca said, "I was fetching this wine for Mark. Have you met Mark Wilding, our student president?"

Mark heard his name and turned to face Wally and Carolyn. He looked like every male student president Wally had ever known: roughly six feet tall, short blond hair, healthy pink cheeks, a studious frown.

"Mark," said Peter, "this is Dr. Baxter, our new visiting fellow from Canada."

"And I'm his roommate," said Carolyn.

Tyler suppressed a giggle, while Dr. Lockridge offered a little smile. Mark shook Carolyn's hand, and Peter touched Wally's arm.

"What did you say your specialty was?" he asked.

"Drinking wine," said Wally.

"Mine too, if we can't find any Cascade," said Mark.

"Cascade?"

"The local beer," said Peter.

"Oh," said Wally. "Back home, Cascade is detergent." Another inane comment! He must be nervous.

At a sign from Dr. Lockridge, Tyler began to line everyone up for the procession into the dining room. He handed out copies of a seating plan. The entourage moved out of the common room, Carolyn walking ahead of Dr. Lockridge, and Wally behind him. Tyler led the way down a hall and up a few steps onto a raised platform (hence, *high* table). The members of the platform party—administration, fellows, Carolyn, some honorary fellows, Mark and Rebecca, and two other student reps—stood at their places while the first-year students filed in. They were all wearing black gowns like Wally's and badges bearing their names. Male and female freshers alike wore garish neckties loosely tied around their necks—like a rope or a leash and not under their collars—apparently one of Jane Franklin Hall's concessions to hazing.

When all the students were at tables, Lockridge went to a microphone set up on a podium and spoke: "*Benedic, Domine, nos sodales et hoc collegium in honorem dominae* Jane Franklin *nominatum, per Jesum Christum Dominum nostrum.* Amen."

Wally joined everyone in answering, "Amen."

"Welcome to Jane Franklin Hall," Lockridge said. "You will learn early in your time here that Jane has gained a fine reputation, not only in Tasmania but also in Australia, though it has existed for only forty-seven years." He suggested that the freshers do all in their power to respect the Jane tradition.

Lockridge introduced Wally as this term's visiting fellow. Not sure what to do, Wally stood and waved. The freshers applauded, some cheered.

"And may I present Dr. Baxter's partner, Ms Carolyn Webb."

Carolyn stood and waved. The freshers cheered more loudly than they had for Wally and some whistled. *Partner.* Well, what else could Lockridge call her?

After the other introductions, Lockridge wished everyone well and sat down between Wally and Carolyn. That was the cue for the servers to move into the hall with the meal: roast lamb. While they circulated, a scuffle erupted near the back. Tyler, who was at a table among the freshers, moved swiftly to settle the kids down. No one on the stage seemed bothered by what was likely typical first-week behaviour. Lockridge chatted with Carolyn; it sounded as if he was asking her what she did in Winnipeg. Across from Wally sat B.J. and Patrick, while Regina was on his other side.

"What did you say your field was?" Regina asked him.

."History and Canadian studies."

"Canadian studies in Canada. Isn't that rather odd?"

"We're so influenced culturally by our huge neighbour to the south, we need to work at self-preservation..."

As Wally spoke, another commotion erupted, this one near the entrance to the kitchen. Three or four freshers were up on their feet, and one was wielding a broom. The object of their attention was a huge black spider—perhaps the size of the one Wally had seen on his windshield that morning—and it was running up the wall above the servery window.

"Looks like a huntsman," Lockridge said, as if he saw them every day. "They are not poisonous."

Tyler stood, ready to move in if required. Wally didn't look to see how Carolyn was reacting, but she hadn't screamed. Some students called out instructions, others cheered, but one swing of the broom ended the excitement, and a young man took the spider away in a serviette. No one at high table knew if the spider was dead.

"I hope it isn't," said Lockridge. "We Australians are usually content to coexist with the creatures that share our planet. Whereas, Canadians seem hostile to theirs, do they not?"

"Didn't I just read that your federal government had declared war on cats?" Wally said.

"*Touché!*" said B.J.

"Cats have become a bit of a nuisance," Lockridge said, chuckling.

At the end of the dinner, Lockridge led the high-table group back to the senior common room. Mark and Rebecca took off to direct their minions in rearranging the dining room and putting up decorations for the dance, which was about to begin. A fresher spoke to B.J. about a problem with the music, and she called Tyler over.

At the common room door, Peter Russell caught up with Wally. "*What* did you say your specialty was?"

"Corruption of youth."

"We shall get on well, then."

Most of the stage party hung around for coffee and what Peter led Wally to believe was a delicacy: choco-late mints. It was Peter's job to give out only one per person, but, because Wally and Carolyn were newcomers, he gave each of them two. They were joined by a fellow named Brewster—Wally wasn't sure what he did at Jane or whether Brewster was his first or last name—and they talked about the number of students expected from the mainland and from other countries. Brewster and Peter gradually drifted away. Lockridge was gone, and Wally hadn't seen him leave.

"Ready to go?" he said to Carolyn.

"If you are."

On their way out, they walked past the dining room, which had now been converted into a dance hall. Some freshers were already dancing, their neckties askew down their backs. Tyler was there, likely as some sort of staff presence. He saw Wally and waved good night.

It was dark outside now, and Wally took Carolyn's hand

as they headed down the hill to the underlodge. The lights of Hobart twinkled in the distance. They heard stirrings in the principal's house above as Wally unlocked the door and let Carolyn precede him inside.

"We have to unpack," she said. She sounded weary.

"We could just leave it until the morning, couldn't we?"

"Let's get settled. We'll be glad we did tomorrow."

"You're right. Okay, you start. You can have first pick of the drawers and the closet space."

He was trying to sound cheerful, and it wasn't easy. Maybe it was natural to feel gloomy when you finally reached the destination you'd been thinking about for months. Or maybe the distraction of the quick tour of the mainland and having Carolyn along with him made a let-down inevitable once they got to Hobart. Maybe he felt obligated to keep Carolyn entertained, and he was already failing. He stepped on another bug when she wasn't looking.

He left Carolyn to unpack in the bedroom, and he went into the study. He didn't turn on the light but instead looked out through his picture window. Part way down the hill was a floodlit tennis court, and some kids were using it, playing tennis on roller blades. He could tell they were freshers because they were wearing ties. Mark Wilding had told him they weren't allowed to take their ties off for a week. He watched them for a few minutes, wondering if it was really all right to wear roller blades on the court.

"Wally?"

He went to the bedroom. Carolyn had pulled the drapes across the French doors and turned on one of the table lamps. Her clothes and her suitcase were put away, and she was wearing a pink nightgown.

"It's … well, it's kind of cozy," she said.

"You're right. It's quite nice. It even smells better than it did."

"I sprayed perfume. Are you going to unpack?"

"Yes, sorry, I was watching some kids on the tennis court."

"Mind if I shower?"

"Not at all."

She took her cosmetic case and headed for the bathroom. She seemed all business, as if doing things would prevent her from complaining or crying. Maybe that was unfair. Maybe it was *he* who felt like complaining or crying. When all his stuff was put away and he was in his pyjamas, he went looking for more bugs. There were none in the bedroom, but he found one in the living room and two by the outside door. He squashed them with a tissue and flushed them down the toilet. He liked the idea of a toilet in a room all its own.

Carolyn came out of the bathroom and said, "It's all yours." She seemed brisk, and she didn't look at him.

After brushing his teeth and washing his hands, he turned out the lights in the living room, and, when he entered the bedroom, Carolyn was lying on her back in bed.

"What, not writing in your journal tonight?"

"I'll work on it tomorrow."

"Okay if I open this?" He pointed to a transom high on one wall.

"Sure."

He opened it wide.

She said, "No window screen, is there?"

"No."

"That space is big enough for a huntsman to get through."

Wally went to the small room where the washer and dryer were and found a mop. He took it back to the bedroom and leaned it against the wall on his side. He turned out the lamp and climbed into bed. He and Carolyn lay side by side, staring at the open transom. After a while, he reached for her and she moved to let him put an arm around her. He held her and he felt her begin to shudder. When she started to weep, he thought he should speak, but he didn't know what to say.

19.

GONE FOR A WALK

A shrill noise. The telephone! Wally's heart leaped, then pounded. Had he slept? He must've. The ringing persisted, filling the underlodge like a fire alarm. Carolyn said something unintelligible as he staggered from the bed, not sure where the phone was. He found it on the kitchen counter.

"Hello?"

"Hello! Is that Wally Baxter?" It was a male voice he didn't recognize.

"Um ... yes ..."

"Wally, it's Dobber. Dobber Dreger? Sorry. I hope I didn't wake you. What time is it there?"

"I'm not sure. Six-thirty? No, going on seven."

"Damn. I thought I'd waited long enough; it's afternoon Thursday here."

"Yes. And Friday morning here. Did you want to speak with Carolyn?"

"Is she up? I could…"

"I'm sure she's awake. Hold on."

He went to the bedroom. Carolyn sat on the side of the bed, rubbing her eyes.

"It's for you," Wally said.

"Who…?"

"Your boss."

"What? Dobber? He promised. Well, it must be important. Don't look at me, Wally. I don't think I slept. Where's the phone?"

He led her into the kitchen and handed the phone to her. Leaving her there to speak with Dobber, he went into the study and looked down the hill. It was becoming light outside, though the sky was overcast. Leaning over the fence to munch on the bushes that grew in profusion on the underlodge side were two goats. Seeing them put him in a better mood. He figured out for himself that, because the hill beyond the fence was steep, you couldn't use a lawnmower to keep the vegetation down; a sure-footed goat or two was a practical solution.

He could hear only certain words in Carolyn's conversation, like "Not distinctive enough" and "White space" and "Did you *read* that copy!" and "They had *three* good looks at it! How can they…"

Wally decided on a shower. It was primitive but tolerable. The flow of water wasn't strong, but Wally achieved a good blend of hot and cold. While he shaved, he killed two bugs on the windowsill. The window glass was frosted, admitting daylight while not requiring a curtain or blind. He put his pyjama pants on and draped his towel around his shoulders. When he opened the door, he saw that

Carolyn was no longer on the telephone. He found her in the bedroom, sitting on the bed and sobbing. Seeing her in this vulnerable state filled him with tenderness and brought on an unexpected erection. He sat down beside her and placed his pyjama jacket over his lap. Her hands covered her face.

"What happened?" he asked.

"Wally ... would you please go away for now, give me a little space?"

"Did something go wrong at work?"

"Please. Just leave me alone for a while, okay?"

"Can I get you a coffee or..."

"*Please*, Wally."

"Okay, okay. Just let me get dressed and I'll..."

She lay down and pressed her face into a pillow.

He felt helpless and oafish and maybe even a little scared. But he grabbed some clothes and went to the study to put them on.

"I'll go for a walk or something," he said from the bedroom doorway. "I'll go for ... what, half an hour or..."

"'Kay."

He left the underlodge, striding out as if this was his usual pre-breakfast walk. One of the goats was leaning over the fence, straining its neck to get at a flower. Wanting to help *somebody*, Wally pushed the branch closer and the goat bit the flower off with one chomp. Wally cursed Dobber for phoning—this was Carolyn's long-awaited and much-deserved vacation, for Christ's sake. But maybe the call had been necessary; maybe Carolyn, in her attempt to do too much before she left, had botched something up. Maybe she'd been worried the whole time they'd been away and Dobber had confirmed her worst fears. Wally walked out of the college grounds and around the perimeter, passing a couple of jogging freshers. After a second circuit and a third, he thought he'd inspect the neighbourhood and find out where the nearest general store and newsagent were.

When he returned, Carolyn was fast asleep, even snoring. He was glad. She might feel better after a sleep and maybe they could talk about how they'd spend the next few days. He closed the bedroom door, went to the kitchen and found some instant coffee, some bread, an egg, and a frying pan. There was a portable radio on the counter and he turned it on, low. A local female announcer was giving a weather forecast: "It's going to be another fine day in Hobart." He wondered what *fine* meant. The sky at present was overcast, with a break here and there.

After eating, he wrote a note and left it on a chair outside the bedroom door. "Just out on a couple of errands. I ate. Leaving at 8:45. Be back soon. Love, Wally." He headed through a residence building, said good morning to a couple of freshers, and found the administration office. As Dr. Lockridge had recommended, he spoke with the bursar, a jolly woman named Elizabeth Hardy, about renting a car. She immediately rang someone and told Wally she would contact him later with the details. On he went over the "heart-starter" hill and down Frobisher Street to the newsagent on Macquarie Street. The first items to catch his eye were sensational magazines, with headlines and photos suggesting sex or scandal or sex scandal. He purchased a map of Hobart and the local newspaper. He checked the front page for a weather report: it indeed was going to be *fine*. Out on the street, he felt spots of rain.

In the grocery store he'd located earlier, he considered buying some snack food or fruit but he settled for a large can of Raid. As he walked with a more sprightly step back up to Jane Franklin Hall, the sun came out.

On the floor inside the underlodge was his note. Carolyn had written under his message: "Gone for a walk. C."

A walk? Where? She hadn't written the time she'd left. Was she feeling all right? Should he go looking for her? What if she got *lost*? Did she have money with her? No, he should *not* go looking for her.

Maybe the whole reason she'd taken off was that she was feeling smothered by him. She needed a break. She needed to do something by herself after their doing everything together on the mainland. Or maybe she was embarrassed about whatever Dobber had called about. She'd screwed up and she needed some time to get over it. Didn't she think she could talk it over with Wally? Hadn't he shown empathy in other matters? Or had he shown too much?

As he worried about her, he looked for bugs. He found some kind of centipede on the linoleum and he zapped it with Raid. He blasted a small spider and a fly. He shot at the creatures as if the can was a six-gun. Take that! And *that!* Then he worried that he was spraying too much of the stuff, filling the underlodge with poison. He picked up the corpses in a paper towel and deposited them in one of Lockridge's garbage cans.

God, was this how a visiting fellow was supposed to spend his time? What kind of a visiting fellow *was* he?

Wally was quite frantic by the time Carolyn returned.

He was sitting in the patio chair just inside with the door open, Raid at the ready, watching for new bugs. She came up the sidewalk looking nonchalant. He was relieved to see her but his first inclination was to tear a strip off her for making him worry. Instead, he said:

"Hi."

"Hi," she answered.

"Nice walk?"

"Very nice, thanks. I see you got your bug killer."

"Works fast. I don't think there's a live one left inside."

"Good."

"Did you eat?"

"Yes. I wasn't hungry at first, but I found a nice little restaurant in Sandy Bay."

"You went as far as Sandy Bay?"

"I heard last night that a lot of students walk from here to the University. I thought I'd see how far it is."

"Wow. Good for you."

"I could use some water, though. I think there's some in the fridge."

"There is."

Carolyn went inside. He closed the door and followed her. He watched her take the top off a bottle of water and swig away.

"I'm sorry about the phone call," he said.

"What?"

"Dobber's call. It obviously upset you. It's okay if you don't want to talk about it, but it might make you feel better if you do. And I won't make any judgements."

She stared at him. "You don't get it, do you?"

"I thought … um … I thought maybe you did something

or *didn't* do something and you were feeling bad because you worked so hard before you left."

"Wally. Okay, sit down. We need to talk."

They both sat down at the kitchen table and she finished off the water.

"Wally, first of all, this has nothing to do with my job. I am bloody good at what I do, and Dobber and the rest of them know it. They rely too much on me and they know that, too. They assured me they could take care of things while I was away. God knows I left them with everything they need. They assured me I'd earned this time away and they wouldn't bother me. So that call this morning made me feel *good*. They need me. I like being needed."

"But, when I came out of the shower, you were crying, and you wanted to be alone…"

"Like a spoiled brat … because I'm here and not there. I'm here, not sleeping and feeling inferior, instead of being there where I'm the fucking *queen*."

"Carolyn, I think…"

"Please let me finish, Wally. This trip seemed like such a good idea, to get away from my house and Winnipeg and see a whole different world, and see it with a nice caring guy. You're such a lovely man, Wally. You really are. And when we first met, I thought you and I were in the same boat: we'd both been married and weren't anymore. But I started to see the big difference. You and your wife *chose* to split up. Stephen and I had no choice. He was taken away when I still loved him madly. I dream about him, Wally, all the time. And the dreams are often horrible. I lose him, and I search, and sometimes I find him, and sometimes I don't. And sometimes, when I do find him, he's not Stephen anymore but someone scary and mean. So many things remind me of him, and I get into a rage inside because he was taken away. But I know it's nuts not to get on with my life, and I think I can have another relationship, and I want to be intimate with someone else—*with* you—but ... God, Wally, I can't even get comfortable enough to have proper sex with you. I mean, how pathetic is *that?* I guess I've been living on my own too long. I can't get used to having you around *all the time*—I mean, I think it was easier when we were at work and seeing each other when we could, when we were dating. I know, I should be relaxing now that I have all this time off, but for that first week we were always headed off somewhere, and I'm sorry, I just *can't* get used to driving on the wrong side of the road. And now we're here at this college with all these academics, and God knows I'm not an academic and I know it shows, and at that dinner last night I felt like a dummy. *You* don't make me feel that way, but those people last night—I don't know—maybe they were *trying* to be nice, but I just felt so *inferior*. Maybe I'm over-reacting to everything because I've been in my own little world too long and suddenly I'm not. And I'm so far away from home. I even feel that they were all laughing at me or looking down on me because I'm not married to you. I know that's nuts. I'm old-fashioned, I guess. I'm this broad who's tagged along with the visiting fellow. I don't even know what a visiting fellow *is!* Whatever you're supposed to be doing here, you'll be doing on your own, and where the hell do *I* fit in?"

Carolyn stopped talking and Wally wondered if now was the time to answer or…

There was a knock on the door.

"I look terrible!" Carolyn said. "Please don't answer it, Wally."

She ducked behind the kitchen counter. Wally could see through the window that it was Dr. Lockridge. He opened the door.

"Hello!" Wally said.

"Slept well, did you?"

"Oh, yes, very well, thank you."

Wally stood there, knowing he should be courteous and ask Lockridge in but also knowing he couldn't.

Lockridge said, "I understand Elizabeth is arranging a car for you?"

"Yes. I'm to hear from her later today."

"Good. I stopped by to invite you and Carolyn for drinks with my wife and me. Tomorrow at six-ish be all right?"

"Oh, yes. Very nice. Thank you."

"By the way, you likely saw it, but there is a reserved parking spot for you on the other side of the lodge. It's marked Visiting Resident Fellow."

"Excellent! Thank you."

"See you tomorrow, then."

Wally caught himself before he said "Jolly good!" He could feel how red his face had become while he pretended that Lockridge hadn't interrupted a crisis.

"It's okay," Wally said, aiming his voice at the kitchen. "He's gone."

Carolyn appeared. "You said we'd go for drinks tomorrow."

"He caught me off guard—just showing up here like that. What else could I do?"

"You could've ... Oh, God, I don't know."

The telephone rang. Wally, glad of another distraction, answered it.

"Dr. Baxter, it's Elizabeth Hardy. I have a car for you, a Toyota Corolla, at thirty-seven dollars per day, and that will include petrol, provided you do not exceed an average of two hundred kilometres per day. What do you think?"

"An offer I can't refuse, Elizabeth. Thank you."

"Jolly good. When would you like to pick it up?"

"Oh ... this afternoon?"

"Right, then. Stop by the office after lunch and I shall explain where you have to go."

"Good. Thank you, Elizabeth."

He hung up the phone. Carolyn was looking at him with an expression he didn't quite understand. Contempt? Despair? Resignation?

"It's business as usual, then," she said.

"Well..."

"I don't know if I'm going to be able to do this, Wally."

"I know. And I want you to be happy. If I'm the problem, then..."

"You're not the problem. Maybe we just don't belong together. Or maybe everything is just happening too fast. I've got my own issues, I know that, and I want to solve them. Maybe we can go along and do the things we have to do—or *you* have to do. I will try. And you can help by trying to understand and by letting me know what you're thinking—about me, about everything."

"All right."

He thought about all the things she did that annoyed him, but he knew enough not to mention them right now. In fact, they seemed trivial now that she seemed less upset.

He said, "I suggest we go for lunch in the college dining room, and then go and pick up the car."

"Please give me some time to shower and get my face in better shape."

"Your face is fine, but do take all the time you need."

20.

LIFE OF CAROLYN: THE SEQUEL

W hen Wally and Carolyn walked to the dining hall, they saw, on the main quadrangle, two fully clothed freshers being dunked in a huge tub. B.J. was among those watching.

"They were caught without their ties," she explained. "On your way to lunch?"

"We are," said Wally.

"So are we." B.J. gestured toward two students along-side her. "Dr. Baxter, Ms Webb, meet Mae, who's from Malaysia. And Andrew, from Swansea, on the east coast of Tasmania. Mae, Andrew, Dr. Baxter is our new visiting fellow."

Wally winced slightly at the introduction, hoping Carolyn wouldn't say "And I'm the visiting fellow's roommate." She didn't.

"Mae was just asking if it ever snows here," said B.J. "I

said there's usually snow on Mount Wellington in mid-winter. That's not far from here."

As they entered the dining hall, Mae said, "I've never seen snow."

"Oh, Mae, you must come to Canada," said Carolyn, surprising Wally with her sudden affability. "We live in Winnipeg, Canada, and right now, we have heaps of snow, this high." She held her hand at shoulder height.

Mae laughed and Andrew said, "How do you *stand* it?"

Over plates of lasagna, they chatted, Mae fiddling with the tie that marked her as a fresher. She talked about Malaysian heat and Canadian cold with Wally and B.J., while Andrew, a lifer, got into a separate conversation with Carolyn. Most of the students having lunch were freshers, and every few minutes one or more of them would break out in loud laughter or song.

After lunch, Wally and Carolyn headed for the administrative office.

"Well," said Carolyn, sounding pleased with herself. "Maybe I'll have something to do while you're *visiting*, after all."

"Oh?"

"Andrew was interested to hear I'm a graphic designer. He says he loves sketching things. He considered studying art, but his parents talked him into law. He wondered if I'd give him a few drawing lessons."

Elizabeth Hardy, the college bursar, gave them instructions on where to pick up the car. They walked the several blocks over to Collins Street and the rental company located in the basement of a state government building. The young man who gave them the keys and the contract spoke so quickly and with such a thick Aussie accent, Wally barely recognized a single word. Wally did think he caught *Shell* and *Mobil* as the two kinds of petrol he was allowed to use, and that was confirmed by the two credit cards in the glove compartment.

"Are you going to be all right in the car?" Wally asked Carolyn.

"No, but I'll try hard, I promise. Please drive carefully, Wally."

"Let's go down to the harbour."

Carolyn squeaked quietly each time Wally made a right turn, but the trip down to the wharf was short. They walked to one end, watching a ferry slowly crossing the Derwent. The wind had picked up, and Wally suggested they go somewhere for a drink. And so they made their way to Firth's Upper Deck restaurant, with its separate bar called The Poop.

Wally felt he needed to talk about their relationship, and this might be a good time. Since this was an odd time of day—three forty-five—there were no other customers in The Poop, but, if Wally thought they were going to have some privacy, the owner had other ideas. He waited on them, told them his name was Tom Firth, and he proved to be a talker. After he had served them Cascade beers, he established that they were Canadians—he said he could tell by their accents—and, when they said they were from Winnipeg, he said he knew exactly where Winnipeg was. "My accountant comes from Winny-peg," he said. "Name is Jack Palson. He's away on a week's vacation right now, but he might drop in here while you're here. Can't stay away, old Jackie." Firth said his restaurant was more than he could handle, and his daughter and son and their spouses did most of the hands-on running of things now. One or two of them would be in pretty soon; he wasn't sure which ones because they were always changing the work schedule. You couldn't blame him for not keeping track of everything because, after all, he also ran a wholesale fish business and that needed him more than the restaurant did. He was only in the bar today because his daughter told him he had to be, just to cover the mid-afternoon period when he couldn't get into trouble. "That's my Cassandra for you." Firth told them they shouldn't miss the Salamanca market, open tomorrow and every Saturday not far from his bar. It was one of the best markets in Australia. He made Carolyn promise that she'd go there in the morning.

They got back to the campus in time for dinner and parked in the spot reserved for the visiting fellow. They ate a meal of roast turkey and veggies in the company of Peter Russell and his wife, Evelyn, and their two small daughters. The Russells lived on campus. Evelyn suggested they visit the casino, and, since they felt like doing something, they went. Using the directions Peter had given them, they found the casino easily—part of the Boardwalk and Wrest Point Hotel complex.

The place seemed more Vegas than Hobart—plush and glitzy, with all kinds of restaurants and shops adjacent to the gaming tables and banks of slot machines. Carolyn wanted to play the slots, though neither she nor Wally understood them. "I used to like pulling down the one arm of the bandit and hearing the clatter of coins in the metal dish," he said. "Now it's all buttons and electronic credits." But Carolyn did something right and came away 267 Australian dollars to the good.

Back on the Jane campus at dusk, there were student stereos blaring from the rooms, clothes drying in open dorm windows, kids out on fire escapes smoking.

Weary, Carolyn wanted to get ready for bed, and Wally let her have her privacy in the bedroom. He sat at the study desk in the dark and watched freshers on the floodlit tennis courts. He thought about the day, what she had told him that morning. He longed to hear her uninhibited laugh; he couldn't remember the last time he'd heard it. Even her winnings hadn't brought it on. He felt melancholy, and the image of Joyce in the Fort Garry bar flashed by him. He shook his head and tried to think about what he was going to do about Carolyn.

"Wally?" She appeared at the study door in her nightgown. "Are you coming to bed?"

"Yup. Right away."

He went into the bedroom, took his pyjamas from a drawer, and moved toward the door.

"You can stay here to change," Carolyn said, pulling the bedcovers back. "I won't watch."

He chuckled, but she didn't. He saw her climb under the covers and lie down with a benign smile on her face. As he took off his clothes and put on his pyjamas, he kept himself turned away from her, even though he knew she wasn't watching him.

After peeing, washing his hands, and brushing his teeth, he returned to the bedroom, got into his side of the bed, and turned off the lamp. He could tell she was still awake. They lay there for a while, on their backs, side by side, several inches apart, not moving.

At last, he said, "I've been thinking."

"What about?"

"Stephen."

"Oh."

"Well, not Stephen, exactly. Your life with Stephen. Which of course I know nothing about. But … I've been thinking of a way to put this … your life with Stephen is like some … some great novel or something, this great play, or movie—maybe more like a movie. And this movie was a huge success, beyond the wildest dreams of the producer and the director and the writer. And the actors, yes, I think even the actors were surprised at how good it was and how successful it was. And now … yes, now … um … the producer wants to do a sequel. Some people think he's nuts. I think the producer is a guy, but maybe not. Anyway, the producer has made it clear that this is not a *remake* of the original, because that cannot be duplicated; everybody agrees with that. Let's see now … where am I going with this? … Okay, the thing is, the sequel has not quite been figured out yet, but it's basically … your life with me. It may not be as good as the original—most sequels aren't—but sometimes … sometimes, they turn out to be better. The thing is, the two shouldn't be compared. And there will always be this great first movie. But the people involved have a right to try to make another damn good one."

He'd said enough. He didn't know if he'd taken a big risk in mentioning Stephen or if Carolyn had been hoping he would mention him. She didn't move, and neither did he.

He didn't turn his head to see if he could see any expression on her face in the dark. He heard her breathing. It didn't sound as if she was crying. He could hear sounds in the distance—a car, a fresher's yell, a dog's bark. After what seemed like a long time, she spoke, so quietly that at first he wondered if he was dreaming.

"Wally, could you please put your arms around me?"

"Oh, *yes*..."

"I mean just that. Your arms holding me."

They turned to each other, and he held her, her fragrant hair against his face, her body against his body.

She didn't say anything else.

After a short while, her breathing became the steady breathing of sleep—quiet, rhythmic, loveable.

21.

OF DICE AND DRAWING

The radio told them, while they were eating breakfast in the underlodge, that it was going to be *another fine day in Hobart*. A good day for the Salamanca market, but first it was high time they checked on Geordie. Ten a.m. Saturday in Tasmania, so it would be five p.m. on Friday in Winnipeg. They had given Carolyn's parents a few phone numbers—the Wooloomooloo Waters, Silky Oaks Lodge, Jane Franklin Hall—in case there was some emergency, but they had heard nothing.

Wally watched Carolyn initiate the call, thinking for the umpteenth time how weird but also how terrific it was that Geordie was billeted with her folks.

"Hi, Daddy!" Carolyn cried. It was always amazing to hear someone's voice from so far away. "Oh, we're just fine, Dad.... We've already seen a lot—the Great Barrier Reef, the Sydney Opera House, a real tropical rain forest.... Well, yes, it *is* a bonus to see everything with a

history prof—he's giving me history lessons all the time."
She winked at Wally. "And now we're in Tasmania—not
far from Antarctica! ... No, it's pretty warm. Dad, we were
wondering how it's going with Geordie.... Really?... So
he's there right now? ... Could you bring him to the phone
so Wally can speak ... Oh! Well, are you sure they ... I
mean ... Dad, just a minute. Yes, hold on just a minute."
She covered the mouthpiece with her hand and said, with
a concerned look, "Geordie's girlfriend Michelle is over
there, and they're in Geordie's room with the door closed,
but Dad says it's all right because he can hear the dice rat-
tling." She smiled even as she frowned. "Is that a good
thing?"

Wally said, "He promised me that he would not take
advantage of your parents in any way. He said he'd help
around the house and he wouldn't stay out late..."

"He doesn't have to stay out late; his girlfriend is *with*
him!"

"Tell your dad I have to speak with Geordie."

"Dad, Wally ... oh, hi, Mum! ... Yes, we're having a
wonderful time. You'd love it here.... Yes, we saw the
Opera House. I sent you a postcard with the Opera House
on it.... Well, yes, it should get there any day now.... Oh,
yes, Wally is spoiling me..." She rolled her eyes. "Right ...
yes, the koalas are so cute! ... Mum, listen, Dad says Geordie has his girlfriend there. Are you okay with that?...
Really? ... That's nice.... Mum, just hold on for a sec." She
covered the mouthpiece again and said, "Mum says she
loves Michelle. The girl is over there for dinner tonight,
and she's already been there twice before, and she brings
dessert!"

"Can I talk to Geordie?"

"You're not mad at him, are you? Sounds like he has all the bases covered."

"Maybe I could speak with your mother?"

"Mum, Wally would like to speak with you.... Yes, hold on, here he is."

"Hi, Mrs. Laidlaw."

"Hello, Wally! Oh, you sound so *clear!*"

"Yes, we do have a terrific connection, don't we? You sound like you're just down the street from here."

"What time is it there?"

"It's ... let's see ... ten fifteen on Saturday morning."

"You mean it's tomorrow morning there."

"Yes. Crazy, isn't it? Listen ... Mrs. Laidlaw, is Geordie ... I mean, is he *behaving* himself?"

"Wally, he is *fine*. It's such a treat to have a young person around the house. And his *girlfriend*, well, she's a delight."

"I'm glad to hear it. Do you think I could speak with him?"

"Of course! Did Louis say you couldn't? He hates to interrupt their hockey games. Just a minute ... oh, here's Louis with Geordie now. Geordie, it's your dad."

"Hi, Dad."

"Geordie! How are you?"

"Fine. How's Australia?"

"Quite outstanding, really. We had a bit of a whirlwind tour of the mainland, and now we're settling into the college life here in Tasmania. Geordie, Mrs. Laidlaw says everything's going well; I'm glad to hear it. I hope you aren't taking advantage in any way, like bringing Michelle over there too often."

"She's really into the hockey game. Her teams are made up of famous movie stars. Like, Johnny Depp is leading in goals. And we've added more stuff to Mr. Laidlaw's rules..."

"Sounds good, Geordie. Just remember, don't get into doing things that the Laidlaws wouldn't be happy about..."

"*Da-ad.*"

"Okay. Glad it's going well. Now, let Mrs. Laidlaw talk with Carolyn again, okay?"

Wally handed the phone to Carolyn, thinking, it's probably easy to roll dice while you're having sex. He wouldn't say that to Carolyn; he'd just sound envious of his son, and she wouldn't appreciate the irony.

On the way to the Salamanca market, they saw fat clouds in the sky and some blue patches. It rained a little, and then the sun came out. Wally had begun to understand that the combination of clouds, blue sky, rain and sun meant *another fine day*.

"I'm not sure where to park," Wally said.

The street was congested, and groups of people were coming from many directions and heading toward the wharf area. Wally thought he could see tents.

"It looks pretty crowded," he said. "Are we sure we want to do this?"

"Why don't you drop me off?" Carolyn said. "You probably have better things to do than follow me around."

He sensed this was one of those times when she'd prefer to be alone, and, besides, he was blocking traffic. "I'd better move. Okay, I'll drop you here, and you can call me at the underlodge when you're ready to be picked up."

"Perfect!" She kissed his cheek and jumped out of the car.

He drove away. As he drove back to Jane, he was surprised to realize he missed her. Or was he just dismayed by the sudden change of plan?

Back in the underlodge, he went into the study and sat at the desk. He stared at a lined pad of paper. Sooner or later, he had to think about the informal talk he was giving some night after high table, and the guest lecture he'd likely give at the University, and the seminar he'd said he'd lead on Canadian studies. As he sat there, Andrew the lifer and two other young men appeared, going past his window to knock on the underlodge door. He went to greet them.

"Good morning," he said.

"G'day, sir," said Andrew. "Could you tell us, please, if Ms Webb is here?"

"I'm sorry, Andrew, she isn't. She's downtown at the market."

"Oh. Dr. Baxter, this is Des Marsden, a member of the Student Committee, and Braden Darwin. Braden transferred here from Brisbane."

"Pleased to meet you both," Wally said, shaking their hands. "Could I give Ms Webb a message?"

Andrew tugged at his forelock. "Uh … she may have mentioned giving art classes?"

"She did say you might like some instruction in drawing."

"Yes … and she said if there were others interested, we might be able to have an informal—or ad hoc—class. I wanted her to know that Des and Braden are both interested, and there may be others."

"I'm working on my degree in medicine," Braden said. "Here at Jane I can finish it more quickly than I could've in Brisbane. And, you know, it's so intensive, art class would be a welcome break, and I think looking at the human body from an art perspective would be helpful to a doctor, don't you?"

"I like doing cartoons," said Des. "Smashing idea, art lessons."

Wally wondered if there was any protocol that needed to be followed in this and if Carolyn's impromptu idea wasn't getting a little out of hand. One problem: Where would the class take place?

"I'll tell Ms Webb at least three of you are enthusiastic." He was about to add, "She may not want many more than that," but thought better of it. Who knew what the hell she wanted?

"Thank you, sir," said Andrew. "Check back with her later, shall I?"

"Fine."

Braden said, "I understand Ms Webb works as a graphic designer. Does she do illustration work as well?"

"She does," said Wally. "She's especially good at drawing people from life."

"Would she do a sketch of me?" said Des. "My mam back in Shepparton would love a nice sketch of me."

"To hang in her loo!" said Andrew, punching Des in the shoulder.

Andrew and Des each said goodbye and started off. Braden hung back.

"You know those detailed drawings of the muscles and the bones and the inner organs that you see in doctors' offices?" he said.

"Yes," said Wally.

"They look so real, don't they, as if the outer flesh has been taken off an entire body. I wonder how those are done."

"Yes, I've wondered too," said Wally.

"I mean, how can anyone be sure that is the way everything looks? Doctors can take the body apart through dissection, but it must be difficult to dissect in layers, don't you think? The artist would have to work with a doctor to have a good appreciation of the human anatomy, like where every part is in relation to every other part, but he must have to apply some imagination."

"I think you're right."

"Have a good day, sir!"

Braden left, and Wally returned to the study. He sat at the desk, again looking at the blank page. He tried to visualize the opening paragraphs of a lecture—a contrast of Canada's early settlers with the boatloads of English convicts, most of them thieves, who were shipped to Van Diemen's Land—but instead what he saw was an artist's rendition of a young model, and the model was Marjorie, sitting in that Paris hotel window all those years ago.

Carolyn called to say she was going to walk home from the market.

"Are you sure, having to lug all your purchases?"

"Didn't buy all that much. It was big, though. Did a lot of browsing. Okay, I'm leaving now. It's straight up Davey..."

"To Elboden. Carolyn, that student—Andrew—stopped

by to see you. He had a couple of other fellows with him who are interested in your art class."

"Great! See you in a few minutes."

At six, they walked around to the principal's front door, which was darkened by an overgrowth of bushes. Carolyn wore a turquoise top with white linen pants and a silver bracelet she'd bought at the market. She had bought a Tasmania cap for Wally, but it didn't quite fit. "It's all right," she said, "it'll fit my dad."

An attractive blonde woman came to the door. Her hair seemed a little out of place, but she was wearing lipstick that matched the red in her dress. She looked considerably younger than Lockridge. "I'm Virginia," she said.

After Lockridge had appeared and introduced the guests, Virginia led them into a comfortably furnished living room—a chesterfield, a loveseat, two armchairs, all in floral design with plump pillows piled in each of them.

"What is your pleasure, Carolyn?" Lockridge asked.

"Oh, white wine would be lovely, please."

"Feel free to ask for whatever you fancy," said Virginia. "Dennis might even let you break into his private stock."

Lockridge eyed Wally. "A little Glenmorangie, perhaps?"

"All right, if you twist my arm. Please."

"Neat or on ice?"

"On ice, please."

"The American way."

Lockridge disappeared. Virginia produced cashews and biscuits and cheese on a tray. As if on cue, a large grey cat came into the room, looked at Carolyn and Wally, and jumped onto a chair.

"You have a cat as well as the two goats," said Wally.

"You've met Jane Austen and George Eliot, have you?"

"A girl and a boy goat," said Carolyn.

"Actually, both female," said Virginia.

"George Eliot was the pen name of a woman writer called Mary Anne Evans," Wally said, trying his best to say it casually, as if it didn't matter that Carolyn didn't know.

"I loved *Middlemarch*. Didn't you?" said Virginia.

"Oh, yes," Wally said, aware that this was just the kind of one-upping chatter that Carolyn would loathe. "Um, which goat is which?"

"The white one is Jane, the black one is George."

"Is it all right to feed them?"

"Now and then—something from the bushes, if you like. But I assure you, they are well-fed. George is the younger one; we adopted her when Emily died."

"Dickinson?" said Wally.

"No, Brontë. By the way, we have two other cats. And two dogs, but they are all tucked away right now."

"They're all very quiet," said Carolyn.

"Virginia has two horses, as well, don't you, darling?" said Lockridge, coming in with a tray of drinks. "She'd keep them here if the board would allow it."

"I do like my menagerie," said Virginia, as each of them took a glass. "Our daughter rides more than I."

"Cheers," said Wally, raising his scotch on one rock.

"Yes," said Lockridge. "Here's to Canada."

All four of them toasted and sipped.

"You've got to tell us what you call the other animals," said Wally.

"Actually," said Lockridge, "we've become rather bored

with English writers. We've started to name them after previous visiting fellows."

Wally laughed, unsure if Lockridge was being facetious.

There was a brief lull. As Virginia passed around the tray of edibles, she said, "Dennis tells me you are a history professor, Wally, and Carolyn, you work as a graphic designer. I assume you have an art background. Do you paint?"

"I've done some painting, yes. A few oils. But I like sketching—more satisfying because it's quicker, I think."

"I've always wanted to do watercolours, haven't I, Dennis? I did some in school and would love to try it again. There is so much beautiful scenery so close to here."

"Maybe you'd like to join my class."

Wally tried not to look astonished. How could she so casually mention her art class, which so far was little more than a whim, *to the principal and his wife?* For all Wally knew, it was against college policy to run some kind of hobby course on campus. Or to distract full-time students from their demanding curriculum. How could she even presume that she could *teach?* And to mention it to the very person whose permission you'd probably need, to mention it as if it was actually happening and not having the courtesy to consult with him in the first place!

Virginia seemed a little perplexed as she said, "Your class." It sounded as if she were trying out the sound of it.

"Let me put this in a little context," Wally said, avoiding Lockridge's gaze. "We were talking with a student the other day at lunch, and he said he wished he could take a few art lessons as a break from his usual studies, and Carolyn said she wouldn't mind tutoring him…"

"And two more students have come forward," said Carolyn, "so if you're interested, Virginia, you could join us."

"What do you think, Dennis?"

"Quite fine," said Lockridge. He showed no anger and even looked rather amused. "Where might this class take place?"

Carolyn had an immediate answer: "In our study. It's the perfect size if we keep the numbers down, and Wally can't be in there all day; he'd go mad."

22.

CAROLYN'S JOURNAL II

Thursday, February 20, 1997

We were met in Hobart by the top dog of the college. He's nice enough. He drove us through town, me in the back seat with my suitcase. He lives on campus, and we parked by his house. He led us down a hill to the back of the house. It became suddenly obvious that our living space was going to be in his basement.

Lockridge pointed out the surrounding scenery. And we had our own entrance. But it's still a basement. With a bed like the one in Silky Oaks. When Lockridge left, I wanted to scream.

It was best just to keep doing things. I don't know how Wally felt. He didn't look at me. We got ready to go to the reception before high table dinner.

Meeting people was a blur. I felt like I was on the set

of an English drama about Oxford. Someone who'd been spirited out of working-class Winnipeg and dropped onto this set. I felt uneducated and boorish. Both men and women looked at me like I was a peasant in an academic gown. I wanted Stephen to come and rescue me.

At dinner, I tried to mind my manners. I worried I might drop something or spill something. I don't even know what I said to people when they spoke to me.

Back in our basement, we unpacked. I saw Wally killing bugs. He didn't say much, and I tried to look pleasant. When we went to bed, I dreaded what he might say. I was worried that he might hate the place as much as I do. I wanted him to speak, but he didn't. When he reached for me, I cried.

Friday, February 21, 1997
I hardly slept. I kept thinking of what I could do: fly home. But that would make Wally look like an idiot. Maybe I could say I caught a tropical disease. I was allergic to the southern hemisphere. I was deathly afraid of huntsman spiders. I just can't be Wally's missus. I don't know what I *can* be.

And then the phone rang. It was like a gun shot, it scared me so much. And wouldn't you know, it was Dobber.

He swore he wouldn't phone me. Okay, so he did. I think I straightened out the problem.

Wally wanted to talk about it, but I wasn't in the mood. I got ratty, maybe because I hadn't slept, maybe because I didn't want to explain anything. I asked him to leave me alone. He finally went out. I can't believe I went back to bed, but I did. I was exhausted. Can't believe he came back and went out again without me hearing him.

I was glad he did, though. I got out before he came back. I didn't know where I was going, but I wanted to walk. And walk, downhill, toward the water. The streets were a maze, and I barely kept track of where I was. I was thinking about Stephen. How he wanted to travel. San Francisco was supposed to be the first of many trips. New York, London, Paris. I wanted to go to those places, too. But I kept putting them off. I was too busy. I couldn't take a long vacation. We went to Chicago for a weekend. And I had a horrible cold the whole time. From too many freakin' nights working. Jeez, I'd give anything to be here with Stephen.

When Wally and I finally did talk, I kind of lost it.

We actually did get to lunch together, though. And I met this kid named Andrew. And he asked me what I did. And he said he'd like to draw ...

Saturday, February 22, 1997
I lay there thinking this morning.

Not about Wally's speech—"Carolyn's Life—the Sequel."

And I wasn't even thinking about Stephen.

I lay there thinking about teaching drawing. Something to *do!*

I was still thinking about it after breakfast when Wally said it was time we phoned home.

Everything's going well. Who cares if Wally's kid is fucking his girlfriend under my parents' noses? Everybody's happy!

I said I wanted to go to the Saturday market. Wally

dropped me off. I <u>thought</u> a lot more about drawing, maybe even having a class.

Wow, talk about positive thinking! When I got back to our place, Wally told me some more kids were asking about drawing lessons.

And, so tonight, I mentioned it to the head honcho and his wife. I was as astonished as Wally was when I did it. I didn't intend to. I guess those people just got to me somehow. And right there I came up with the underlodge study as the place I'd use! But it felt good, you know? To speak up like that. Fucking good.

23.

TUTORING

On the way out the door with Carolyn, Virginia described a watercolour that had won her a prize in school. Behind them, Lockridge touched Wally's arm.

"A word?" he said.

"Yes, sir?"

Lockridge watched the two women go around the bushes, out of sight. "Ms Webb—Carolyn—shouldn't place too much importance on this watercolour thing. Virginia is quite the dilettante, I'm afraid. She won't want to work at it, and tomorrow, when she realizes she'd be in a *class* with Jane students, she will not be so keen."

"I see."

"Also ... I did not want to dampen Carolyn's enthusiasm, but ... there is no budget for this sort of thing. And the board won't want her to charge the students."

"I think this is purely voluntary, sir. But I'll make sure she knows that."

Wally mentioned this over dinner at the Hog's Breath Café, a downtown restaurant recommended by Virginia.

"Of *course* I don't want any money," Carolyn said. "I'm on a paid vacation, and part of my motive is to keep me thinking. I will need some art supplies, and I totally expect to pay for them myself."

Sunday morning they thought they'd venture into the scenic countryside. On the way to the car, they saw a group of perhaps forty freshers assembled outside the dining room. There were three rows, the front row crouched on the grass, the second row sitting in collapsible chairs, the back row standing. The photographer looked professional, with his camera on a tripod.

At the point when he believed everyone was ready, he said, "Wallabies!" instead of *cheese*, and five or six lifers stationed on the roof dumped huge buckets of water onto the freshers. Peter Russell was there to watch, and he told Wally it was a caper that worked every single year.

They talked about the drenching as they drove south, headed for a wildlife park about seventy kilometres from Hobart, near the town of Cygnet. Carolyn had brought along her video camera and thought it might help her deal with her jitters. Only when a twist or turn came too quickly did she cry out, and then she would apologize. Wally suggested she try looking into the distance, let him concentrate on the road. There'd be an emerald-green hill with a dark-green forest beyond that, and then a turquoise expanse of water. Around every corner, it seemed, there was another beautiful vista. Wally would slow down or stop so that Carolyn could shoot what they agreed was *the best view*, only to have a better one appear a minute later.

The park was small, marked by hard-to-see signs, but the young proprietor was friendly, and, for a mere six dollars, you could see what you expected to see in Australia: wallabies, kangaroos, koalas, even a cheeky emu that wanted to stick its beak into Wally's pockets, snooping for the bag of feed the proprietor had provided. Carolyn was talked into holding a fat and furry wombat, and, after a minute, she didn't want to give it back to the smiling park staffer. They were able to pat a Tasmanian devil; it looked like a large mole, not at all like the Disney version. This was the first live devil they'd seen; Wally had noticed several dead ones on the highway. They fed the ducks and the peacocks and kept their pockets away from a one-horned deer. They left the park feeling it was well worth the visit, stopped at a pub on the way home for what were referred to as *tubs* of beer (half-pints), and were back at Jane in time for dinner.

"I held a wombat this afternoon," Carolyn told the group they joined.

"At that park near Cygnet," said Wally.

"Well, we now have a cat," B.J. announced. This might've sounded like B.J. meant owning a cat trumped holding a wombat any day, but, coming from the good-natured B.J., it came across like she was settling for second best.

Patrick, beside her, looked smug, as if he felt he could now leave town knowing his wife had a companion.

"Aww!" said Amy, one of three students at the table. "Is it male or female?"

"Female," said B.J.

"So the government hasn't banned cats yet?" said Wally.

"Not yet," Patrick said.

"What are you going to call her?" a student named Marie asked.

"Elizabeth? Helen of Troy? We don't know yet," said B.J. "Perhaps Cleopatra."

"Do you like cats?" Marie asked Wally.

"I do. They have such personalities. They can be aloof when you try to be affectionate, and then they're all over you when you least expect it."

"That's the way I'd like to be," said Amy. She dared to aim her flirtatious smile at first Wally and then Patrick, and then she laughed with the others. She was on the short side, with a pretty face, dark hair, and an hourglass figure, endowed in a way that Wally's high-school mates used to call BFC (built for comfort). "Marie, we had better go and decide which teddy bears we're taking to the slumber party. And which pyjamas we're wearing."

As they left the dining hall, they met Braden, who asked, "Are you hoping to start up the art classes this week?"

"Most likely Wednesday," Carolyn said, "if I get my supplies tomorrow."

"I have a class I can't miss at one on Wednesday, but after that..."

"I'm going to try three o'clock. We may have to move it around if there's no perfect time for everyone. Say, Braden, are you going back to your room right now?"

"Yes."

"Mind if Dr. Baxter and I have a peek?"

"I'd be honoured to show you my room. Follow me."

Wally had said nothing to Carolyn about wanting to see a dorm room, but he was glad of the chance. And he soon saw why Braden was so pleased to show them his: uncluttered desk, spotless computer and keyboard and printer, single bed made up as tightly and crisply as that of an army private expecting an officer's inspection, clothes all hung up or put away in drawers. The single window that overlooked the campus quadrangle was clean. As Wally and Carolyn left, offering compliments, Des was coming down the hall, and, chuckling, he offered to show them his room. It was twice as big as Braden's—a perk of being on the Student Committee—with a double bed, but it looked as if vandals had ransacked the place a few minutes earlier. Perhaps they had.

Monday morning, Wally drove Carolyn downtown and she bought paper, art board, drawing boards, easels, pencils, and erasers. When they returned to the campus, she insisted that Wally stay in his study while she went to the admin office to arrange to borrow chairs and to leave messages for Andrew, Des, Braden, and Adam Flynn—a friend of Andrew's—telling them the first drawing class would definitely be on Wednesday at three. Wally had to work on the talk he was giving that night after high table. He tried not to appear annoyed as Carolyn brought chairs, one at a time, into his study. She didn't speak, but he could sense her excitement as she set up the boards, easels, and chairs all around him. Though she had enough for seven work stations, she set up only four, and he felt they were crowding him out.

Those present at high table—Dr. Lockridge, selected fellows and board members, a few Student Committee reps—settled into the senior common room after dinner to hear Wally's talk. He began with the provocative observation that Canada had long been dominated by American culture—books, music, movies, television—but, since Expo 67 in Montreal, Canada had fought hard to nurture its own artists. He spoke about some who had achieved international reputations—writers like Robertson Davies, Margaret Atwood, and Alice Munro. He went on to talk about the current literary scene, the boom in children's fiction, the fact that Canadian bestsellers were usually literary works, the advent of big-box bookstores, the problem of consignment for small publishers, the battles to change the copyright laws. He saw some listeners yawn—they included Carolyn—but some asked questions, wanting to compare the Canadian scene with the Australian. They gave him polite applause and Board Chair John Powell came up to Wally to invite him and Carolyn for dinner, and Official Fellow Bill Merton invited them to take part in a golf tournament.

And then there was Rebecca from the Student Committee, picking a moment to speak with Wally when others were turned away from him.

"I thoroughly enjoyed your talk," she said, shaking his hand. "I'd like to go to Canada someday, perhaps even to live. I'd like to learn more. Do you think you might tutor me?"

Wally looked at her young, immaculate face, framed in *drop-dead gorgeous* shoulder-length blonde hair. "Of course!" he said.

From the senior common room, Wally and Carolyn and others headed to the music room for a short concert: Patrick on the violin and B.J. at the piano. Wally contemplated the importance of the violinist's chin. In Patrick's case, it held the violin in place and allowed him to use both hands to manipulate the bow while turning the pages of sheet music. Patrick's face was devoid of expression; he conserved air in his cheeks and puffed it out through his mouth at intervals. The wayward lock of B.J.'s hair kept falling over her eye, but she was adept at flipping it back in mid-melody. Once, the music sheets slipped down across her hands as she played, and both she and Patrick continued on, unruffled. Their performances—a solo by Patrick and two duets—were lovely and much appreciated by the small gathering.

Over refreshments, Wally and Carolyn met Joan and Stan Radcliffe, who offered to take them on a "convict" tour on Saturday. All four of them wished Patrick *bon voyage* because he was leaving for Montreal in the morning.

A phone call came from B.J.

"Wally, do you think I could borrow your car? I don't have one, and I have to take the cat to the vet for shots. I don't fancy taking him on the bus."

"I was just going out myself. Could I take you there?"

"If you don't mind, that would be awfully good of you."

"I'm ready to go any time. Did Patrick get away all right?"

"Bright and early yesterday. I'll come by the underlodge right now, shall I?"

"Perfect."

B.J. arrived with a cardboard box. She opened it to show Carolyn and Wally a grey tabby with a wide-eyed kitten face.

"She's so cute!" said Carolyn. "We should get one, Wally."

Her exuberance was increasing as the drawing class drew closer, and her delight at seeing and holding the cat must've seemed exaggerated even to B.J. And her comment *We should get one* suggested closeness as a couple that was not translating into intimacy. Wally felt more and more like a brother. When he'd told Carolyn about Rebecca's wanting to be tutored, she had said, "Oh, I'm so glad for you! Wally, she's *gorgeous!*"

The vet wasn't far from Jane. Wally went inside with B.J., and a nurse took B.J. and the boxed cat into a back room. Wally sat in the waiting room, watching people come and go. A genial middle-aged woman came in with her sheltie. A sour-looking couple came out of the back with two puppies and left. A biker couple entered with a hefty malamute. A woman eating a bag of French fries came in to make an appointment for her dog. A short woman with a heavily madeup face came in and asked the receptionist for directions. Wally was disappointed that no one appeared with a pet indigenous to Australia—a kangaroo or a koala.

B.J. emerged, looking embarrassed and carrying the kitten. It looked alert and healthy.

"She's a boy," said B.J. The young vet came out behind her, smiling. "Patrick was so sure it was a girl."

"Does this mean Cleopatra now becomes Caesar?" Wally asked.

"I honestly don't have a clue what to call her ... him ... now."

"Maybe *Patrick?*"

"Oh ... Patrick will object, but, for now, why not?"

When they returned to the college, B.J. said, "I can't thank you enough for the lift. If there is anything I can do for you..."

"Rebecca wants me to tutor her in Canadian history. I thought it might be good to meet somewhere while Carolyn is using the underlodge study. Any suggestions?"

"When do you want it?"

"This afternoon at three."

"Why not use my flat? I'll be in the music room at three."

B.J.'s flat was in the same building as the music room. It was barren—no rug on the wooden floor, no furniture except for a futon, a narrow table, and a few odd straight chairs, two of which likely came from a bridge set. In two corners of the white ceiling were splotches of bright-coloured paint, one scarlet, the other deep blue. B.J. told Wally she'd been trying out new colours to liven up the place, and she hated both. The paint cans and brushes were still out in the middle of the floor.

Andrew had arrived at the underlodge twenty minutes early, partly to announce that two more of his buddies were coming to the class. He helped Carolyn set up two more stations. Where the study had been spacious, conducive to free thinking, it now looked cluttered and stifling. Carolyn seemed unfazed, but Wally was happy to get out of there.

Though he offered to look after the cat, B.J. took it with

her, as well as the litter box. "I would not want you or Rebecca to have to contend with an accident," she said.

Rebecca arrived two minutes after B.J. had left. She had her blonde hair pulled back in a loose ponytail, and she wore white shorts that showed off her long legs.

"Good. You got my message," Wally said, trying not to look too dazzled by the tall young woman as she walked past him into the flat.

"Yes. Thanks," she said. "I love the stripes." She was gazing at the paint on the ceiling. "Where would you like me?"

Wally scanned her as she looked around. Her breasts nuzzled the pink material of her blouse.

"Let's use these bridge chairs," he said.

Wally opened the file folder he'd brought with him, and Rebecca opened her loose-leaf binder to a blank page. She wrote something in the middle of the first line and he read it upside down. Dr. Baxter: Canada.

"We … um … can make this pretty informal," Wally said. "Why don't you tell me where you'd like to start."

"Oh. I would like to know a little about the early days, some of the heroes. And then I would like you to touch on the highlights from then until now. I don't know how many meetings we shall be able to have but, really, anything you can tell me will be valuable."

"Why don't we begin with Jacques Cartier? And the importance of the French? He was a French mariner who, in 1535, was sent by his king to the land that became Quebec. I've always thought of him as the most important figure in early Canadian history. And quite underrated. Here …I have a picture of him, a painting, with the Iroquois chief Donnacona…"

24.

CAROLYN'S JOURNAL III

Sunday, February 23, 1997
We went to this wild animal park near Cygnet, and the animals were livelier than the ones we saw in Sydney. I liked the koala bears, but I fell in love with the wombat. A park staffer saw the fuss I was making over this fat and hairy guy. He asked me if I'd like to hold it. I hesitated, but he talked me into it. He set it in my arms, and the wombat instantly cuddled. I got all teary eyed.

Stephen and I never had a pet. We wanted a nice dog, but neither of us thought we'd give it enough time. This wombat fella was like a big warm fur coat all rolled up. With the cutest face! I didn't want to leave him.

At dinner tonight, all I could talk about was the wombat.

A lot of the girls were going to a slumber party after chapel. I wished I was going with them.

Monday, February 24, 1997

Went shopping for art supplies today. Not a bit sure what I needed. I thought back to my college days and what we had to get for classes. I probably got more than I need.

Got some chairs, told Wally I didn't want his help. It's important I do everything myself. I really don't want to be a nuisance. Never let it be said that I interfered with the visiting fellow.

I intend to have the first class on Wednesday at three.

I almost forgot the visiting fellow was giving his talk tonight after high table. He hadn't told me much about it. Well, nothing really. He spoke well. I think his topic was a little boring, though. Canada. Maybe it's just because I'm Canadian. Some important people were there, like the board chair. He invited us to dinner.

I was glad Wally got some kudos. He deserves them, I think. He's been putting up with a lot from me. He seemed to be in his glory when this young blonde babe gushed all over him.

And then we went to hear B.J. and Patrick do a duet. Patrick's an intense fellow but easy to look at while he fiddles. (Should that be <u>violins</u>?)

Tuesday, February 25, 1997

I spent most of the day figuring out what my first class should consist of. I woke up thinking I was nuts doing this, but I got more confident as the day progressed.

I did my best to stay out of Wally's way. He tried to concentrate on something at his desk.

I kept moving easels around. And looking at different angles for the student seating.

Wally eventually went somewhere else.

Wednesday, February 26, 1997
I did it!

Scared as I was, I put those guys through a two-hour workshop. They didn't want to leave. Had them do sketches, anything they saw around them. The desk, the window, each other. Even the goat they could see outside (Jane or George). I gave them objects to draw. A handbag, a carton, a clock. Trying to get them to understand perspective.

First off, I asked them to do a few quick drawings of faces. Des did cartoony stuff. Andrew did about seven sketches of me. Not very good. Hey, maybe I look like that to him!

One or two of them showed they had a pretty good idea of depth or proportion. Braden and one of the new guys, Joe or David. Andrew was probably worst.

They took the whole thing seriously. Des laughed a lot, mostly at his own cartoons. He kept at it, though. I'll give him that.

We didn't take any breaks. I did give them a choice of juices half way through. Des wanted a Cascade. A couple of the others wondered why we couldn't have wine. Twice, Joe or David went out for a smoke.

I had them try drawing something without looking down at the paper. Most found that pretty awkward. I didn't mind if they sneaked peeks. A couple of them did all right.

I demonstrated. I drew the goat without looking at the

paper. It came out okay. Probably more my idea of a goat, though, rather than actually Jane. (Or was it George?)

I got into the swing of it, talking about drawing with six young men, all different shapes and sizes. Stephen would be proud of me. He always said I'd be a good teacher.

I handed out sketch pads and gave them homework. I told them hands were the hardest things to draw. I asked them to draw their own hands and bring me the work next class. This coming Friday!

I had to draw my own hand for the entrance portfolio I did to get into advertising art at Red River College. You draw the one not holding the pencil, so I did my left. The way you draw hands can be a game-breaker. My drawing instructor told me I did hands better than anyone he knew. Maybe he was just sweet-talking me. Instructors used to date students in those days, the steamy seventies.

That assignment made me think of Stephen's hands. His slim fingers and his trim nails. How he didn't touch me much when we were dating. He was pretty religious that way. Wanted to wait until we were married.

So, yes, we're going to try to get the group together again on Friday. Saturday, if that works better for everybody.

Andrew hung around after class. Helped me move the easels against the walls. He asked me if we might do some life drawing. That's the academically acceptable term for drawing nude models. I said I hoped we could.

And he volunteered!

25.

SOLITARY

Joan and Stan Radcliffe arrived at one thirty Saturday afternoon in a four-door four by four. Wally and Carolyn soon learned that Stan had developed his historical expertise—a repertoire of stories about the English sending convicts to Tasmania in the early nineteenth century—for teaching Elderhostel, the American program that had tourists taking classes in the places they visited. Stan spoke with authority, his running commentary beginning in the Female Factory, not far from Jane Franklin Hall. Joan patiently chipped in remarks from time to time.

There was not much left of the Female Factory—four crumbling stone walls—but it had once housed the female convicts who had been exiled to Van Diemen's Land. A plaque mounted on the site told of a day when the women were assembled for inspection by Lady Jane Franklin, and they flashed their bare bottoms at her in some kind of protest. The last line of the text said that, although this report was investigated, it was never confirmed—a rather bizarre statement to engrave on a plaque.

From there, Stan drove them to the historic town of Richmond, about twenty-five kilometres from Hobart. They toured a prison where repeat offenders had been incarcerated in the mid-1800s. Wally stepped into one of the solitary-confinement cells and closed the door to experience what it was like to be alone in a narrow space without light or furniture. He felt a tingling of creepiness. What if the others left him and he couldn't get the door open? He didn't admit to any weird chills as he rejoined the others in the yard, where, they were told, prisoners had been flogged. Information on a display told him that relegation to a solitary-confinement cell was much more effective for breaking the spirit than flogging. He believed it.

Another display told of Ikey Solomon, a London thief and supposedly the model for Dickens's Fagin. Solomon became a respectable businessman in Tasmania.

After a snack in a Richmond wine-and-coffee place, Stan led them to The Old Hobart Display, a recasting in miniature of the way Hobart Town once was, with people and animals in the proper scale. Last in the Radcliffes' itinerary was a drive through the narrow streets of Battery Point. It had become so trendy, said Stan, that some of the tiny houses were selling for half a million dollars or more.

Through the pleasant afternoon, Joan and Stan often held hands, even kissed. This was apparently the second marriage for both of them, and fairly recent. These showings of affection were too brief and natural to make anyone feel uncomfortable, but they *did* make Wally feel uncomfortable. Because he was envious. Or inadequate. Or stupid. Envious because he craved that kind of affection—that mutual attraction that caused two people to touch each other for no reason other than their liking to be together, that caused two people to hug each other in odd places like shops and ancient prisons. Why couldn't Carolyn be like that? Inadequate because, even if deep down, Carolyn *was* that kind of person, he didn't bring it out in her. Stupid because he had believed that Carolyn could be that way with him, that they had progressed through what he thought was a meaningful wooing period, and that they had dramatically shown how they felt about each other on that three-circled night in December. He supposed for her it had been lust, plain and simple. But he had gone ahead and invited her on an extended vacation, only to discover that she wasn't the kind of person he thought she was. Or, if she was, she couldn't be that person with him. And now she was getting her kicks not out of seeing the world with *him* but from teaching a bunch of Aussie adolescent boys how to draw. No wonder he longed for the next class with Rebecca and her pretty frown of concentration, her attentiveness—her legs—as he related the story of the adventurous and fearless nurse Mademoiselle Jeanne Mance and her part in the early life of French Canada.

"Thank you so much for the tour," Carolyn was saying to the Radcliffes. "What an enlightening afternoon!"

"It was truly our pleasure, Carolyn," said Stan, giving her a quick hug.

"I think we learned more about Tasmania in this one afternoon than in all our time so far," said Wally. He shook Stan's hand.

"Now, you be good to this lady," Stan said. "Don't you dare let her get away!"

They had barely enough time to change their clothes for a dinner party at the Lockridges'. There were five other guests, including B.J. and Tyler, and, prompted by Virginia, Carolyn was soon talking about her drawing class. A nervous-looking woman named Helga seemed troubled by the knowledge that the class was all male, causing Virginia to say that was precisely why she wanted to get in on it. The truth was that Virginia had not followed up on her watercolour interest, perhaps confirming what Lockridge had told Wally about her tendency to flit from hobby to hobby. Carolyn gradually won over the attention of Lockridge, Tyler, Virginia, Helga, and Helga's husband, Scotty, with her stories of how the class had come about and what exercises were more constructive. Wally, amazed and perhaps a bit jealous, turned to listen in on what B.J. was telling a woman named Susan. B.J. had only recently married Patrick. The wedding reception had been held in her parents' home in Brisbane; the number of guests had to be limited to thirty-six—only six were friends of B.J.'s—and she wore multi-coloured shoes with her white dress, carrying a bouquet that matched the shoes.

Carolyn was just as big a hit at the Powells', where Board Chair John and his wife, Dolly, kept asking her questions over a delicious roast-beef dinner. The Powells lived up one side of Mount Wellington, in the last habitable area before the slope became rugged and densely treed. Wally wanted to hear about the fire that had swept through the area in 1967, destroying homes and killing over sixty people; or about John's work as a psychiatrist designing more humane nursing homes and training staff to use the facilities to their fullest potential. Wally did get John to describe how patients felt so much happier and unthreatened because the place was more like home, not an institution, how Alzheimer societies in Florida and Ontario were planning facilities around his idea. Carolyn showed interest, but Dolly kept bringing the conversation back to graphic design and drawing, and John seemed happy just to listen to Carolyn talk, as if her spontaneous decision to offer art classes was the best thing that had happened to Jane Franklin Hall in years.

"I couldn't draw a straight line," John commented, and everyone laughed.

And it wasn't only Carolyn's drawing class that impressed people. She and Wally were entered in a ten-hole Stableford golf competition at the Kingston Beach Golf Club, at the invitation of Jane Franklin Official Fellow Bill Merton and his wife, Irene. Club regulations dictated that you had to wear spiked golf shoes. Carolyn was able to borrow a pair from Joan Radcliffe, but Wally was at the mercy of the club pro shop. Bill assured Wally they'd find something, and, after Wally tried three pairs that didn't come close, the pro-shop attendant dredged up a tattered and muddy pair that fit; they just *looked* terrible. Joan's shoes, on the other hand, looked stylish on Carolyn—surely a sign of how the afternoon was going to unfold.

The first hole was 159 metres long, and Wally drove

into long grass in a gully to the left of the green. The others drove to spots on the fringe. It was Carolyn who found Wally's ball. Embarrassed that he'd had such a lousy drive and that Carolyn had found the ball before he did, Wally channelled some of his anger into a nine-iron shot that dropped within two feet of the pin. He sank the putt for a par three. The others were impressed, all eventually settling for fours. That, however, was the extent of Wally's brilliance.

His game was a disaster from then on, and Bill wasn't much better. Irene played well, hitting the ball straight with an unorthodox swing. Carolyn played superbly, claiming it was all luck as she stayed out of trouble on the fairways and sank ridiculously long putts. The day was hot and sunny, and Wally was gasping for beer before the ten holes were half over. He thanked the Lord for the lift device—called an inclinator—that took them up the steep hill between the seventeenth green and the eighteenth tee.

"*What* did you say your specialty is?" Bill asked Wally, as they settled down to tubs of Cascade in the clubhouse.

"*Not golf,*" said Wally.

After a tasty chicken dinner with wine, they waited to hear who'd won the top prizes—one for men, one for women. The prize was supposed to be two chickens, but the club had substituted bottles of wine. The ladies' winner, with twenty-four points, based on an intricate handicapping system, was … Carolyn Webb.

And her star rose even higher two days later, when Lockridge took them sailing. He drove them to the Kettering Marina, close to the dock where you caught the ferry to

Bruny Island, where the famous Captain Cook had once landed. Scattering cormorants and seagulls, Lockridge led the way to his thirty-foot yawl, moored among many others and accessible from the dock, unlike those that had to be reached by dinghy. Lockridge did all the fussy things that a skipper had to do before setting out. He turned down Carolyn's offer to help—"Best if I do them; I shall need you on board later"—so she shot some video footage.

When Wally stepped on board, he felt the way he always felt when he got onto someone's boat—awkward. There seemed to be too many odd ropes lying around and too many curved surfaces. Like a bull in a china shop, or a bear in a boat, he brought his feet down heavily in the wrong places, just missing the table and the seat that Lockridge cautioned them not to step on. To get out of the way, Wally went below-deck—and banged his head. Perhaps he should stay in the cabin for the duration of the trip. Where was the poise he'd gained on Joyce's Jet Ski? Meanwhile, Carolyn wasn't experiencing any difficulty moving around on deck and staying out of Lockridge's way, even with the video camera glued to her eye. Lockridge enlisted her help in untying the mooring ropes, while Wally watched from the stairwell, and then Lockridge started the in-board engine he used for manoeuvring the boat out of its slip and the tight fit of the marina. Carolyn steered with the wheel that was mounted on deck beside the stairwell, while Lockridge unwrapped the main sail and handed Wally the cover to be stashed in the cabin. Lockridge ran the sail up the main mast. The wind was, according to Lockridge, "a prevailing westerly," and it filled the sail, pushing the yawl out into D'Entrecasteaux Channel toward Barnes Bay and Bruny Island.

Once they were out among the many other sailboats, Wally could hear the crackling of sails in the wind. Some of the boats were heeling at a forty-five-degree angle. Dennis said that would happen to his boat if it was under full sail, but, given the neophyte status of his crew and the fact that they were progressing nicely and were in no hurry, he would stick with a single sail. Wally thanked him for taking it easy.

Lockridge took them into quiet Barnes Bay. He had Carolyn steer while he pulled the sail down and walked carefully up to the bow to drop anchor. He then went below to make coffee.

Carolyn doffed her tracksuit jacket and took several deep breaths. "Wally, breathe in the sea air! It's marvellous!"

They enjoyed coffee on deck while at least four other boats came into the bay to anchor and take a break. This interlude was quiet and calming. Wally watched Carolyn as she asked Lockridge some nautical questions, and he thought how beautiful she looked out here on the water—beautiful and unattainable.

When it was time to lift anchor and head back, chores had to be repeated. Lockridge started the engine so they could chug to a safe distance from the other boats. He ran up the main sail again and unsnagged the red ensign, while Carolyn helped him release guide ropes. Out into the wind they went, this time heading into it—what was called *beating*.

After minutes of barely moving forward, Lockridge said, "We're not going to make much headway with only one sail. I'm going to put up the jib."

Carolyn steered while he crept forward and untied the

jib cover. He handed the cover to Wally but had some difficulty unfurling the jib properly; he said he was used to having Tyler—his usual crew—do it for him. From his precarious perch on the bow, he eventually freed the jib-boom—or whatever the diagonal crosspiece was called—from one of the side ropes. As Wally watched Lockridge grapple with the jib, he had anxious thoughts, like What do we do if Lockride falls overboard?

Wally soon wished Lockridge had never unfurled the jib. The extra sail, though working at a different angle from the main sail, not only increased their speed but also made the boat more prone to heeling. It leaned way over—thirty degrees, forty degrees, forty-five degrees, said the inclinometer (not to be confused with the *inclinator* at Kingston Golf Course)—and Wally had to scamper to the high side, not to balance things on the boat (it was too big to be affected by the weight of three people) but to prop himself up with stiffened legs rather than hold onto something for dear life with his arms. Once Lockridge returned to the helm and they were drawing closer to the marina, there had to be a lot of *coming over*—switching the boom from one side to the other—and that meant Wally had to shift every time. Carolyn found a spot in the stern, between the flagpole and some taut ropes, where she could wedge herself in and hold on tightly while she continued to film. On one of his coming-over shifts, Wally didn't make it to the opposite side fast enough, and his ass and most of his body dropped through the cabin entrance, his legs splayed and his hands grasping for anything that was nailed down. Lockridge had assured them that the yawl could not tip, and Wally had faith in his word; but, what if, under that cool and confident exterior, the college principal was terrified? He'd taught himself to sail; what if he'd missed an important lesson? Wally should've been worried about falling overboard himself, but he was more worried about Lockridge. Did a yawl *always* right itself? Wally felt tense—no, *scared*—as the boat heeled and righted and heeled and righted, while Carolyn, looking happily calm and even regal, kept filming like some confident and ambitious movie director determined to bring home a nautical classic. She stopped filming only to take over the wheel for some of their forty-five-degree-angled progress to let Lockridge work at hauling down the jib and tying it up, and then the main sail. It was Carolyn, finally, who took them into port.

Back at Jane, Lockridge invited them to his place for a drink. They regaled Virginia with an extensive report on the outing, and she laughed when Wally said that, on the return trip into the wind, he'd worried that Lockridge might have missed a lesson. Lockridge laughed at that, too. His praise, though, was heaped upon Carolyn.

"She handled the wheel like a veteran sea captain," Lockridge said.

Carolyn smiled and said, "Deep down, I was probably more terrified than Wally."

Their routine each night, even after social evenings and after the adventure at sea, was for one of them to prepare for bed while the other worked in the study, Carolyn writing in her journal or preparing a drawing lesson, Wally brushing up on his Canadian history or working on his Canadian studies treatise. One of them was often asleep when the other went to bed. Occasionally, they might cuddle—*just cuddle*—but, when they did, Carolyn would move away in a minute or two, saying she was too warm to cuddle. In their first few days at Jane, Wally had seen Carolyn as a fledgling he needed to pamper, but she had suddenly taken flight and was revelling in her new freedom. When they did something together, he wanted them to be seen as a couple, but more and more he felt they were not a couple, and they certainly weren't coupling. As she blossomed, Wally wilted. He believed he had made a mistake. He had thought they were ready to go together on an extended trip, but they weren't.

As she napped beside him after the seafaring afternoon, he lay there feeling as solitary as a convict in Richmond Prison. As a visiting fellow, he was *just visiting* in the life of Carolyn.

26.

STUDENT OUTING

On a day when neither of them had a commitment, Carolyn wanted to venture out into the countryside again. Perhaps the jaunt on Lockridge's boat had made her ready to conquer her skittishness on the road. Wally saw this as a sign that she wanted to spend some time with him, just the two of them. There were places like Freycinet and Devonport that he wanted to see, but they were a fair distance away. It might be best to go somewhere closer, with less traffic, and he could drive more slowly. He suggested they try the Tasman Peninsula, on the other side of the Derwent.

Before they left, they received a call from B.J. "I have been meaning to ask if you and Carolyn are free tonight after dinner. It's the night the RFs (the resident fellows) and the RAs (their student assistants) take their houses on an outing. We have buses booked, one for each house. Ours will be going to the beach for games and then on a cruise. We would be delighted if the two of you could come along."

Wally explained to Carolyn, and she said, "Sounds fabulous!"

"You heard that?" Wally said. "We accept."

B.J. said, "I assured my RAs that the two of you are not prudes."

"What does *that* mean?"

"Things can become rather wild and risqué. Nothing outlandish. Our bus will pick all of us up at the Davey Avenue entrance around seven forty-five."

They left for the Tasman Peninsula in mid-morning, driving through downtown Hobart and over the grand Tasman Bridge. Once they got past the airport, they were on winding roads through marvellous scenery, passing quaint towns like Sorell, Dunalley, and Eaglehawk Neck. There were so many dramatic twists and turns, Wally felt he was pulling the steering wheel left and right and left as if he was driving a dodge'em car. Often, when a car appeared on the crest of a hill and there was no centre line marked on the road, he had a split second of fear and indecision about which side he should be passing on. He hoped he was managing to hide the fear from Carolyn (and to stay on the left side of the road), and she seemed less uneasy, though she still tensed up at intersections when they were making a turn. At no time, whether they were confronting a scary bend or viewing a magnificent landscape, did she clutch his arm, and he chose to believe this was a symptom of their drifting apart.

They came to a sign for The Remarkable Cave.

"Oh, let's try that," said Carolyn.

By now, they were close to the southern shore of the Tasman Peninsula. Wally turned off the main road onto a narrow lane through scrub bushes and sandy hills. At the end of the trail, they had to get out of the car and walk down a path and down a few sets of wooden stairs. There was nothing touristy about this place, no commercialization—no hotdog stand or souvenir shop like what you find in the United States. There were permanent signs leading you to The Remarkable Cave.

They came to a wire-fenced platform. There was a gate that allowed you to go down more stairs and under the platform; instead of standing overhead and simply looking into the cave, you could walk into it. Wally did, and Carolyn followed several paces behind. They could see through the cave to the open sea beyond. Water came crashing into the cave, rolling up the sand and rocks and then receding. While Carolyn filmed, Wally ventured further in, stepping up onto a slope of sand and fantasizing that, if the tide came in quickly, he could be marooned, cut off from the main cave opening where Carolyn stood. This thought suited his current mood: would Carolyn even care if he were swept out to sea?

A rush of water poured in, and, although Carolyn backed up quickly, she still got her shoes wet. Wally scampered further up his slope, so that now Carolyn's view of him was cut off by a vertical ridge of rock. The water began to recede.

"Wally?"

He waited until the water had fully retreated before he stepped around the ridge and said, "This truly is a remarkable cave."

"I couldn't see you. Were you trying to scare me?"

"Naw."

"Come on," she said, taking off her shoes. "Let's find a place for lunch."

Dressed in jeans and sweatshirts, Wally and Carolyn joined B.J. and her thirty or so students at the meeting place. B.J. introduced her two residential assistants, Colin and Bobbi, who were more or less in charge of the evening. Wally looked around for Rebecca. He'd been polite and businesslike in their few tutoring sessions, and he hoped she would be there for this night of fun. He didn't ask about her. He resigned himself to the fact that she was not in B.J.'s house.

When the bus pulled up, the students boarded, scrambling to pair off. They saved a double seat for Wally and Carolyn, and B.J. sat beside Bobbi. Colin stood at the front and introduced Charlie, the driver. Before Charlie pulled away, Colin set the rules.

"Rule one: If the bus makes a right turn, all of you wave your arms in the air. Rule two: If the bus makes a left turn, all of you wave your *legs* in the air." Everybody groaned. "Rule three: If I give a blast of this whistle, all of you must *change places*. Now, we have not quite figured out the fourth rule. If a car overtakes us, what should we do?"

"*Moon it!*" a number of students yelled.

"No, no, we better not," said Colin. "We don't want to get Charlie into trouble."

"We'll all point at it and hex it," one young fellow said.

"And make faces and yell!" Carolyn cried out.

B.J. applauded. The students yelled, "Yes! Yes!" and that

was what they decided to do. Some complained—the idea was pretty juvenile—but it avoided total mayhem.

The bus driver shifted into first gear.

"Go, Charlie, go!" Bobbi shouted.

That started a chant, "Go, Charlie, go!"

The bus made a right turn. The chant switched to "Hooray!" as everyone waved both arms.

The bus turned left. With some kids nearly on their backs, everyone attempted to shake both legs in the air. Wally ducked to avoid Carolyn's kicks.

Colin blew the whistle. Freshers and lifers alike leaped around the bus, diving for new places. Carolyn, well into the spirit of this, leaped into the aisle and disappeared in a crowd of off-balance young bodies. The bus was on a long curve, and bodies tumbled and fell and rolled sideways. Wally bounced off a seat, a chrome pole, and nine or ten students before being thrown into the arms of a girl who was gasping for air, she was laughing so hard.

"I'm so sorry!" he said as he tried to get up. This was as bad as sailing under full sail. He tumbled into the aisle and a large young man helped him up.

A car passed. On a cue from Colin, everyone stood, leaned over to the windows and yelled. A girl beside Wally used her fingers and thumbs to distort her face as she let out a sound like a loud fart. She collapsed into a seat with a roar of laughter. There was another left turn, and the busload erupted into a show of legs. Colin blew the whistle, and a girl sat on Wally before he could get up, and a guy hurtled past Wally's head. Bodies bounced all over. Charlie kept his composure and held the bus on the road. Just as Colin blew the whistle again, a car overtook them, and kids yelled and threw themselves about, all to the right side of the bus. They waved and grimaced and yelled, and one girl in a heap of bodies did manage to hang a moon.

After more turns and whistles, Colin seemed to sense that the antics should be tempered. Wally didn't know where Carolyn was, but he now sat beside an attractive lifer named Annabel. He smiled at her through his puffing. She tossed her long auburn hair around, keeping time to some rhythmic beat in her head.

As Charlie pulled into the beach at Kingston, Colin and Bobbi explained that they'd break into groups of six and make something creative in the sand. Dr. Baxter and Ms Webb would be the judges, and there were chocolate bars for the winners.

The groups quickly formed and got busy on the beach. Annabel's group decided to build a giant breast, the three boys in the group enjoying the molding. They soon added a second breast, and Annabel sculpted the nipples. Someone added a head and shoulders, and another started on the hips.

Another group created a huge face with an over-sized nose. A third group made a man with a real head—that of a live student with his body buried. The fourth fashioned a shark with a massive penis and testicles. The fifth constructed an underwater scene that featured a variety of fish and an octopus with one its tentacles wound around the breast of a mermaid.

"How do you want to judge these?" Carolyn asked Wally.

"I'll go with whatever you say. You are the artist."

"Come on, go with your gut."

With twilight fading fast, the students' handiwork was becoming hard to see.

"I like the underwater scene," he said. "It's the most ambitious and the most whimsical."

Carolyn smiled. "I like the fish, too. Want to announce it?"

Wally announced the winning team and was greeted by cheers and boos, the loudest boo coming from Annabel, who then laughed and stomped all over her sculpted woman.

The next competition was an egg toss, the players wearing academic gowns, won by Annabel and a skinny chap named William.

Colin led everybody back to the bus for the trip to Franklin Wharf.

"No more bouncing about," Colin told everyone. "We have enough bruises. Time for a chant."

Wally expected something like the old bus-trip song, "Ninety-Nine Bottles of Beer on the Wall." When most of the kids had settled into seats, Charlie moved the bus out of the parking area, and Colin yelled, "Monday is a happy day!"

Students, B.J., Carolyn, and Wally responded in unison: "Monday is a *happy* day!"

Colin: "Tuesday is a whore day!"

Everyone: "Tuesday is a *whore* day!"

Colin, in a louder, menacing voice: "*Tuesday is a whore day!*"

Everyone, in the same tone: "*Tuesday is a whore day!*"

Colin took the chanting back to Monday, through

the two versions of Tuesday, and on to whatever anyone wanted to suggest for Wednesday.

A young bloke at the back cried, "Wednesday is a working day!"

"Wednesday is a *working* day!"

Back to Monday, the two versions of Tuesday, on to Wednesday and an impromptu suggestion for Thursday: "Thursday is a smoking day!"

"Thursday is a *smoking* day!"

Back again over the week and at last and inevitably to what everybody expected Friday to be: "Friday is a fucking day!"

"*Friday is a fucking day!*"

This was louder than ever, and Wally watched Annabel's sweet mouth cry out the word that had once been taboo and was now the most popular word in the English language; Annabel, with eyes sparkling, watched his mouth do the same.

It was an oddly subdued lot that climbed aboard the cramped little cruise vessel. Nearly everyone stood out on deck as the boat moved upriver, under the colourfully lighted Tasman Bridge. Wally thought about the drunken sea captain who had knocked down the original bridge. There was no booze in evidence on this jaunt. B.J., Carolyn, and Wally watched as the students formed a queue inside for muffins, potato crisps, biscuits, apple juice, hot chocolate. Outside, they lined up for sausage rolls heated on a barbecue.

"May I get something for the three of you?" Bobbi asked.

"We'll share a plate of whatever you want to round up for us," said B.J.

Annabel came out eating a muffin. "Everything's gone so quiet. You'd think we'd all been drugged."

"You haven't, I hope," said Carolyn.

Annabel laughed and held her muffin up to Carolyn's mouth. Carolyn declined but Wally leaned forward and took a bite.

"You two are awfully good sports," Annabel said. "Ms Webb, I hear your art class is super."

"Please call me Carolyn. Thanks for saying so, Annabel. I'm looking for models. Are you interested?"

"Are you *serious?*"

"Very much so."

When the boat docked, an hour and a quarter after it had set out, B.J. offered Wally and Carolyn a ride to Jane Franklin Hall. The bus wasn't rented for the return trip, and most of the students were walking back.

"It's a beautiful night," said Wally. "Would you like to walk?" He looked at Carolyn, and he thought she must see something meaningful in his face.

"Yes, let's," said Carolyn. "But thank you for asking, B.J."

"And thank you for including us tonight," said Wally.

"The students loved having you. Good night, then."

The trek through the empty downtown streets was mostly uphill. A large group of students led the way, while Wally and Carolyn brought up the rear, about a block behind. Between them and the leading pack, a lone girl walked. She was carrying a backpack. No one in the lead group dropped back to walk with her, and she didn't try to catch up.

"What do you think?" said Carolyn. "Is she being rejected?"

"She could be showing an independent spirit."

"You mean she might be the loner who's going to make it because she didn't go along with the crowd."

"Could be."

"I still feel sorry for her. Do you think it would embarrass her if we catch up with her?"

"I wouldn't think so."

"Should we, then?"

"Let's let her be." He stopped walking and looked at Carolyn. "Let's concentrate on you and me."

They resumed walking, and Wally felt Carolyn slip her hand into his.

They agreed the night had been fun; it was so good to be treated like kids by the kids themselves. When they reached the underlodge, Carolyn looked weary, and Wally felt that way too, so, though he'd felt a new closeness as they walked, he was not surprised when they fell into their usual routine: Carolyn getting ready for bed while he puttered, zapping a bug or two with Raid, adjusting windows, checking the tennis court (dark tonight), making sure his car was locked, writing himself a note to phone a Canadian studies professor at the Uni in the morning. In his pyjamas, he brushed and flossed his teeth. Carolyn had sprayed the bathroom and toilet stall with a lovely lavender scent.

A lamp was on in the bedroom. Carolyn lay there on

her back—not her usual sleeping position—with her eyes closed and the covers pulled up and tucked under her chin.

"Chilly, are you?" he said, keeping his voice low in case she was asleep.

"No," she said, opening her eyes.

She tossed the covers off—way off—and there she was, gloriously naked.

For a second, he didn't understand. He hadn't seen her this way for what seemed like an eternity. In fact, he knew he'd *never* seen her *this* way, with her arms held out to him. He was so relieved, so grateful, he wanted to fall on his knees and express his thanks, if indeed this wasn't a mirage. And he did get on his knees, but only after he'd torn off his pyjamas like some kind of crazed Clark Kent, and he knelt not on the floor but on the bed, and, because she was offering herself so brazenly, he bent his mouth to her and was enraptured by the taste of her.

27.

PILLOW TALK

G ood morning."
    "Good *morning!*"
"It looks like it's going to be another fine day in Hobart."
"Oh, I hope so."
"How do you feel?"
"Excellent!"
"That's good."
"What time did we go to bed last night?"
"It was after midnight."
"Friday, then. So they were right."
"Who?"
"The students on the bus."
"About what?"
"Friday *is* a fucking day."
"And it's still Friday."
"Did you think I'd never be in the mood again?"
"I … I wasn't sure…"

"Last night was lovely, Wally."

"It was, indeed."

"Oh, Wally, I'm sorry I've been so ... I don't know ... in a funk or something. I thought a lot about what you said ... you know, about getting on with the sequel.... I kind of liked that."

"Good."

"But ... I guess I thought I still needed time ... and I thought I needed to do things ... and I went off on this drawing-class caper. I have to say it's been a distraction—but a *good* distraction, don't you think?"

"I ... um ... I do."

"You're not so sure. I know, it was distracting me from *you*, as much as anything. And you've been so *patient*."

"Maybe it looked that way. I was starting to think maybe we weren't suited..."

"Aww..."

"And I think I was getting jealous or something, which didn't help..."

"You know what I think turned me around?"

"Having fun with all those kids last night?"

"And seeing what a good sport you were ... but what I think affected me too was that girl. You know, the one we followed when we walked home. I saw myself; not myself when I was her age, myself now. Being a loner. Being this widow who's been taken out of her world and dropped into foreign territory. And she's feeling sorry for herself."

"Surely you've got past that; you've been the life of the party everywhere we've gone."

"Didn't it seem like I was trying too hard? The person

who pretends to be an extrovert to hide the fact that she's scared stiff?"

"You sure put on a convincing act."

"Maybe so. But last night I had this great revelation when you stopped me in my tracks and said we should worry about *us*. I'm *not* alone. How about that? My god, I'm on the other side of the world with a guy I like, a guy who says he loves me. Enough to put up with my moods. So I have to tell myself, stop wallowing already!"

"Sounds good to me."

"You know what?"

"What?"

"Last night, when I saw the way you and Annabel were looking at each other, I felt really jealous."

"Really?"

"Yes, really."

"Carolyn, she's a student and I'm a prof. Back home, I'm surrounded by girls exactly like her all the time."

"Doesn't make you immune, though, does it?"

"I know the difference between…"

"It's all right. We don't have to worry about that, because we're going to drive each other insane with pleasure."

"I can't argue with that."

"And Wally, the drawing class, I'm so grateful to you for supporting me."

"Speaking of that, are you really going to get Annabel to model for you?"

"Sorry, you can't sit in on that class. No, I don't think she's the type. Maybe nobody is. I shouldn't have mentioned it to her. You have to be careful when…"

"Let's not think of that right now."

"No."

"We should concentrate on having fun."

"Yes. We don't need anybody's permission to have fun."

"Right now!"

"Oh. Right now, I'd really like to have a shower."

"Why don't we shower together?"

"That would be a first for me."

"You've never showered with someone?"

"Nope."

"Then we have to."

"Can two of us get under that spray?"

"Rats, we might have to get close."

"Let's go!"

"Okay, but first, a confession."

"Oh, no. What?"

"I've never showered with anybody either."

28.

CAROLYN'S JOURNAL IV

Thursday, February 27, 1997
We did a bit of sightseeing today, drove over to the secluded Seven Mile Beach. No wonder it was secluded; there was a cold wind. Came back to the underlodge to write a few postcards, and then we went downtown to post them.

Friday, February 28, 1997
I had another class today. The boys were a little less serious, likely because it's Friday. Des showed up with a Cascade in his bag, and I had to get strict. I would not let him drink it. He grumbled, went out and came back with a peculiar grin on his face.

The rest of them worked. Braden has been copying a cut-away drawing of a human heart. He has doubts that it's accurate.

I don't know where Wally went. I didn't ask him. I don't think he tutored Rebecca today. So he was moody.

Tonight was the night of the student pub crawl. Nine buses came to pick the students up. We weren't invited.

Saturday, March 1, 1997
The Radcliffes took us on what they called "a convict tour." They were so nice to each other, the way Stephen and I used to be, not afraid to show affection in public. I liked the model of old Hobart they showed us. And the prison in Richmond.

Stan really gave us a load of information. I thought there might be a test at the end, but no, he let us off the hook.

Dinner party at the Lockridges'. Virginia got me talking about the art class. I guess I got so into it, I could hardly shut up.

Sunday, March 2, 1997
Here we are, living in the midst of nearly 200 young people, and we almost never hear them. When I go out, I usually always see some, maybe two or three, sometimes nine or ten. Walking purposefully. Kibitzing. Playing tennis on roller blades. Carrying a fresher off for a dunking. Sitting out on a fire escape having a smoke. Or heading to the building across from us for a tutoring session. Most of them say g'day or hi.

This is the last day of their orientation week. Tonight the freshers will officially become members of the Jane Franklin community. It's Commencement night.

Talked to lots of people tonight but too tired to write about it.

Monday, March 3, 1997
We took a ferry to Bruny Island to see where Captain Cook landed.

Wally and I are getting along okay. He seems more relaxed, somehow. I think he has a crush on Rebecca. We actually had a few laughs waiting for the ferry to go back. We had to call the Powells to tell them we'd be late for dinner.

The Powells were lovely hosts. He likes the idea of me giving kids art lessons. Nice to have encouragement from the chair of the board. I think Wally is impressed.

Tuesday, March 4, 1997
Buckets of rain today.

I've sort of got away from writing. I feel I have to do the assignments I give the guys. So I'm drawing. It's kind of liberating. I haven't done any serious drawing for a long while. I don't like distracting Wally, so I'm drawing in the porch.

Did a good one of the goats, Jane and George.

Wally thinks I should frame it and give it to the Lockridges.

Wednesday, March 5, 1997
Great class today!

Des has come up with a comic book hero. Sooper

Cooper! Mild-mannered Reg Cooper strips down to his jockey shorts, or are those swimming trunks? Anyway, he's already knocked off pages of adventures.

The others are more serious. David did a gorgeous drawing of a girl he fancies. (Listen to me, already talking like an Aussie!)

They are all doing well. I just hope the drawing isn't taking them away from their studies. It's meant to be a pleasant break from their usual routine.

Wally is off tutoring.

Thursday, March 6, 1997

Golfing with the Mertons today.

Wally started off so well, but it didn't last.

My goodness, I haven't golfed in so long, and yet I had some decent shots.

All those women out there, so serious. It was almost embarrassing. <u>I beat them all!</u>

I thought Wally might be a little pissed off with me. But, I don't know, he seemed genuinely proud of me.

I bet Stephen was beaming, looking down on me from wherever he is. He always thought I had a classic swing. I just needed to practise, he said.

Friday, March 7, 1997

Some of them are painting.

Des did a beautiful colour portrait of … Sooper Cooper!

They're asking when they can do their first live model.

Saturday, March 8, 1997
Sailing today!

Dr. Lockridge let me take the wheel. I felt like Captain Cook.

It was gorgeous out there. When I wasn't helping, I was shooting video. I never knew sailing could be so much fun. But you have to keep your wits about you. You see people sailing and think they're just lying in the sun. It's work!

I couldn't thank Dr. Lockridge enough. I mean Dennis. He wants me to call him Dennis. I blushed when he told his wife how much help I was.

I'd go sailing again tomorrow if I could.

Sunday, March 9, 1997
Special Sunday class.

The guys are so into this that they wanted to give up their Sunday afternoon. I thought we could be bold and strut our stuff outside. (Mostly because Wally had decided to tutor Rebecca in the study.)

We set up the easels on the hill outside the Frances Parsons Building. We worked on drawings of our surroundings.

Naturally, we attracted a lot of attention. Girls stopped by, some of them wanting to model. They balked when Des said we could only draw them if they were nude. Some kids tried to distract us, but the guys were pretty mature. I think they feel sort of privileged.

Monday, March 10, 1997

B.J. invited us to a party she was hosting for her "house." Wally and I were happy to accept. An outing with the kids sounded great.

But first we went sightseeing over on the Tasman Peninsula. We found this intriguing place called The Remarkable Cave. The tide came crashing into the cave when you least expected it. For a minute I lost sight of Wally and thought he might've been washed away. I soon saw he was just fooling around. On the way back, I had some dark thoughts: I'd felt curiously free when he disappeared for those few moments ... I'm terrible.

At high table, a lifer named Melanie sat beside me and asked about the art class. Seems like everybody knows about it.

We had to change quickly to get out to the bus.

What followed was a crazy series of activities. I can't begin to list all the stuff we did. The bus, the beach, the bus again, the cruise. It was insane!

No more insane than the sudden feeling I had on the way home. I saw how much of an idiot I'd been. As far as Wally is concerned, I mean. It wasn't just the girl walking all alone ahead of us. It was something more. A jolt of something.

It was like I'd just discovered him.

29.

NEITHER YOUR PLACE NOR MINE

One Sunday morning, while working in the study, Wally looked up and saw the largest ship he'd ever seen entering the Hobart harbour.

This must be the USS *Kitty Hawk*, the most famous aircraft carrier in the American fleet; the local newspaper had said, in a special section devoted to it, that it was due to arrive that day before noon. According to the paper, the *Kitty Hawk* carried seventy-five airplanes, twenty-four missiles, and 5500 people—5300 men and 200 women. It had been at sea for six months, and the Tasmanian premier had stated the obvious in his welcoming message: "The crew is no doubt looking forward to some rest and relaxation." The ship would be in port for five days, loading up with everything they'd need for another six months. With all the sailors visiting on shore, Wally wanted to cry to the people of Hobart, "Lock up your daughters!"

It was Athletic Day, when Jane competed with other

university colleges at a track-and-field facility called the Domain, on the other side of town. When Wally and Carolyn drove B.J. there in early afternoon, American sailors, in uniform, were everywhere downtown, walking in pairs, standing on corners, stepping into cabs.

"They seem to have spread out so fast," said Wally. "I'm surprised to see them so far from the ship so soon."

"They're hungry for local colour," B.J. said, with a straight face.

"Will they descend on Jane?" Carolyn asked.

"Not likely. Judging from previous visits by American naval vessels, they are under strict orders to behave. The difficulty for us will be keeping our girls away from the ship."

They dropped B.J. off and said they would pick her up later. Wally would've gone to the track meet if he hadn't had something else on his mind. In the few days since their outing with B.J.'s house, life with Carolyn had been stimulating. It was, in fact, everything Wally could've wished it to be. It seemed time for him to *do* something.

They drove north on Highway 1, a thoroughfare that was wide and relatively straight as Tasmanian roads went, meaning Carolyn had fewer jitters; or perhaps she was getting used to the "wrong" side of the road. Or perhaps she was preoccupied with wondering what Wally was being so mysterious about.

They stopped at the Huntington Tavern in Kempton. It was just the kind of cheerful-looking place Wally had hoped he'd find. Though they were expected back at Jane for dinner, they ordered from the specials on a blackboard—chicken pie with chips and salad. Wally picked up two Cascades from the squire at the bar. There were other people in the dining room—a smartly dressed woman who was apparently the squire's wife having lunch with her mother, two other groups of locals, and a fellow who looked like an engineer travelling on an expense account. The place had a homey feel about it, and what added to this—and added to Wally's mood—was the music being played: Sinatra, Rosemary Clooney, Tony Bennett.

"You're wondering why I called this meeting," Wally said. He was nervous.

"And why we came out here—though I have to say, I *love* the place."

"I just thought … because I have something important to say, it was best to get away from the underlodge and the college and the city."

"Well, you've got me interested, that's for sure."

"This trip may have been a bit—I don't know—premature or something. I mean, because it threw us together maybe too suddenly. But there's no doubt in *my* mind that you and I should be together. I don't want to rush you by proposing marriage. I'd like to. I *will*, if you want me to. It completely depends on how *you* feel. The thing is, this trip will be over soon, and we'll be going back home … and I don't want to go back to two separate places."

Carolyn smiled, seemed on the verge of tears, and held up her glass. "I'll drink to *that!*"

"You agree, then…"

"I don't want to go back to *my* place and I don't want to go back to *your* place; and I don't want you to go back to my place or *your* place."

"We'll get a new place together."

"This may sound crazy, but, when we get off the plane in Winnipeg, I want to go … some place different…"

"We'll go to a hotel! Until we find a place…"

"Yes!"

They both laughed, loud enough to make others turn to look at them. Wally laughed mostly with relief; he thought everything was moving too fast, they weren't thinking anything through, but then he did hate his apartment and…

"Wally." Carolyn placed her hand on his. "There's something else. I … I want to have a baby with you. I wanted to have one before I met you, and the reason I didn't wasn't *me*. Now I'm nearly forty. If you agree, Wally, I want to go off the Pill. *Today.*"

Wally tried his best to hide his shock. He didn't want to spoil the mood; but did he really want another child? He smiled; he laughed; he even leaned over and kissed Carolyn right there in the tavern.

They picked up B.J. and delivered her to her flat, and, when they returned to the underlodge, they made celebratory love. They were late for dinner, but by then they had ravenous appetites for the delicious lasagna. They sat with Regina Dales and several female students—Rebecca and Amy and Marie were among them. The topic of lively conversation was the arrival of the *Kitty Hawk.*

"I think it's brilliant that there are bars offering free drinks to women accompanied by sailors," Marie said.

"*I'd* like to see the inside of the ship," said Amy. "Where's the harm in getting to meet one or two sailors and asking them for a tour?"

"Some advice," said Regina, staring into Amy's eyes

through her thick glasses. "If and when you go downtown for the express purpose of meeting sailors, make sure that you take condoms with you, and demand to see medical certificates before you become too involved with anyone. That goes for all of you."

Rebecca glanced at Wally as she said, "I shan't be meeting sailors, but if a lot of you are going downtown, surely there is safety in numbers."

"Doesn't the navy insist they be on their best behaviour?" said Carolyn. "They can't risk an international incident."

"Best to be safe," said Regina, as if that was the last word, and she stood up to leave.

"I must go, too," Rebecca said, again looking at Wally. "You said your test is going to cover…?"

"My test! Of course, I'm giving you a test tomorrow. Up to 1900. Concentrate on Macdonald."

"Bit of a drinker, wasn't he?" Rebecca winked and started off.

As the others dispersed, Carolyn had a tête-à-tête with Amy. Wally waited for her, and, when she was through, he said, "Dare I ask what that was about?"

"I admire her spirit," said Carolyn. "I think she's the right young woman to model."

Wally wasn't keen on having any of the students posing naked in the underlodge, but he didn't say so.

"She loves the idea," Carolyn said, slipping her arm under Wally's. "I think it might take her mind off the sailors."

30.

FROM HERE TO FRIENDLY
BEACHES

High table continued to be a highlight twice a week—
meeting new honorary fellows and official fellows
and student reps—even a fire drill one night that forced
everyone to evacuate the dining hall. Sometimes, in the
senior common room prior to dinner, the libation provided was port or sherry instead of wine, and both went
down well despite normally being after-dinner drinks.
Chatting with the others was always pleasant, but no one
ever wanted to prolong the evening; the high-table entourage might assemble back in the common room after dinner for another drink and a chocolate mint, but everyone
soon drifted off.

One morning, while Carolyn sat in the quadrangle
sketching, Wally walked the route the students usually
took to the University's main campus. He was meeting a
Dr. Marcus Bainbridge there and conducting a seminar

on Canada—more precisely, a comparison of Canada's ten provincial governments with Australia's seven state governments. The way Wally went was mostly down the Lynton Avenue hill that rivalled anything in San Francisco for steep grade. En route, he took note of the houses, mostly quaint, some of which had been converted into professional offices. He picked up a campus map, and, after some confusion, he found Bainbridge's office and was a few minutes ahead of schedule. Bainbridge was younger than Wally expected, perhaps in his thirties, with curly brown hair, and wearing baggy trousers and a ratty grey cardigan. Bainbridge asked for a few minutes to finish something on his computer, and Wally was grateful for time to compose himself and look around. He saw many signs—posters, books—of Bainbridge's leftist sentiments.

The seminar went well. There were eleven students who seemed to know a lot about Canada and, likely finding Wally's material too basic, asked some detailed questions that made Bainbridge beam with pride. Wally was able to answer fully, even adding colourful details, like Prime Minister Mackenzie King's consultation of supernatural sources, and the infamous October Crisis of 1970, when a Quebec cabinet minister was murdered and dumped into a car trunk by home-grown terrorists.

And then there were the tutoring sessions with Rebecca. She was beautiful and intelligent and apparently fascinated with whatever Wally could tell her. At first, she seemed assured, vital, completely at home in her young body. But lately, Wally sensed a little sadness, most noticeable in her large blue eyes.

"When is it you're leaving?" she said after one of the sessions.

"At the term break," he said. "At Easter."

"I shall miss this," she said, and, as she turned away, her hand grazed his arm.

Surely she wasn't upset about his coming departure. He believed there must be a major reason for heartache—perhaps an unrequited love, a problem in her family. The next time they met, he said things to make her laugh, and he was glad when she did. He wanted to comfort her, and he cautioned himself to comfort her with words and words only—not just jokey comments but lessons that were packed with solid information, as well as compliments on her fine marks and her wise questions and thoughtful answers. *Words*. And then what did he go and do at the end of the class? Touch her bare forearm with a gentle, comforting hand.

Carolyn's classes were progressing; she'd added a seventh young man, named Bron, and Des was proving to be a serious student; he'd learned to do a brilliant likeness of his left hand. As the week of the *Kitty Hawk*'s visit wound down, Wally had no idea if Amy had modelled yet, and he didn't want to know.

They made time to see the countryside as often as they could. The morning they drove to Gordon Dam was the first time they'd gone due west. The highway was almost deserted, so, despite the usual curves and the absence of a centre line, there was less cause for panic. They passed hops fields, the flower-bedecked yards of Westerway, thick forests, and tree-shaded meadows reminiscent of New

England. At the dam on Gordon Lake, there were look-outs set up for spectacular views, one looking down on the dam from a great height. The lake behind the dam was vast, with miles of untouched, uninhabited shoreline and no beach. It led Carolyn to voice one of life's mysteries: how do they dam up the water while they're building the dam?

On the way back, they stopped at a small pub in a tiny town oddly named National Park. The one customer, a man sitting up at the bar in a shirt that had had its sleeves torn off, and the shapeless barmaid both stared at the new arrivals as if this were the Ozarks and they were hillbillies resenting intruders from the city. They brought to Wally's mind the rude image of Tasmanians given to him more than once by Australian mainlanders: "Look closely and you'll see the scar on their shoulder where they've had the second head removed."

Midweek in *Kitty Hawk* week, they ventured on their longest jaunt so far. It was going to be another fine day, despite the shower that greeted them as they stepped out of the underlodge door. They headed north up the highway that went to Launceston, the comparatively straight Number 1. Once they left the main road and headed west, the driving became trickier. They wanted to find a coffee place, but they had to continue non-stop through a narrow, winding stretch called Elephant Pass. With Carolyn quaking and Wally antsy for a break, they came upon a huge drawing of a coffee cup mounted on a sign that read *200m on the right*. A quaint restaurant advertising pancakes materialized, and they turned off the crazy road.

The place was full. When some people left, more arrived. Wally and Carolyn weren't the only tourists who needed a break from Elephant Pass. But many had not yet been waited on. Only one server—a woman—seemed to be doing all the work, and, scowling, she went out back and brought in a man—possibly her husband—and gave him hell for being somewhere else. He waited on Wally and Carolyn, eventually serving them pancakes that were folded over fat and tasty blueberries like crêpes, with whipped cream and syrup. The man looked sheepish, and, when Wally paid him and gave him a tip, the man said, "Normally we'd put this in a staff pool, but today it will go to a fund for maitre d's with Alzheimer's."

They reached the eastern coast at Chain of Lagoons and drove south along a scenic road to Bicheno. The penguin watch was available only at night, so they walked down to the water where instead of sand they found slabs of rock. The formations reminded Wally of those at Peggy's Cove in Nova Scotia, and, ironically, they were not far from a part of Bicheno called Peggy's Point.

They continued on to a narrow road marked C302 and made the twenty-seven-kilometre jaunt to Freycinet National Park, bypassing a gravel road into the Friendly Beaches. Carolyn paid the eight dollars that allowed them to take the car into the park. The winding gravel road climbed and descended for several kilometres, taking them to Cape Tourville: a lighthouse and a cliff with a panoramic view of the Tasman Sea. Down the road was another viewpoint overlooking Sleepy Bay, and, on the way, they spotted a wild wallaby that Carolyn photographed before it hopped into the bush. At Sleepy Bay, there was a sign that pointed down to the beach and said it would take fifteen minutes to go there and back. They parked the car and followed the trail—as much vertical as horizontal—climbing down steps formed by tree roots and rocks. They emerged from bushes onto a sheltered wedge of beach and a mound of rock that invited further climbing. A young couple lay together on the sand.

"Oh, that's what *I* want to do," said Carolyn. "Find a secluded beach and ... and relax."

Several hikers arrived in the next few minutes, some with giant backpacks.

"Let's go and check out the Friendly Beaches," Carolyn said.

They returned to the car. Wally drove back to the gravel road and took that to a kilometres-long stretch of beautiful secluded sand with blue waves rolling in.

"Did you ever see *From Here to Eternity?*" said Carolyn.

"Yes, more than once."

"It's one of my favourites. I want us to be Deborah Kerr and Burt Lancaster in the famous beach scene. Come on!"

"It'll be too cold, won't it? And we don't have bathing suits."

Carolyn was already out of the car. The sun was sinking behind them, and some of the beach was already in shadow, but the incoming waves sparkled in the sunlight. It looked inviting, and there was no one anywhere to be seen.

Carolyn was running to the water, stripping off her clothes as she ran, leaving them where they fell on the sand. She stopped to kick off her sandals and pull off her jeans and bikini briefs. She waved to him to *come on!* and she ran into the water and dove into an incoming wave.

Wally watched from the car, transfixed. Who *was* this woman? She'd turned into a wanton free spirit. Would he ever understand her? Did it *matter* if he *never* understood her?

He stepped out of the car. Again he looked up and down the vast beach for signs of other people. She called to him, but he couldn't tell what she said. There was nothing else he could do but join her.

He walked to where she had dropped her jacket, and he put his there, spreading the two out as a makeshift blanket.

She called again and waved at him as she cavorted in the waves that were rolling in, lifting her, dropping her.

He felt chilled, but, as he watched her, he grew oddly, wonderfully, warmer with each item of clothing he took off. He ran into the water, gasping at the feel of it, finding it not as cold as he expected. First a wave, and then the undertow, took away his balance and he tumbled, face down, into the salty sea. He fought the tide to get up, coughed out water, and, discovering his buoyancy, he launched himself toward her.

"Isn't it marvellous!" she cried.

She eluded him, half-stroking, half-leaping back toward the shore.

Okay, so he was going to be the Lancaster character, and she the captain's wife. She wore a bathing suit in the film. Well, it was a fifties movie, and this was the nineties, and, if Carolyn was going to play the scene naked, who was Wally to complain?

She seemed to have little trouble projecting herself out of the water. She knelt on the hard flat sand that waves kept flooding before they receded. He staggered through the undertow and dropped to his knees beside her.

"The scene's in two parts," she said. "If you remember, he's lying here as the waves come in on them. She bends over him and kisses him, surprising him, and she gets up and runs to the dry sand—to the blanket—and he comes after her."

"I think I remember," he said, and he lay back on the hard sand, just as a wave came in and broke over his legs.

She knelt beside him, and, instead of bending to kiss him, she lowered a breast to his mouth as if it was ripe fruit. This isn't in the script, he might've said if he wasn't enjoying another of her surprises. A wave crashed over them. She laughed her melodious laugh—how fabulous it was to hear it again!—and she withdrew from him, stood up and ran to the spread-out jackets and lay back on them.

Feeling energized, as if he'd sucked a magic potion from her, he got up and rushed to her, dropping to his knees beside her as Lancaster had in the movie, gazing down at her for a second, seeing the happy look on her face, and he bent to kiss her, trying to tell her through his lips how much he appreciated her.

"I never knew it could be like this," she said, her voice soft, urgent. "Nobody ever kissed me the way you do."

"Really?" he said.

Carolyn laughed. "I was quoting Deborah Kerr."

Wally laughed too, but, instead of saying anything, he kissed his way down her body, stopping here, here, here, and at last tasting the salt mingled with her own warm wetness, there on the beach at twilight, feeling her hand on his head, her smooth thighs cool against his ears, venturing far beyond the film, moving up now, oblivious of the trees and hills and open space around them and ignoring the sand, concentrating only on satisfying the woman beneath him, finding their mutual rhythm, and knowing there was nothing in the world better than *this*.

They cleaned up as best they could but still felt like vagabonds risking being denied entry into the Swan Inn, a restaurant in Swansea. They did get in—the staff had no doubt seen worse—but they made a point of sitting in a corner where most people wouldn't notice the smudges, wet patches, and wrinkles. They devoured meals of roast lamb, carrots, potatoes, stir-fried veggies, ice cream with chocolate sauce, and coffee. The drive back to Hobart in the dark was aided by red reflectors on posts on the left and white reflectors on posts on the right, and white lines on the shoulders. Occasionally, there were passing lanes (Keep Left Unless Overtaking). Yet there were still enough curves, narrow sections of road, and too-fast vehicles meeting them at treacherous places to make this a white-knuckle trip. Luckily, though, only one of them had white knuckles, and that was Wally, who tried to be even more careful than usual because his head was full of their Friendly Beaches interlude. Carolyn was exhausted and, for the first time in their travels, she fell fast asleep in the car.

When they arrived home at the underlodge, there was a message on their answering machine: "Just thought you'd like to know that your son is now a criminal."

The voice was unmistakably Marjorie's.

31.

CAROLYN'S JOURNAL V

Wednesday, March 12, 1997
We welcomed another student—a tall, well-built guy named Bron. He looked a little stunned by the serious way the others got down to business. Once he got going, though, he did a brilliant likeness of his left hand.

I missed a couple of days of writing. Somehow, it doesn't seem necessary anymore. I feel different all over, including in my head.

Sunday, March 16, 1997
I guess I'm only going to write in this thing when the spirit moves me, and tonight it did. I'm sort of excited about Amy wanting to pose. Probably this coming Wednesday. She's got the flair for it, to say nothing of that body. The

guys deserve a treat. (Which of course is not the right attitude for an art instructor.)

Wednesday, March 19, 1997
God, I'm still shaking. What a horrible fiasco!

It started out fine. The day Amy was going to model. It was going to be a big surprise for the class.

I met with her in her dorm room. I didn't want her to chicken out. I thought a little chat would help prepare her.

She couldn't wait to tell me about a party she'd been to. An older woman named Roxanne, a friend of Amy's, invited her. Apparently Roxanne had an "impossible" boyfriend. Out drinking with his buddies all the time. Roxanne welcomed the Kitty Hawk sailors, partied with a different one every night.

More girls than guys at the party. Amy played a game that's popular in the pubs. She had to take a frozen Mars bar and move it up a sailor's leg. Up to the top of his leg. Inside his trousers, at the front! Move it over his abdomen to the top of his other leg. And down the leg and out. Without damaging the Mars bar!

And Amy did it. She did it again with another sailor!

She made me laugh. Took my mind off Marjorie. Fuckin' woman spoiled our day at Friendly Beaches. No! She didn't. I won't let her.

I feel bad for Wally. But he's got to deal with it.

On this afternoon, though, he was giving a guest lecture to the local Canadian Studies Association at the Uni.

So there I was in Amy's room. I think I was more nervous about the class than she was.

Said she'd posed before. For a photographer in Melbourne.

I asked her how she felt about posing for the likes of Bron and Des and Braden. She said they were young. They'd be more nervous than she was.

I showed Amy the poses I wanted. Typical classic poses. Sitting, her back to the class, in a half-turn from the waist. Semi-reclining. Face mostly turned, never looking directly at the artist. Legs always together. Natural poses to show muscles in neck, shoulders, arms, legs, ass, back. No intention of trying to hide her big breasts. Just let them follow the natural flow of the body.

She said she understood. She looked forward to it.

Did she have a robe? Yes, she had a nice purple bathrobe. I told her to bring it to put on when she needed a break. She packed it in her backpack.

We left her room at twenty to three. The class was scheduled for three. We thought we'd avoid the quadrangle, take the back way. Through the parking lot, behind the dining hall, past the front of the lodge.

I heard voices. Laughter. Male laughter.

At the corner of the lodge, we stopped. Oh my God. The hill down to the underlodge was covered with young men. Grouped around the underlodge door. Along the fence where we usually saw the goats. Down to the newest building, over to the nearest residence. Past that, almost to the administrative office. A crowd of young men! Chatting, laughing, a few smoking, some kibitzing with each other.

They were all sailors. They were in civvies, didn't have to wear uniforms after the first day, but you could tell by their haircuts. Still more were arriving!

I felt scared. My heart pounded.

"You told them at the party!" I said to Amy. "You told them you were going to model!"

She had been smiling, but now she was crying. "I told one! Maybe two! No more, honestly!"

One of the sailors recognized Amy. "Here she is!" he shouted.

The others broke into a chant: "Ay-mee! Ay-mee! Ay-mee!"

I told Amy to run for it.

I stood there, sweating like a pig. I'd spoken to groups before, but nothing like this.

I spoke as loudly as I could. My voice shook. I said I was sorry but there had been a terrible mistake.

They booed. They grumbled. I think one or two went looking for Amy.

I worried about Wally's reputation. Jane Franklin's reputation.

I spoke again, in my strongest voice, the one I use for presentations to clients. I told them this was a college and we needed to get it back to normal.

Some of them swore.

Some of them laughed.

A few moved close to me and suggested I could model.

A few more suggested I could buy them all a beer.

Maybe they saw the fear in my face. Maybe some felt sorry for me.

They started to leave.

I thought, they truly don't want an international incident.

Tears came into my eyes when one said he was sorry if

they'd scared me. Would I like to go for coffee? I told him I'd love to but I couldn't.

Some wandered across the quadrangle. Some stopped to chat up a few girls. Some stragglers were still there when Andrew and Des arrived for the class.

"What's with all the blokes?" said Andrew.

"Sailors, aren't they?" said Des.

"Bit of a tour of the campus," I said. They must've noticed how badly I was shaking.

I have no idea where Amy went.

Friday, March 21, 1997

We survived the naval invasion. Amy came to apologize and promise she wouldn't brag about it. She said she wouldn't go looking for any more sailors, but I wouldn't bet on it.

I am feeling odd. Different. I suddenly have this idea of how cool it'd be to get pregnant in Australia. It's ridiculous, but now it's all I can think about.

Well, it can't be. Lots to do in the class.

Wally says he'd be happy if I ... I hope so. God, I hope so.

I've stopped drinking, just in case. At B.J.'s the other night, we took the wine, but I drank juice.

Tuesday, March 25, 1997

Tomorrow is the big day. The guys make their final presentations. And maybe we'll do a bit of life drawing ... we'll see.

313

I'm going to miss them. I'm sure I'm going to get all choked up. I want to keep in touch with them.

It's been a bit of rollercoaster ride, this trip to Tasmania. Can't believe Wally's been so patient with me; I don't deserve him.

He's off with Tyler tomorrow to see some place called Mystery Creek. I hope it's an amazing place.

If I'm pregnant, I'm going to think of Tasmania as the most amazing place in the world.

32.

MYSTERY CREEK

Marjorie was back from her African safari. Wally wasn't sure how long she'd been back—maybe just a few days. She'd lost little time in getting to him, aggravating him.

It was part of Wally's nature to expect something bad to happen after he'd experienced something good. Life tended to balance out like that, he thought. But the ecstasy of Friendly Beaches had been so intense, he felt his fortunes had taken a permanent turn for the better, only to have this cryptic message waiting for him about his son. Perhaps he deserved it. He'd nearly forgotten he *had* a son.

For Carolyn, who'd slept so peacefully all the way home and who likely wanted nothing more than to continue her sleep in the arms of her lover, the message was a rude reminder that Wally had an ex who was very much alive.

"You'd better call her now," Carolyn said. "How do I know she won't blame my parents for whatever happened?"

"It's only six-thirty in the morning there," said Wally. "Please call her."

"If something happened when he was staying with your parents, *they* would've called."

"That's logical, but we don't know that. *Please* call her."

The woman who'd brought him such ecstasy—and basked in it with him—went into the bedroom and shut the door.

He took a deep breath and dialed. The phone rang and rang, and he expected it to go to the answering machine, when a male voice said, "Hello?" Bill Horton.

"Hello, Bill. It's Wally."

"Oh ... Wally! Hello, Wally. It's been a long while. How are you?"

"Um ... fine."

"Well, we've both been away, haven't we? I believe you're *still* away, aren't you. Amazing, really, you being down there in Australia and your voice is coming through so clearly, you could be in the next room."

"I'd like to hear about your trip, Bill, but ... is Marjorie there?"

"Well, she is, but I think she's sleeping, Wally. It's not quite seven in the morning here; what time is it there?"

"Nearly midnight."

"Isn't that fascinating! Time zones have always fascinated me. I know when we were in Africa, I kept tabs on what time it was here in Winnipeg just so that—"

"Bill. Bill, Marjorie left a message here. It sounded urgent, about Geordie..."

"Oh ... yes, yes ... she did say she was going to call you. She was pretty upset, I can tell you that. I don't think I should get into it with you. You know, I think she'd like to explain everything herself, and I … just a minute. I heard the toilet flush. I do believe she might be up. I'll see if she can come to the phone. Wally, can you hold on for a minute while I go and see?"

"Yes, Bill."

"All right, then. Hold on."

Wally heard Bill Horton set the receiver down and give a little cough as he went to check on Marjorie. The wait became excruciating. He was worried about Geordie, worried that he hadn't been there for him or found a way to bring him to Tasmania.

"Wally."

"Marjorie. What's up?"

"Took you long enough to call back."

"We were out all day. What happened to Geordie?"

"He got *busted*."

"Busted. With what?"

"He and Michelle, stopped by the cops and caught with an ounce of pot. He tells me the easiest place to get drugs is in his school. *Anybody* can get them. He was seeing way too much of that girl. I know that. While he was staying with your artist's parents, she was there all the time. Christ knows what they got up to over there, playing some stupid fuckin' hockey game, he says; but that's a little hard to believe."

"Marjorie, what is he charged with?"

"Simple possession, the police say. If he pleads guilty, he'll get off with a reprimand. The cops said, if they'd had more, he'd be charged with trafficking. They said they're more interested in where Geordie got the stuff and who that person got it from."

"Where is Geordie now?"

"Where the fuck do you think he is? In his room. And that's where he is going to stay. He needs his dad now, Wally. When are you coming home?"

"In about two weeks. April second."

"I hope you're having fun with your artist and the kangaroos and Crocodile Fucking Dundee. I know Bill and I had a great time, and I got used to it. Time for you to take over. I'm sure you'll love it."

"Can I talk to Geordie?"

"What good would that do?"

"Marjorie?"

She didn't answer, and Wally thought she'd hung up, but then he heard voices.

"Hello."

"Geordie! Geordie, it's your dad."

"I know."

"Geordie, your mother told me what's happened. I'm sorry I'm not there. I just want you to know that I love you. I'll be home pretty soon and we'll talk about you and I doing more things together."

"Dad, it's..." Geordie's voice wavered. "It's not as bad as..."

"I know, Geord. Just try to hang in there, okay? We're going to get through this."

They talked for a few minutes more. Wally tried to avoid getting too emotional. Again he told his son he loved him and would be home soon.

"You must go caving at Mystery Creek before you leave," Tyler Chipman said.

He was having dinner with Wally and Carolyn in a group that included Bron, Andrew, Rebecca, and B.J.

"Oh, yes," said Rebecca. "You'd love it."

"Not far from here," said Bron. "Maybe an hour or so."

"You can drop down into the main cave by rope," said Tyler. "Or you can take the long way through the creek bed."

"I've heard it's quite amazing," said B.J. "I've never been. I'd like to go along, if you're going."

"I've been, and I'd love to go again," said Rebecca.

"When?" said Carolyn. "We're only here another week."

"How about tomorrow?" Tyler said.

"Bron and Andrew and I can't," said Carolyn. "We have a grand finale—everyone presenting the major drawing they've been working on. But, Wally, you could go tomorrow."

"I could," said Wally.

Tyler said, "B.J. then, Rebecca, and Dr. Baxter. We'll need your car, Dr. Baxter. I shall bring hard hats for everyone. Remember to wear clothes you don't mind getting dirty. Let's meet at the visiting fellow's parking space at … what … nine-thirty tomorrow morning?"

Though he was much younger than Wally, Tyler had become a friend. Twice they had had beers together at Knopwood's Tavern, and one night at B.J.'s, Tyler and B.J. helped Wally and Carolyn polish off the bottles of wine they'd picked up one day at a place called Marion's Vineyard. He said his job as resident tutor was the best in the world; he had absolutely no bills that weren't covered by Jane.

Half an hour before they were to leave, B.J. called Wally to say she was sorry, but she was unable to accompany them—something about one of her music students.

Carolyn was busy rearranging things in the study when Wally left. He had told her about Geordie's plight, and she had called her parents, not to tell them but to hear how the rest of Geordie's time with them had gone. They still thought of him as a fine young man, who had thanked them on his last night with them by buying them dinner (at Salisbury House). Carolyn had no intention of spoiling her parents' image of Geordie, and Wally chose not to mention—not yet, anyway—Marjorie's desire to unload their son.

Tyler arrived at the meeting place at the same time as Rebecca. He was carrying a pair of well-worn heavy boots, along with white miners' hats—only two of them.

"I must apologize, and I feel bad about this, but I'm afraid I can't take you to Mystery Creek. I have things to do for Dr. Lockridge. But I assure you that Rebecca is more than capable of guiding you."

"I'm flattered," said Rebecca.

Stunned by this dramatic change, Wally said, "Are you sure you want to, Rebecca?"

"Certainly! We can talk about Canada."

"Take these." Tyler gave a pair of boots to Wally. "You can change into them when you reach the entrance to the forest. And do wear the hat in the cave. The light goes on like this." He demonstrated.

Rebecca was dressed in a heavy pullover. She was already wearing boots, and she carried a small backpack.

"We'll be off, then, shall we?" she said.

"Right," said Wally. He pulled out the car keys. "Would you like to drive?"

"Oh, yes, please!"

"Again, I'm so sorry I can't take you," said Tyler, "but, believe me, you are in good hands."

Once Wally had adjusted to the idea of being accompanied by only Rebecca, he talked about Canada: the rich Quebec culture, the endearing quirks of Newfoundland, the fresh-water lakes, the wines of Niagara and the BC interior, the flat prairie breadbasket, the Aboriginal influence, the grandeur of both coasts, the world-wide appeal of PEI's *Anne of Green Gables*.

They stopped at a bakery for good plunger coffee and pasties—similar to large sausage rolls. The road gradually became gravel, and, near a village called Lune River, Rebecca pulled into a small parking area.

"Time to change your footwear," she said. "This is where we go into the forest."

He opened the passenger door and turned sideways to change into the boots Tyler gave him. They fit. Rebecca placed one of the hard hats on his head. It sat on top.

"Oh, oh," she said. "Your head is too big."

"Swelled from being treated so well."

She laughed. "Let's see. I think the inside band is adjustable."

She worked at it. He looked up and saw the sky was becoming overcast, threatening the shower that seemed to be a part of every fine Tasmanian day.

"There. Try that."

Wally took the hard hat, and it felt tight, but it fit.

"Thank you," he said.

"Let's go, then. I have sweets and water in my backpack if we want them."

There was an opening in the trees where a beaten path began. Rebecca led the way. A short distance in, they came upon a wooden shelter, no more than an inverted-V-shaped roof over a lectern that held a ledger-sized notebook and a pen on a string. Anyone entering the forest was supposed to sign in, presumably to let rangers or cops know who'd gone in and when. As far as they could tell from the register, no one had gone in today, but Elvis Presley and Adolf Hitler had gone in late yesterday and had not come out. Wally and Rebecca entered their names and the time of day.

The path followed an abandoned rail line that Rebecca said had once been used for taking rock from a quarry. You could still see some of the ties, though they were now mostly covered by leaves and branches, and other vegetation. Had there not been the raised track-bed path, the going would've been far more arduous, since the trees were so plentiful and so close together. Wally was glad of the hard hat for warding off low-hanging branches. Rebecca said the whole forest had been replanted in the twentieth century, but every so often you'd come upon an ancient tree that had fallen and not been taken away. One of these lay across their path. It was easily a metre in diameter—too big to jump over, too rough to scale—and steps had been carved into it to make it easier to cross over.

"This is convenient," said Wally, extending his arms the way a tightrope walker would as he climbed up and down.

He turned to give Rebecca a hand coming down because the steps were so narrow.

"Thank you," she said.

There were other fallen trees and stretches where bushes and underbrush hindered their progress. In places, the mound of the rail line had sunk and the ground was mucky. They did their best to tread on a fallen branch or a piece of rotted tie or a clump of wild grass to keep their feet out of the ooze. Overhead, clouds dominated the sky, but there were breaks where the sun's rays came through and struggled to penetrate the web of branches on the tall trees. Some rays did reach the path and light the way. Wally felt giddy, free, cheered by the filtered brightness and the warmth. He was in a primeval forest with a young woman he felt at ease with. It was like the other day with Carolyn on the secluded beach, except that instead of being Burt Lancaster and Deborah Kerr, they were Adam and Eve.

"How come we don't see any wildlife?" Wally said.

"I don't know. I'm surprised. I think, if we had a good look above us and around us, we might see a koala."

They came to the edge of a steep bank. Several metres below was a creek, the one Rebecca said led into the cave.

"We have to make our way down there," she said. "It's about a thirty-metre drop. The bank is slippery. Those jutting rocks and tree roots will ease your climb down if you step in the right places. I shall go down first and point out where you should step."

"Ready when you are."

"Want a sweet?"

She gave him a wrapped hard candy. He unwrapped

it and popped it into his mouth. Licorice flavour. She unwrapped another for herself.

"Here we go," she said.

Rebecca eased herself down into a sitting position and used the slippery grass on the edge of the bank as a slide. The grass was coated with greasy mud. This was not a place to worry about keeping clean.

She looked up at him. "When you come down, aim your foot at this rock and get a foothold on it." She pointed.

He did as directed, feeling less clumsy than he had on Lockridge's boat. He slid down faster than she had, and his right foot went hard into the rock. The rock did not give. She moved on to a jutting tree root then showed him how to negotiate the small space under the trunk of a fallen tree, pushing her backpack ahead of her and then imitating a limbo dancer. He followed. The trunk knocked the hard hat off his head, and it tumbled down to the creek below.

"Don't worry about that," she said. "We shall pick it up when we get down there. Now shift your weight in kind of a jump here. Give me your hand."

Her steady hand reassured him. In the next giant step, he felt he had the correct rhythm, and he landed on the next rock just as she left it to make room for him. Step here, duck there, slide on your bum here … and, out of breath but gaining confidence, he arrived safely at the level of the creek.

"Good on you!" she said, patting him on the back.

"I can't get over how agile *you* are. Like a cat."

She fetched his hard hat, brushed it off, and set it on his head.

"I think the water level is going to be fine," she said.

"There's an indicator back there that says we can walk into the cave without being in danger of getting swept up in a current or a sudden wave."

"We have to walk in the creek?"

"Tippytoe from rock to rock, if you like. Some rocks are below the present water level, so you're going to get your feet wet."

"I'm taking your word for it that this is worth the effort."

"You are going to love it!"

Again Rebecca gave precise directions about which rocks to step on. Their route would criss-cross the creek several times before they reached their destination well inside the cave. They started out, hopping from rock to rock, Wally again following Rebecca's lead. Each hop or step was different from the previous one; each rock was a different shape, and you couldn't figure out which kind of foothold you needed until you were there. Some rocks were smooth and slick, others were slanted at such an angle that any foothold was precarious. Again, Rebecca's guiding hand proved essential.

At the entrance to the cave, on a secure boulder that accommodated both of them, Rebecca turned on the light on each of their hats. Wally's worked, despite the fall. As they continued on, Wally felt like a miner, his hat lighting the way into a mine. The light was none too bright, but its beam did give him an idea of what was to come and where to put his foot next. He realized how important it was to wear a light-bearing hat. He could never have carried a flashlight, needing to have both hands free to help keep his balance and to pull himself forward as they proceeded from rock to rock. To get past one overhanging rock formation, they had to squat and lean back, again like limbo dancers.

The criss-crossing of the creek became more and more difficult as they moved farther into the cave and their route became darker and darker. It was harder to judge how far your foot needed to go to find a safe purchase. Sometimes, it was better to hop without help; at other times, Rebecca's hand seemed crucial, a lifeline. On a few moves, they worked together in tandem, as if in some demanding dance competition, executing a step that required perfect timing and each partner relying on the other. He couldn't remember ever growing to trust someone as quickly as he had grown to trust Rebecca.

They reached an outcropping of rock with one section where Rebecca could sit and another where Wally could lean back. Rebecca turned off his light and then her own.

"Close your eyes and keep them closed for about a minute," she said. "They must adjust to the darkness. I shall tell you when to open them."

Wally closed his eyes. He felt at ease. Trusting. He was a little boy again, keeping his eyes shut tight until he was told to open them, and when he did, there would be a big surprise. As a kid, he had never cheated in these situations. He liked to believe in magic. He had never ever wanted to know how a magician did a trick. And now he waited, feeling pleasantly exhausted from the trek and the climb and the skipping from rock to rock.

"All right," said Rebecca. "You can open your eyes now and look straight up."

He opened his eyes. What he saw were hundreds of tiny lights. It was like being in the countryside on a clear night, away from streetlights—out in a field in rural Manitoba at midnight in January—and looking up at the Milky Way. But each light was more distinct than the stars in a night sky.

"Every one of those lights you see is a glowworm," said Rebecca.

The longer Wally looked, the more lights he saw, as his eyes adjusted even more to the darkness. There had to be thousands. The ceiling and the upper walls of the cave were covered with glowworms.

"This is incredible," he said. "What do they live on?"

"Their lights attract insects and, I suppose, other creatures."

He looked around. There were glowworms everywhere.

"Now, close your eyes again," said Rebecca.

Without questioning it, he obeyed. What could the next surprise be? Would the lights change colour, or...

He felt a soft pressure on his lips. Rebecca's lips, pressing on his, her face right *there*, her *scent* right there, her lips so soft and moist, pressing a little harder on his, her hand on his face now, gently, her body touching him, pressing against him, leaning on him. He didn't understand. He didn't want to understand. His back supported by the flat rock wall, he yielded to her pushing into him, and still she kissed him, teasing him now with her tongue, and, emboldened by the darkness, he raised his hands to touch her, to run his hands over her sweater, to embrace her.

33.

A SPECIAL WAY TO SAY GOODBYE

S he backed away from the kiss.
He said, "That was…"
"No need to say anything."
"I don't—"
"Please. We must start back."
"Can't we stay and at least—"
"No. Come on."

She turned on her light. She made no move to turn his on. Shaken, he began to speak again, decided not to, took off his hard hat, and fumbled with the switch. The light didn't go on. Rebecca lowered her head so that the beam of her light illuminated the hat in his hands. He fiddled with the bulb and jiggled the battery, and the light went on. He put the hat on his head.

They retraced their steps along the creek bed. Wally felt shaky, less secure, but Rebecca still offered a steady hand. He tried to concentrate on the steps and the rhythm, the rhythm of the steps, and tried not to be distracted by the question *What happened back there?*

It seemed easier, working your way toward the daylight instead of into the darkness. He misjudged one rock, and his foot slipped into the water, ankle deep, but he stayed upright.

"I thought we'd lost you there!" Rebecca said, laughing.

Wally felt relief at the sound of her cheery voice. He wondered what the embrace had meant. Had she planned it, or was it spontaneous? Had she developed a crush on him, or had the spectacle of the glowworms simply caused her to seize the moment?

They didn't need their lights anymore, and, once they had emerged from the cave, they had to climb up the steep bank. Wally had a second wind. He went ahead and offered Rebecca *his* hand.

When they reached the top of the bank, their clothes spattered with mud, they started along the path without a word, as if they needed to preserve energy. There was a new tension between them. How stupid could he be, thinking nothing had changed between them. *Everything* had changed between them.

Back at the car, they both took off their boots and put on sneakers.

"Can we stop somewhere for a snack and a beer or something?" he asked.

"Of course we can," she said. "Shall I drive again?"

"Please do."

It was mid-afternoon when they pulled into Ye Olde Franklin Tavern. There was no one in the pub except a middle-aged woman who claimed to be both the bartender and manager of the restaurant next door. Hanging from the pub ceiling were some odd items: a cow's skull, a life preserver, a sign saying it was 8000 miles to Wall Drug in South Dakota. There were stools, and there was a lot of space for standing, but there was only one table, in a far corner.

"All right if we sit at the table?" Wally asked.

"Suit yourself," said the woman. "What is your pleasure? Cascade draught, Cascade draught, or—in the can—Cascade draught?"

"Cascade draught, not in the can," said Rebecca.

"I'll have that, too," said Wally. "And could we get some fish and chips or something?"

"If you don't mind me going next door to cook them," the woman said.

She gave them their beer and went into the restaurant. They sat at the pub table. Wally looked at the young woman sitting beside him.

"Rebecca, what happened back there in the cave? ... It was beautiful."

"I thought so, too."

"What did it mean?"

"It meant our sessions are over. And you'll be leaving and going back to Canada. I wanted to ... say goodbye in a kind of special way."

"Thank you."

"I'm sorry I didn't get to know Ms Webb better. She seems a lovely person."

"She is."

"I..." Rebecca wiped a tear from her eye.

"What ... ?"

"It's all right," she said.

The woman appeared with the fish and chips.

"There we are, then," she said. "Another Cascade?"

Carolyn greeted Wally at the underlodge door looking buoyant.

"How was it?" she said.

"A bit gruelling, I have to say. Trekking through a forest, climbing down to a creek over rugged rocks—before we even got to the cave."

"Sounds like good exercise, anyway."

"Oh, it was! But what we saw in the cave was more than worth all the effort. Thousands and thousands of glowworms."

"I've never seen glowworms."

"It was an amazing sight."

"Well, things went well here. They all made their pre-sentations—some really fine drawings! I think Braden's is good enough for a medical textbook. Bron did a fine perspective of two of the residences, with the face of Jane Franklin hovering over them. Some of them wanted me to keep what they'd done, but I insisted they start portfolios. They can send me photos, if they like. Well, then I gave in to Andrew. We hung blankets over the window and he posed."

"I'll bet they wished it was Amy."

"Yes, well … that's another story."

"What is? You mean she…"

"Surely you've heard rumblings."

"You mean she's already…"

Carolyn told Wally the story.

Wally didn't know what bothered him more: the fact that the sailors had swarmed the campus, the fact that the situation could've been explosive, or the fact that nobody—not even Carolyn—had told him about it.

"I was *going* to tell you. I was embarrassed. I was sure you'd hear about it from someone, but when it blew over, I pretended it hadn't happened. I guess I was lucky. And Amy ran away, and I don't think she's been bragging about it. I think she was scared."

All right, she'd jolted him with the sailor story, but now it was his turn to jolt her.

"I have something to tell you," he said. "Let's sit down."

They went to the dining table. On it was a folded sheet of art paper. Wally opened it.

"What is this?" he asked.

"My drawing of Andrew."

"Carolyn, it's terrific."

"Yes, I think so too."

"Well. Rebecca was the only one who went with me to the cave."

"I knew B.J. couldn't go. You mean Tyler didn't go either?"

"He brought us the hard hats and boots but said he had business with Dr. Lockridge."

"Well, wasn't that nice for you. I'll bet Rebecca planned it that way."

"She couldn't have."

"You don't think so? I think you underestimate her. She's got a crush on you."

"No..."

"You mean she didn't make a move on you?"

"I wouldn't call it a *move*. She did kiss me, though. A farewell kiss."

"Aha. Must be an Aussie thing. Andrew kissed me goodbye, too."

"What?"

"It's all right. He had his clothes back on by then. Nice young guy, really. I'm going to miss him."

34.

DAD QUALITIES

Thursday morning, the day before Good Friday and two days after the jaunt to Mystery Creek, Wally found an envelope in his mail. *Dr. Baxter* was written on it in familiar handwriting. There was a bulge in the envelope … caused by a small, wrapped chocolate Easter egg. It was accompanied by a letter. He smiled at Elizabeth Hardy and hoped he didn't look too flushed as he left the administrative office and stopped in the hall to read:

Dear Wally:
(I hope you don't mind if I call you that!)
    I shall be gone from the campus when you read this. I'm writing to tell you again how much I have enjoyed your company. This is a rather sad time for me because my parents separated a year ago at Easter. I know our family structure is better off changed, but somehow the little girl inside of

me wants to cry for the loss of the security I felt I had before. I have friends but no one I can call a soulmate. I have been feeling lonely. I know I'll look back on uni life as good times but lately I've been missing my dad so much. I want to be loved and praised, and I want to feel that sense of unconditional support I used to have. At first, I think I was attracted to you for your dad qualities, and I wanted to learn from you, and you'd be proud of me. But then you turned out to be such a pleasant companion, and I felt that you were learning from me, too. You've helped me to feel more independent. I'm not used to looking at myself and liking what I see. In the cave, I think I was feeling more than gratitude. I've been confused. I hope you won't think any less of me for what I did. I'm glad we had that time together.

I hope you have a safe journey home. Perhaps we shall meet again in Canada one day.
Take care.
Love, Rebecca.

"Fan mail?"
Peter Russell walked past on his way to the office. Wally gave a little grunt in response; he was too choked up to say anything.

He folded the letter and returned it to the envelope. As he carried it back to the underlodge, he took the chocolate egg out, unwrapped it, and ate it.

Carolyn was dismantling easels, restoring the study to its original spaciousness.

"You should read this," Wally said.

"Nice handwriting," said Carolyn.

She checked the name at the end of the letter and then read the letter. Twice.

"My god," she said. "She sounds like a troubled young woman. Just how chaste was that kiss?"

Many students had gone home for Easter, leaving only a small contingent for dinner that evening, so they moved tables together, with Wally and Carolyn more or less in the centre. Des came in bearing news that Dr. Lockridge and Tyler had gone sailing around the Tasman Peninsula and up to Maria Island, and they would be back Friday night in time to say goodbye. Bron and Braden were there, saying they intended to work on a computer-programming problem at Jane most of the weekend. They gave Carolyn their email addresses.

Annabel arrived drunk, with two friends steering her in. She wasn't the least bit obnoxious; she stared into the mid-distance and smirked. Her boyfriend set a plateful of food in front of her, and she toyed with it but didn't try to eat it. Regina Dales and Peter Russell came in and sat on the periphery of the group, as if to give the visiting fellow this one last hurrah.

Most had finished eating the main course when Amy made a grand entrance, looking her voluptuous self in a form-fitting sweater with a deep V neck.

"Not staying," she said, "just stopped in to say goodbye."

She headed for Wally. She had him push away from the table so that she could plop into his lap and hug his head to her generous bosom.

"Bye, Dr. Baxter," she said, kissing his forehead. "Bye, Carolyn. Come and see us again."

It seemed such behaviour was expected from Amy, and in a minute she was gone.

It rained most of Good Friday. Wally spent time catching up on his notes for a future paper, while Carolyn wrote in her journal and sorted through her belongings in preparation for their departure the next day. Virginia Lockridge came to the underlodge door in late afternoon to tell them that the morning storm had seriously affected Dennis and Tyler's sailing excursion. Gale-force winds had snapped the front mast, and they had no choice but to limp into shore at Port Arthur.

"Wally," she said, "Dennis wanted me to tell you that you were right. He *did* miss a lesson—the one on how to sail in a gale."

She laughed and said she had to drive the 100 kilometres to pick them up on Saturday morning and they would likely not be back in time to say goodbye.

"They give you their love and best wishes," she said. "It's been lovely to have you here. Do have a safe trip."

B.J. had invited them for dinner on their last night, and they were surprised to find she had other guests, not people from Jane, but good friends: the Hutton family. Or was it Sutton? Charlotte, a pleasant woman with her brown hair done in tight curls, and her shy husband, Cedric, who spoke quietly with such an Aussie accent that Wally couldn't understand a word he said, were accompanied by their two sons, six-year-old Devon, and eighteen-month old Clive, or Clyde. Devon sat on B.J.'s futon reading a book that was beyond his years, while Clive (or Clyde) sat in his mother's lap colouring at the table. The flat was as spartan as ever, the only homey touch provided by the cat and his toys. The cat ventured out on occasion through the living-room window, which B.J. left open for that purpose.

"Wally was with me when we found out Patrick was a male," B.J. said.

"I presume you mean the cat," said Charlotte, "and not your husband."

Carolyn and Wally had brought all their leftover wine and beer, and they were happy to see that it was appreciated. Through dinner, they talked about what the Huttons (or Suttons) did to make sure Devon could read early, what Tasmanian sites Wally and Carolyn had visited, how Patrick (the husband) was liking Montreal, and where exactly Winnipeg was in relation to Los Angeles. Wally picked up nothing Cedric said but seemed to get by with nods or murmurs when answering him. B.J.'s dinner was both tasty and substantial—lamb, potatoes, and salad in large helpings.

When the evening wound down and the adults were preparing to leave, Devon was playing with Patrick.

"You want to buy him a cat," B.J. said.

"We have talked about a pet," Charlotte said. "Cedric thinks we should have a dog, don't you, Ced?"

"Mmgmdpffrr," Cedric said.

"Good night, Wally," said B.J. "Do have a good trip home. And do drop us a line." She gave him a vigorous hug.

"I will, I will," he said.

"Good night, Carolyn," said B.J. "So very nice to have you here at Jane." They hugged.

"Give our best to Patrick," Carolyn said. "Nice to meet you, Cedric and Charlotte. G'night, young fellows."

"Say good night, Devon."

"G'night."

Wally and Carolyn headed back to the underlodge. The moon, almost full, seemed brighter than usual after such a rainy day. Moonlight shimmered on the Derwent. They stood on the hill and looked out over South Hobart and Wrest Point and the harbour. This was the last time they would see this sight. Wally thought he'd like to stand there looking for a long time, but Carolyn wanted to take him to bed.

Their flight to Melbourne didn't leave until one fifteen Saturday afternoon. They had returned the rented car on Thursday and were going to take a taxi to the airport. They had time to kill, so they decided to walk down to the newsagent for the newspaper as if it was a normal day. They walked out through the back parking lot to Davey Street, down Davey and Weld to Macquarie and the newsagent, where Wally picked up the *Mercury* and paid the woman, who said, as always, "Thank you, sir." They walked up the hill, remembering to *look right* before they crossed Davey. They walked along Elboden, passing the open gate of a walled house, where they glimpsed signs of wealth— a uniformed maid and a parked Jaguar. Old cars, bikes, broken windows, and cluttered yards suggested the other large houses on the street had become rooming houses.

They continued onto the Jane property, through the lower parking lot that was almost empty, up "Heart-Starter Hill," past a residence building and its empty games room, and down to the underlodge yard, where they fed some lavender to the goats one last time.

Over breakfast, Wally read in the *Mercury* about a flash flood caused by yesterday's downpour. Damage to a shopping mall in Kingston was estimated at a million dollars. They finished off the orange juice, the cereal, the jar of instant coffee, the brown bread, and the dish of jam, having portioned these out over their final days. ("I have measured out my life with coffee spoons," says Prufrock in the famous T.S. Eliot poem that Tyler Chipman could quote at length.) They washed the dishes, killed a few morning bugs, pulled the blankets and sheets off the bed in readiness for the major cleanup Shirley the cleaning woman would do prior to the arrival of the next visiting fellow, and finally they got down to some serious packing.

The taxi arrived just after eleven. They left the underlodge keys on the dining table and hauled their suitcases out the door. They waved goodbye to the view of the harbour, the campus and the goats, and they wheeled their luggage over the flagstone sidewalk and up the hill, where they were met half way by the cabbie. He was middle-aged but tall and wiry and quite capable of lifting the bags into his trunk (or boot). He was talkative, the right type of guy (or bloke) to take you away when you hated to leave. They told him they had a one-fifteen flight, and he said, "No problem. We could have a flat tire and change it and still get there with lots of time to spare." He liked to talk so much, he kept his speed down so that he could talk longer.

When they reached the airport, he parked in front of Qantas and carried their bags all the way inside to the check-in counter.

Staying four nights in Melbourne had seemed like a good idea when Wally was planning this trip. Not only was it where they had to leave from—the flight home was from Melbourne to Winnipeg via Los Angeles and Calgary—but also it should be as worthwhile seeing as Sydney was. Now, however, they were anxious to get home. It wasn't Melbourne's fault. They wanted to hurry up and start looking for a house.

But, if they had to stay in Melbourne, they might as well enjoy it. They were booked at the centrally located Grand Chancellor Hotel. To get acclimatized, they took the City Circle tram, which ran around the perimeter of the downtown area. They attended the comedy festival that had just opened. They wandered around the Greek festival, which was loudly located near their hotel.

Mostly, they talked about their immediate plans. For dinner on Easter Day, they went to Brunswick, a street of trendy cafés, and picked a restaurant that was just funky and eclectic enough to be popular. Not a great place to talk, but it made them feel young. Wally thought it was a good time to mention Geordie.

"One thing we need to discuss," he said.

"There are *lots* of things we need to discuss," said Carolyn.

"Let me get this one out in the open. I guess it comes under the heading of *my baggage*."

"And you don't mean suitcases."

"Right. This is about Geordie. It might be time for him to live with me ... with *us*."

"Hallelujah! It's about time, I'd say."

"You wouldn't mind?"

"I *love* the guy. He's at the stage of his life where he needs his *dad*."

"Well, that was easy."

"We'll put him in a room over the garage."

"Let's drink to that. What would you like?"

"I ... I'm not sure. Nothing alcoholic."

"Come on! It's Easter."

"I'm serious, Wally. I feel ... not sick, exactly ... different. I can't say what it is, I have no experience with this, but I think ... I think I might be pregnant."

"Already?"

"Why not? Potent guy like you. And we haven't exactly been abstaining."

"Wow." Wally wasn't sure what else to say. Was he ready for this?

"It's really too early to be sure. If it's true, though, Geordie can be our live-in babysitter."

35.

WALLY: OCTOBER 2013

It's a gorgeous October afternoon—you could say, it's another fine day in Jordan Station. I've just been for my daily walk, and I picked up some peaches and cherries from Larry's fruit stand. They are to die for, let me tell you.

Jordan Station is a hamlet in the wine country between Hamilton and St. Catharines, a bucolic little paradise hidden away just a minute south of the QEW highway and Lake Ontario. Carolyn and the girls and I moved here when I retired. I didn't need to retire, didn't want to retire, but the offer of the house was too good to pass up. Carolyn's old aunt Ethel couldn't look after the place anymore but wanted to keep it in the family. So we moved, just over five years ago now, when I was a sprightly fifty-five. The house we had in Winnipeg—a two-storey in Charleswood (with a room over the garage for Geordie)—was in such good shape, it sold within a couple of days.

First thing we did when we arrived here was have a barn

built, something that fit in with the agrarian surroundings. Not that we needed a barn for grain or livestock. We
wanted a nice space for Carolyn's studio. You should see it.
Big enough to display all of her paintings and drawings,
and big enough for her to hold a class in when she wants
to. She picked up the teaching bug in Tasmania, and now,
every few months, she puts on a ten-week class, and folks
of all ages sign up. She restricts it to twelve. Mostly sketching. As far as I know, she hasn't had anybody posing nude
yet.

There's a luxurious loft in the barn. It's great for guests,
but mostly it's for us—a comfy place to fool around in
when the mood hits us.

Carolyn still does a lot of design work, mostly freelance.
She has contracts that take her into Toronto for meetings,
but these days she does most of the work at home on her
laptop. It's unbelievable, what she can do with today's tech-
nology—masters every new model of iPad and iPhone as
if she had invented them. And she's in demand, which
means she brings in big bucks—always welcome when
you have teen-aged girls.

She says one of the toughest things she ever did was
leave Dobber Design. They were so good to her when she
was expecting and when the kids were little. If we had a
daycare problem (turned out Geordie didn't do a heck
of a lot of babysitting), they'd let her work from home.
She gradually did more and more that way as comput-
ers became more sophisticated. Dobber even thought she
could do her work from *here*, but, after a couple of trips
back to Winnipeg to meet with clients, she believed it was
time to cut ties. Dobber sold the business shortly after that.

The most I do on my computer these days is send email messages. I am working on something that might be a book someday—need to spend a bit of time browsing in the National Library and doing some interviewing. I want to save Prime Ministers Kim Campbell and John Turner from oblivion. Right now, though, most important is cleaning up my backlog of email. Over 1000 sent messages I can't seem to part with, and over 500 in my inbox. A few of them are related to my project, but too many are exchanges with old friends, or with Geordie.

Here's the one I sent to Geordie this morning:

From: Wally Baxter
Sent: October 6, 2013, 10:14 a.m.
To: Baxter, Geordie
Subject: Congrats

Hi, Geordie:
Congratulations on hiring two new people! Your business is taking off. And so good of you to credit Carolyn's dad with giving you some of the skills so essential to what you're doing. He would have been tickled to think his old hockey game could spawn such creativity!

I'm amazed at how well you're making your way around London. Not an easy place to navigate, but you're doing it!

Rachel sounds like a lovely young woman; and she's a graduate architect as well! It sounds like she has caught on with a good firm. Tell her not to worry about the "go-for" work she's getting now—

the big bucks (or pounds) will come. I can under-stand why she'd like to move in with you, to save money, but might it not be premature? Mind you, that is only my opinion.

Make sure you're not having her move in just so that you can tell your mother there is no room for *her*. Your flat sounds tiny. If your mother wants to visit, we both know she can afford a hotel, or her oilman can, anyway.

I do know they moved to a better part of Cal-gary after their condo was flooded in the spring.

I received a long message from Bill Horton the other day. He's been determined to keep in touch with me ever since your mother left him—what, ten years ago? Since he retired back in 2005, he's been working on a novel, and he says he's finished it now and would like my opinion. It's called *Im-petuous*, and I'm worried it's about your mother, but he claims it's about today's society.

I'm glad you liked the logo Carolyn did for your company. I thought it was pretty cool!

By the way, Carolyn's mother has moved into a new assisted-living place in Niagara-on-the-Lake. Do make sure you get a card and a letter off to her in lots of time for Christmas. She is always thrilled to hear from you.

Carolyn and I are planning to take the girls over there to see you next year—maybe in their spring break? Let me know what dates would work best for you. It won't hurt the girls to miss a bit of school, they're both doing so well.

Thank you for your latest cheque, but no need to pay off the loan too fast. Keep some breathing room.

Next time you're at Kensington Palace, say Hello to Will and Kate and George for me!

Love, Dad.

I hear a car pull up. That will be our dinner guests.

"Carolyn, I think they're here!"

I go out through the kitchen door. A silver Cadillac SUV has pulled up beside our white Hyundai Sonata. The SUV has British Columbia licence plates and is flying a Vancouver Canucks flag. The driver's-side door opens, and a tall, good-looking, dark-haired man steps out. He's wearing sunglasses, a red polo shirt, and black trousers. He turns to the back door, leans in, fiddles with something—likely a seat belt—and backs out to make room for a pretty blonde girl about seven years of age. She doesn't cling to his legs or show any shyness. She takes a couple of steps toward the house.

"Hi there!" I call.

Out of the other side of the SUV emerges the woman I've thought about more than a few times in the last sixteen years. This is the first time I've seen her since that day we went to Mystery Creek.

"Hello!" she calls. "Dr. Baxter, this is my husband, Jason Kirkwood."

"*Wally*, please," I say.

Jason takes off his sunglasses, shakes my hand, and says, "I am so glad to meet you at last, sir. I really want to thank you for stirring up Rebecca's interest in Canada."

"Oh, I, um..."

I feel myself blush. I look at Rebecca, who is striding toward us dressed in a white shirt with the sleeves folded back and skimpy mauve shorts that show off her long, gorgeous legs. Her shoulder-length blonde hair shows a trace of dishevelment. In the next second, the brightness of her hair, her face, her shirt seems blinding, and I long for the darkness of the cave as she says, "So lovely to see you again," and hugs me tightly, leaving no doubt about the feel and shape of her body. The exquisite yet earthy scent of her is exactly as I remember it. But this time there is no kiss.

"And who is *this?*" I say, directing my attention to the little girl.

"This is Jessica," says Rebecca. Her voice bears only a trace of an Australian accent. "Jess, this man, Dr. Baxter, was my teacher a long time ago in Australia."

"Hi," Jessica says.

Carolyn comes out, followed by our two daughters. Carolyn is wearing light-blue Capri pants and a blue sweater. Given who our guests are, I suppose her competitive instinct has prevailed. She's put on a little weight in the last few years, but in the right places, as they say. Her looks are every bit as appealing as those of the much younger Rebecca.

The girls—the brunette Freya and the blonde Deborah—have made every effort not to look alike. Freya is wearing a crimson cammie with a sheer top and red skinny jeans, while Deborah has on a black tank top under a yellow sweater with black leggings and black-framed glasses. Both are beautiful in a self-conscious adolescent way.

Carolyn never really knew Rebecca that well, but it was Carolyn whom Rebecca found on Facebook some months ago, and it was the two of them who planned this day when Rebecca knew she and her husband were going to take a cross-Canada vacation.

After the introductions, Deborah offers to take Jessica into the house to amuse her.

"Jess," says Rebecca, "why don't you show Deborah your friend Saige? Jason, Saige and her wardrobe are in the green bag."

Jason goes to the SUV and finds Jessica's doll and a doll-size suitcase. Saige is wearing the same kind of sparkly red dress as Jessica.

"Oh, she's so *sweet!*" says Deborah, and Jessica lets her hold the doll as Deborah leads the way into the house.

"We're really into the American Girl craze," says Rebecca. "You won't believe the number of outfits Saige has."

Jason smiles and says, "We even go down to Seattle some weekends just to have Saige's hair done. The American Girl stores have beauty parlours and rooms where you can take your doll for tea."

"Mom," says Freya, "I'll check on the turkey, and then I'm phoning Craig, okay?"

"Fine," says Carolyn, "but let me know when to start the vegetables."

"It's such a beautiful day," I say, "we thought we'd stay out here until dinner. What can I get everybody to drink?"

"Ahh," says Rebecca, "do you have a chardonnay from around here?"

"I do."

"I think I'll have the same," says Jason, who has maintained a sanguine look through all the preliminaries.

"That makes three of us, Wally," says Carolyn.

"Well, I'll be the exception," I say. "I'm having a rum."

Jason helps Carolyn assemble the lawn chairs, while I fetch the drinks. In the kitchen we have a vintage barber chair that Carolyn's aunt picked up when a relative closed his shop. Freya is sitting in it, texting Craig on her iPhone, her thumbs a blur of movement on the tiny keyboard. Remember when *all thumbs* meant a *lack* of dexterity? She's the first of the two girls to have a boyfriend. Texting keeps the conversation quiet; why do I always think she's plotting something? I suppose it's only a matter of time until we compete for the loft.

When I've distributed the drinks, Carolyn says, "I'd like to drink a toast to you, Rebecca, for getting in touch with us."

We clink our glasses.

"Oh, Wally," says Rebecca, "this is lovely wine."

"Grown about twenty kilometres from here," I say.

"Do you ever hear from any of the Jane people?" Carolyn asks.

"Annabel, occasionally, and Bron," Rebecca says. "Did you know Bron and Amy got married?"

"That's wonderful," says Carolyn.

"Three kids, they have. Oh, and you'll remember Tyler Chipman. He came to visit us a few years ago when he was travelling in Canada. He lives in Jakarta now. I think his wife is an Australian diplomat. I've lost track of Dr. Lockridge, but Tyler told me he moved to the mainland to be a university president."

"I liked both of them," I say. "I should try to contact them."

"I'll give you Tyler's email address," says Rebecca.

"Good. Thank you," I say. "Now. Tell us how and when you made your move to Canada."

"Oh, dear." Rebecca glances at Jason. "You may remember, Wally, how *down* I was at Jane. I didn't like my family, I didn't like my life. Jason has a hard time believing it, but that's the way it was."

I remember the letter she gave me. For a long time I wished I'd done something to help her. But of course, I had my own big adjustments to make. Over time, I thought I should throw her letter away. I almost did until I realized Carolyn was keeping the drawing of Andrew. Well, I guess it's not the same, is it? Kind of childish for me to think so. And now she has the drawing *framed* in the barn. And I still have the letter.

"My father married again, and I never saw him, except he did say he would give me money on my twenty-first birthday," says Rebecca. "After I finished my arts degree at the uni, I tried to settle in Brisbane, and I worked there for a while, but I knew I had to try Canada."

"You were always hooked on Canada, weren't you?" I say.

"I think I was. And your tutoring only made it more fascinating. I saved that money from my father and finally made the move. I flew to Vancouver and didn't have enough to go any further, so that's where I stayed."

"And I'm so glad you did," says Jason.

"At first, I lived in rooming houses and took any old job. Eventually, I was working at something I liked, with a law firm. I took some legal-assistant courses and considered going on to law, but along came Jason—"

"To the rescue," Carolyn says.

"Yes, and we put my career aspirations on hold. Jason is doing very well and I'm enjoying life as a mother. We have a smashing home in West Vancouver."

"Where did you two meet?" Carolyn asks.

"I'm embarrassed to tell you. Jason, you tell them."

Jason smiles as if recalling the day they met. "In a place near the airport," he says. "A bar called The Outrigger."

Carolyn and I look at each other and laugh.

"It *is* awful, isn't it?" says Rebecca.

"No, no," says Carolyn. "We're laughing because we met in a bar. In Winnipeg."

Jason laughs. "And look at you," he says. "Your marriage turned out well, didn't it? Nothing wrong with meeting in a bar."

"Actually," says Carolyn, "we were both married before. My husband died young, and Wally and his wife divorced. Wally has a son who lives in England now. And do you know? We haven't yet got around to having a wedding. If we have one, would the two of you come?"

"You're on!" laughs Jason.

"But you do have two *lovely* daughters," says Rebecca. "How close in age are they?"

"They're twins," says Carolyn. She smiles at me and says to Rebecca, "Do you remember the lovely pristine beach at a place called Friendly Beaches in Tasmania?"

"Yes?"

"That's where they were conceived."

"Oh!" says Rebecca, looking shocked.

"The first to arrive we called Freycinet after the beautiful park next to the beach," Carolyn tells them. "We call her Freya for short; I have an old friend named Freya."

"And Deborah?" says Rebecca.

"That's a little more obscure," says Carolyn. "There's a famous love scene on the beach in an old movie called *From Here to Eternity.*"

"I've seen it," says Jason.

"Yes, well, the actress is Deborah Kerr," says Carolyn.

She's always liked to believe the girls were conceived on the beach. If you do the math, it isn't possible, but, God, it's romantic.

Rebecca touches Jason's forearm and says, "I wish the name we chose for our daughter—Jessica—had a more exotic origin. She's named after Jason's mother."

Jessica bursts out of the house, saying, "Mommy, Mommy! Can I stay with … with…"

"Deborah," says Deborah, coming out behind her.

"With Deborah tonight?"

"Oh, no, honey, we can't expect—"

"Hey," says Carolyn, "Deborah is the world's best when it comes to looking after kids. She has a thriving babysitting business."

"We don't want to impose," says Jason.

"We'd be happy to have her stay here," I say.

"You know," says Rebecca, "Jason has a meeting in Buffalo tomorrow. We have to come back this way anyway. If she still wants to stay when we're leaving…"

"Yay!" Jessica cheers.

"Maybe we could even sleep in the *loft*," says Deborah.

"Well," Carolyn says, looking at me with a broad smile, "sounds like it's all settled."

ACKNOWLEDGEMENTS

I am indebted to Alison Preston for closely reading the manuscript, providing vital feedback and offering such thoughtful suggestions. Thank you to Carol Dahlstrom for her astute editorial work. And thank you to Turnstone Press for producing and promoting this novel, magically turning it into that most endearing and enduring of creations—a handsome book.

Many thanks to the people at Jane Franklin Hall in Hobart, Tasmania, for inviting me to spend some time in their midst and providing the setting where many of the fictional events in this novel take place.

Chapters One and Three of *Visiting Fellow* appeared in slightly different form as the short story "Harassment" in *Prairie Fire* magazine, Spring, 2009. A longer version of Chapter Four appeared as the short story "Lightening Up" in the collection *Accountable Advances* (Turnstone Press, 1994).

Information on English explorer Sir John Franklin and his wife Lady Jane was gleaned from Ken McGoogan's excellent biography, *Lady Franklin's Revenge* (HarperCollins, 2005).